Praise for *Death in the Family*

"*Death in the Family* is a terrific suspense novel in the classic Agatha Christie tradition. With a masterful hand, Tessa Wegert combines slices of serial-killer thriller with a locked-room mystery . . . simultaneously claustrophobic and hauntingly beautiful. Wegert offers an intense read that will grab your attention and not let go, even after the last page is turned."

—Christine Carbo,
bestselling author of *A Sharp Solitude*

"Intricate plotting and a razor-sharp narration keep the pages turning in this up-all-night murder mystery. Menacing and atmospheric, *Death in the Family* will have you on the edge of your seat rooting for Detective Shana Merchant to uncover the truth and triumph over the scars of her own dark past."

—Wendy Walker, *USA Today*
bestselling author of *Don't Look for Me*

"A deliciously complicated locked-room mystery that would make Agatha Christie proud. Add a savvy sleuth battling her own demons and the result is an up-to-date and thrilling ride. *Death in the Family* definitely deserves a place on your must-read list."

—Margaret Coel, *New York Times*
bestselling author of *Winter's Child*

"Tessa Wegert's *Death in the Family* assembles delicious ingredients—isolation, a ticking clock, family secrets—and creates a mystery at once familiar a[.............................]
good comfort food."

—Andre[.....]
The Res[.....]

"Tessa Wegert expertly ratchets up the tension, turning an idyllic island claustrophobic as the characters' tangled pasts unravel and the killer closes in. Compulsively readable and utterly satisfying, with an ending that will leave you desperate for Shana's next case."

—Erica O'Rourke, author of
Dissonance and *Time of Death* as Lucy Kerr

"This locked-room thriller has all of the requisite tangled motives and deductive crime-solving, along with a riveting introduction to edgy survivor, Shana, and Tim, her steady, easygoing foil."

—*Booklist*

"*Death in the Family* marks a bold beginning to an addictive new series."   —*BookPage*

"*Death in the Family* has it all: an immersive atmosphere, a cinematic setting, and a deliciously dubious cast. But what elevates this book above the pack is its thoughtfully crafted protagonist."   —Crime by the Book

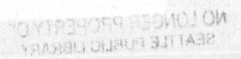

THE DEAD SEASON

Tessa Wegert

Berkley Prime Crime
New York

BERKLEY PRIME CRIME
Published by Berkley
An imprint of Penguin Random House LLC
penguinrandomhouse.com

Library of Congress Cataloging-in-Publication Data

Names: Wegert, Tessa, author.
Title: The dead season / Tessa Wegert.
Description: First edition. | New York: Berkley Prime Crime, 2020. |
Series: A Shana Merchant novel
Identifiers: LCCN 2020022052 (print) | LCCN 2020022053 (ebook) |
ISBN 9780593097915 (trade paperback) | ISBN 9780593097922 (ebook)
Subjects: GSAFD: Mystery fiction. | Suspense fiction.
Classification: LCC PS3623.E422656 D42 2020 (print) | LCC PS3623.E422656
(ebook) | DDC 813/.6—dc23
LC record available at https://lccn.loc.gov/2020022052
LC ebook record available at https://lccn.loc.gov/2020022053

First Edition: December 2020

Printed in the United States of America
1   3   5   7   9   10   8   6   4   2

Cover image © Carmen Spitzmagel/Trevillion images
Cover design by Erin Fitzsimmons
Title page photograph: Shutterstock/Sarah Mika
Book design by Elke Sigal

For Karl, Leila, and Karel with boundless love

Swanton, Vermont
August 1995

The forest circled John R. Raleigh Memorial Field like a scythe, its tree line cutting an arc into the park's sun-scorched grass. The grass was where I played Little League, back before I decided there were better ways to spend my time in Swanton.

There was no game being played on the day we walked those woods, but there had been. Just two hours earlier, dozens of children and their parents had swarmed the field, mothers chasing toddlers through the silver dust blowing in from the limestone quarry at the end of the road. Nodding absently when their older children, fed up with watching baseball, begged to explore the woods. That's why what we found there was so alarming. Whoever left it intended for kids to see it. Kids like us.

"Check it out."

I stopped. He was a few steps ahead of me, and his body blocked my view, but I was conscious of a new sound linking up to the chatter of crickets at our feet and warblers in the leafy, wind-jostled canopy of trees overhead. The flies, mechanical in their buzzing, hovered just beyond where he stood. I closed the distance between us and looked down, first at the toes of my size-three Keds, filthy now—Mom would be pissed—and then at the box. Large. Plastic. Containing something that made my insides squirm.

"Ew," I said, pressing my chin against his shoulder. He smelled sweaty, which was new; at nine and a half, six months younger than me but tall for his age, he was well on his way to puberty. "What is it?"

"A cat, I think," he said, still staring.

"Weird." It was more than that. The animal was wrapped in a makeshift bag, clear plastic bunched at the top and bound with the green paper twist ties I liked to swipe from the grocery store. One furry white leg stuck straight up, and the animal's pink toe pads were pressed against the inside of the sack. In my mouth, my saliva had turned to glue. "Is it . . ."

"Dead?" I could feel his heart thumping through his back. "There's blood."

I swallowed hard and stepped out from behind him for a better look. Through the plastic I could see the white fur around the cat's left ear was dark and matted with blood.

"If it's dead," he said, "that means it got murdered."

"Fuck." Using the illicit word gave me a thrill, and tweaked his mouth into a smile. He studied my face.

"I heard a story. This old guy in town, lives over by the river? Crissy told me. He tortures animals and stuff."

"But Crissy's a liar." That was fact: she made shit up all the time, mostly so she could sneak out with her friends.

"She's not lying about this."

"My neighbor has a cat," I said, contemplative. "It digs in our flowers and drops dead mice on the porch. Mom hates it. One time she was so mad she said she could kill it. I bet a lot of cats make people mad like that." I waved my arm at the box to support my argument. Flies lifted like a cloud of black confetti.

"This isn't like that."

"Well, *somebody* did this. We've gotta figure out who." It was the first thought that came to mind, not *We have to tell my parents* or *Let's get the cops.* I loved a good mystery, even then.

"We'll look for clues." There was an undercurrent of excitement in his voice. Try as he might to be solemn, I could see he was delighted. "Footprints and stuff. And we can ask around to see if anyone saw him."

Wanna play? This was our new favorite pastime. The games our fellow fourth-graders liked—four square, cops and robbers—held no joy for us. We yearned for more. Usually we had to concoct mysteries for ourselves, but here was a real one, right at our feet, and we aimed to solve it. We were natural-born detectives, he and I. That's what I told myself, and I believed it.

"I'll look here. You take the field." He flashed me a grin as he crouched on the dirt path and swatted a fly from his shin. He was so tan his legs were three shades darker than the skin visible where his sock, the elastic stretched out from wear, had slipped down.

"Okay," I said, keeping my head real still. Trying not to let him know I'd spotted the bracelet on his ankle, a neat braid of green paper twist ties lying flat against that band of pale, secret skin.

ONE

B ullshit."

"Nope." I turned over the cards on the table between us, and there it was: three aces take the game.

McIntyre groaned. "I hate playing with you. You're so damn lucky."

"Me and my charmed life," I said, deadpan, as I gathered the cards in a stack and tapped their rounded corners into place. Across the table, McIntyre tried and failed to catch my eye. "This has got to stop, Shay."

She was talking about my mood. It had been black lately; she wasn't wrong about that. Four months since my rebirth in the Thousand Islands. Three weeks since it all went to hell. Tim once told me things were simple around here, but that was before the murders and the drowning, before the fiancé I kicked to the curb. If that was what passed for simple in Upstate New York, I didn't want to see things get complicated.

I reached behind me, pulled a blanket from the back of my chair onto my lap, and smoothed the fabric over my knees. There was a quilt for every patron on the covered patio at Nelly's Bistro, thoughtfully placed for Clayton's chilly mornings. I was only a little cold, didn't need the throw any more than I needed a third cup of coffee, but the card game was over and I found I couldn't quiet my hands. "I know," I told Mac. "It's not that easy."

"Who cares about easy? You're Shana Merchant, the bad-ass who solved the bloodiest case these parts have seen in years."

Baptism by fire, as they say—or in my case, water. "Cue the ticker tape parade."

"Great idea," she said. "Only instead of ticker tape we'll shred those damned corruption case files from my desk and blanket Church Street in confetti. Bear claw?"

I looked askance at the pastry in her hand. "Isn't it taboo to chase breakfast with dessert?"

"It's my birthday."

"Not yet it's not."

Extricating a slice of almond from the frosted dough, she swiped at me, catlike. "Close enough—and when you're fifty, you get to do whatever you want. I'm thinking about chasing this dessert with that hunky Canadian border guard."

I laughed, had to, because I knew which guard she was talking about, and he was more scrumptious than any pastry Nelly's could produce. Where would I be without Maureen McIntyre and her uncompromising humor? It still came as a shock to me that we were friends, especially when I thought of her in the context of her work. If someone manufactured Sheriff McIntyre posters for fangirls, I'd have taped one to my bedroom wall—if I had a wall to call my own, that is. Mac was my professional idol, but she was also the person without whom I'd be homeless. Most of my things were in storage, but thanks to the sheriff of Jefferson County I had a La-Z-Boy couch and the best company a person in my situation could hope for.

When I moved out of the apartment I'd shared with my ex-fiancé into McIntyre's place in nearby Watertown, she made a point of telling me she wouldn't push it. *Talk when you're ready,* she'd said, just as she had in July when, brand-new to the job, I'd opted not to tell my closest colleague about my variegated past. She hadn't forced me to share my secret pain with anyone. This was more of the same.

The chin-up routine Mac kept rehashing had to do with my ex, and the betrayal I endured by his hand. Despite her intuition, though, Carson Gates was the last thing on my mind. The thin line on my fourth finger, left behind by my engagement ring, was proof I'd once loved him. Soon that would be gone.

No, Carson wasn't the reason why—as McIntyre dove into a story about the couple who spent an hour in her office arguing the innocence of the four Watertown officials accused of misconduct—I couldn't stop sizing up every man in the room. *That one with the wife and kids is too short, but his gaze cut to me twice after he sat down, and his voice when he ordered sounded tight for a Saturday morning. The guy who just walked in with his girlfriend is the right height and build, but the features are off.* My eyes lingered on the stranger's face anyway. With a prosthetic nose and some liquid latex, available online for less than twenty bucks, it would be a convincing disguise.

Beyond the covered deck where we sat, wind raced toward us across the river and assailed the clear plastic flaps that enclosed the outdoor seating area. When the man caught me staring and his mouth crimped at the sight of my scar, I couldn't help but go rigid. For half my life I'd looked in the mirror at the skinny white mark that ran from the crook of my mouth all the way to my left ear, yet I often forgot it was there until I saw it reflected in someone else's expression of distaste.

I turned my attention back to my plate to find I'd finished off my breakfast without realizing it. Stress-eating session complete, I surveyed the St. Lawrence River. Nelly's shouldn't have been open this late in the season, but unusually high temps had convinced the owner to push on. Our luck was running out. With a cold front on the way, Nelly's was about to trade those patio flaps for plywood boards until next summer. There was no more pretending it was fall. The lusterless sun and biting breeze added up to one conclusion. Winter was on its way.

I swallowed the dregs of my coffee in one bitter gulp and said, "I'll miss this place."

"Ah." Mac drew the word into a sigh. "I keep forgetting you're still a newbie. You're not used to it yet, but this is how things are around here."

"Temporary?"

"Cyclical. When the tourists pack up, all that's left is us townies. Not enough folk to support the local economy, including, sadly, places like this. But come late spring, everything will open up again. New season, fresh start. You'll see."

I nodded. Spring was months away. Where would I be by then? I honestly didn't know.

"Don't look now," Mac said, "but we've got company."

Every hair on my freckled forearms lifted, and it took an embarrassingly long time for me to realize Mac was grinning over my shoulder. I turned to see yet another man striding across the restaurant, this one carrying two mugs of coffee from the self-serve counter near the entrance.

I hadn't seen much of Tim Wellington in recent weeks, with my suspension and the therapy sessions I was required to complete, plus the fact that I was actively avoiding him. The sight of him trying not to dribble coffee onto the floor made me smile, but the corners of my mouth quickly fell back into place. Tim wasn't alone.

"Sheriff." He shook McIntyre's hand. Then, "Long time, Shane."

The nickname, a reference to an old western movie, was starting to grow on me. I considered grumbling about it anyway, for old times' sake, but my gaze slid to the woman by his side. I didn't recognize her. She was in her early thirties like Tim and had a small face and perfectly round eyes, not unlike those of a creepy Victorian doll. She accepted one of the coffees from Tim and their hands brushed for an instant before she curled hers around the mug. *Eight a.m. on a Saturday morning's a strange time for a date*, I thought. Tim was keeping a respectable distance, but his cheeks were pinker than usual, and there was stubble on his jaw. Not a date, then. Just breakfast.

Well, well. Good for Tim.

As happy as I was to see him, I wasn't happy to see him now. I'd intended to deal with my demons and arrive back at the station the detective I was before Tim, before Carson, and most importantly, before Blake Bram. I didn't want any of my investigators asking me how I was doing, especially not this one. Especially not in front of a doll-faced woman and Mac.

"This is Kelsea," Tim said. The woman rattled off a greeting, commented on the unseasonal weather. *A local, like Tim.* When she was done, Tim turned to me. "Looks like you need a refill. I'll come with."

I eyeballed his fresh pour, fragrant and steaming in his hand, and the woman he was about to abandon. "Right," I said, getting to my feet.

We left Kelsea with Mac and made our way into the anteroom, where we found the coffee bar unoccupied. Tim, who hadn't thought to leave his overfilled mug behind, cursed under his breath as the hot drink sloshed onto his wrist.

"It's good to see you," he said, grabbing a wad of paper napkins as I reached past the thermal carafe of decaf for the good stuff. "That's looking better."

He was talking about my hand. The burns I'd sustained

during my last case, caused by a pot of boiling water and a troubled teenage girl, were healing well. Before I could make a joke about swearing off cooking for life, Tim said, "How are things?"

"Good. Things are good."

He raised his thick eyebrows. "Well? When is it?"

So this was why he wanted to talk. "What, my fitness-for-duty psych eval? That old thing?" I stirred cream into my coffee, licked the straw. "Next week."

"And you feel ready?"

"It's not the SATs."

"No, I know, I just—you've been slacking off long enough, is all. I could really use a hand back at the station."

As the senior investigator for our unit, I head up our team. All the guys answer to me. But the time Tim and I spent on Tern Island investigating the Sinclair family altered the dynamic between us, and with a pang of regret, I realized how much I'd missed our special brand of repartee. "Been busy, have you?" I said. I meant it as a joke—A-Bay in the off-season is as action-packed as a grade school in summer—but Tim's face lit up.

"You have no idea. Last Thursday? We had a drug deal go south in a hurry, this divorced couple fighting over who gets to keep the clients. The hubby goes out to sell from their mutual stash and his wife tips me off, failing to realize she's implicating herself in the process."

"Dear God."

"But wait! There's more. A motorboat got stolen from that RV park on Swan Bay—you know, over by the Price Chopper? Shittiest vessel you've ever seen, and someone felt the need to nab it while the owner was onshore buying groceries. She calls herself Miss Betty, and she calls *me* daily to ask why I haven't found it yet. Says I'm a disgrace to the legal system."

I laughed so hard I had to stabilize my mug. "Did you point out you're not a lawyer?"

"Not yet, but I'll be sure to mention it when she calls again on Monday, and Tuesday, and Wednesday. To be honest, I'd rather take calls from Miss Betty than the paper any day. Looks like Cunningham's finally moved on from the Sinclair story. I was starting to feel like I had a stalker."

"You and me both." When Tim and I went to Troop D headquarters to report on our last case, the *Watertown Daily Times* features writer tailed us all the way to Oneida. The resulting article led to more calls, more requests for a comment, which I promptly ignored.

"Anyway," Tim said, "I'm glad you're here."

"Mac insisted we squeeze in one last breakfast burrito before this place closes for the winter."

"Here in the county, I mean."

The atmosphere around us fizzled. "Where else would I go?" I said it lightly, but Tim's expression was somber.

"You know where. I've been thinking about our talk. That day in Oneida."

I remembered it well. While we'd managed to close the

Sinclair case, it hadn't been the cleanest of solves. I knowingly barreled onto the scene a liability, and did some serious damage. Our witnesses could easily have built a police misconduct case against me; it was a wonder they hadn't. The fact that I'd worked the case on Tern Island while still wrestling with PTSD was irresponsible on every level. Over the last few weeks, the magnitude of what I'd done had settled on me like barbed wire biting into flesh. Little wonder the big guns wanted to know how it all fell apart, and how my conduct turned a missing persons case into an unholy mess.

Behind us, a boisterous group of teenagers walked in and descended on the coffee bar. Tim cupped my elbow with his hand and guided me to a cluster of empty tables at the back of the room.

"You've had some time on your hands these past weeks."

"Should I have knit you a hat?"

By the look on Tim's face, the time for jokes was done. "So you're not looking for him?"

Him. No need to specify who Tim was talking about. "Bram's gone," I said.

"Maybe." Tim's tone was hard to read, and I sensed a trap. "After he got away in New York, Blake Bram had every reason to leave the state. He could have changed his name. He's done it before. Or maybe he went home. Back to Swanton."

"I don't think so."

"You don't think so because that behavior doesn't fit? Or you don't think so because you know otherwise?"

Nearby, the teenagers cackled as they filled their mugs.

Under his jacket and heavy crewneck sweater, I could see Tim's shoulders were tense. "Bram could be gone," he said, "or he could be here. I should have brought the wrath of God down on Cunningham for printing your picture in that story. How did they even know we'd be in Oneida?"

"No idea," I said with a pang of guilt. "The man's thorough, I'll give him that. Look, I don't know where Bram is, or where he's been since I left New York. There haven't been any more murders that match his MO. That doesn't mean he's done."

"But you are, right? With him? Because you still haven't actually answered my question."

The teens split into groups and took two tables, one on either side of where Tim and I stood.

"You should get going," I said. "I don't want to keep you from your friend."

I'd always thought of Tim's eyes as gray, but in the November sunlight that leaked through the restaurant's front windows, they presented as starbursts of blue and white. He blinked at me, nodded, and advanced on the patio door.

As I fell into step behind him, I overheard one of the waitresses talking to the group of teens. "Last bear claws for a while," she said. "Better eat your fill while you have the chance."

Nelly's last weekend. The dead season was coming. And there wasn't a thing I could do to stop it.

TWO

Breakfast settled in my stomach like a hunk of cement, and thanks to my talk with Tim, I was running late. I made the half-hour drive from Clayton to Watertown in twenty-one minutes and jogged down Arcade Street with a stitch in my side.

My destination was well concealed, tucked between a pizzeria and an art studio at the back of a courtyard, but I took a moment to survey the street before ducking under a brick archway. The paint on the walls of the building was flaking, and the pavement under my feet was tacky with grime, but it drew me in all the same. I'd gotten good at cultivating my anger so that when I entered the studio, my limbs were primed like a nocked arrow on a raised bow.

The small foyer that led to the dojo was sparse and clean. There was a check-in counter on one side, a water fountain and a couple of benches on the other. The walls were lined with posters of Bruce Lee and Jet Li, and the lighting was dim in a way that reminded me of a subterranean cave. I winked away the sunspots burned into my retinas, slipped off my shoes, and rummaged through my gym bag for my belt.

"You're late," Sensei said as I yanked the thick, curling strip of fabric free and shoved my bag and shoes against the wall. The belt was brown, just a few stripes away from black, but I didn't deserve it. On my last case I'd been assaulted and had failed to employ even the most basic self-defense techniques. I was out of practice; until recently, I hadn't attended a karate class in more than a year. My new sensei was a burly guy called Sam, and he wasn't going to let me forget the lapse. "Twenty-twenty-twenty," he said before I could finish peeling off my socks. "And ten extra push-ups for being tardy."

I dropped to one knee and wrapped the belt around my waist, cinching it tight over my belly button. "Sorry," I said. "Work stuff."

Sensei Sam raised an eyebrow. "You're back at work?"

"Not yet. Soon."

He stepped aside so I could bow and enter the dojo. Then he closed the door behind me and watched as I paid my penance: jumping jacks, crunches, and push-ups. The extra ten I did twice as fast, and by the time I was finished my arms were buzzing. When I paused to wipe my brow, Sam shook his head.

"Roundhouse kicks, side kicks, back kicks, four times

each way. Two-knuckle punches from horse stance until I say stop."

I wound up into a kick and made my way across the mirrored room. I'd gotten used to Sam's brusque style, had even grown to like it. Sam didn't coddle me. Back in Manhattan, my karate classes had been social affairs, a dozen adults of varying ranks practicing their pinans and katas, blocks and counterstrikes. My time was spent memorizing combinations, but there was just as much palling around. Sometimes we'd go for drinks afterward at the bar around the corner. The private class I was taking in Watertown couldn't have been more different. Here, I was entirely focused on advancement. Readying myself for what was to come.

"Faster," said Sam, as I faced the mirrored wall and punched the air with quick, sharp thrusts. Against the peachy skin of his neck and forearms, Sam's gi was extraordinarily black. I'd asked him once how he came to be a Shaolin Kempo master rather than, say, a professional caber-tosser. He told me he used to watch karate movies with his father before the man died of cancer. His rank, the culmination of a decade and a half of hard work, was a tribute to his dad. I hadn't pried into his personal life since.

"Soon, huh?" he said, assessing my form. "You sound confident you'll be cleared."

I tried not to let him see me grimace. It was the second time today someone had brought up my psych evaluation, and all the meddling was starting to grate on me. Sam knew little about my situation, just enough to understand why I was here. *Abduction. Trauma. Recovery.* That last part was a work in progress, but he'd already given me some solid instruction. In some ways, I was getting more value out of my karate classes than the meetings with my state-appointed therapist.

"Gasko is . . . hard to . . . read," I panted as I punched. "But he seems happy with my progress."

Silently, Sam crossed the room to the padded targets piled in the corner. My eyes followed him in the mirror as he selected a kick shield and retraced his steps. When he got back to where I was, he peered down at me. "What about you?"

I swiveled to face him and shook out my arms. I could feel my pulse in the tips of my fingers, and what remained of my burn throbbed. "It's not like I have an actual problem. The flashbacks are gone. I'm back to normal. As normal as I ever was."

Sam grunted noncommittally and instructed me to kick the pad.

My first few kicks were strong, but the pad didn't budge. "Gasko's acting like I'm going to start hallucinating the second I'm on a new case. According to him, if it's a kidnapping or a homicide, I'm screwed."

"Kick *through* the bag."

I pivoted on the ball of my foot and channeled all the power I could muster into my right leg. Sam didn't even wobble. "Apparently women are at greater risk of PTSD after a traumatic event, so Gasko's convinced I'm still a mess. But I'm not checking those boxes, not anymore. I know the signs."

Sam narrowed his eyes. "Bring that leg back to chamber every time." He arched an auburn eyebrow. "So no problems sleeping, then."

Kick. "I'm sleeping fine."

"No bad memories you can't control."

Kick. "Not a one."

"You don't avoid conversations that force you to think about your trauma. You're not suspicious of strangers. No anxiety or amplified startle response."

"Jesus, Sam." I kicked the bag three times in quick succession, and this time Sam momentarily lost his balance. My thighs were on fire—and what the hell was this? I hadn't confided in him about my attack so he could throw it back in my face. I didn't mention the mandatory therapy sessions so he could mock me. The last thing I needed was another person psychoanalyzing me. When I told him as much, Sam only shrugged.

"I'm asking," he said, "because it's relevant to what we're doing here. It matters, Shana. You can't train your body to be alert without also training your mind."

It happened fast. The padded shield hit the floor with a muffled thud, and Sensei Sam went from a pillar of stone to a cyclone. I had just enough time to plant my feet before he was behind me, his right arm wrapped tight around my neck. The muscles in his forearm strained against my sternum and the soft underside of my chin. His left hand clasped his wrist to lock the hold into place. I could feel his breath in my ear and his sweat on my cheek as he pressed the length of his body against my back.

Instantly, I saw it for what it was: a test. *I know this one,* I thought. *Seize his forearm and twist my head toward his hands to escape the hold. Side kick to the gut, hammer strike to the head, and run.* We'd practiced the drill dozens of times—and yet, my body refused to respond. *Suspicion of strangers. Anxiety. Startle response.* The room was suddenly stifling. Under my ponytailed hair my scalp was aflame and my pulse pounded in my ears, all dense noise and blood-whoosh. I fought against Sam's grip like a squirming child, every action driven not by intent but desperation. Throw it against the wall. Thrash and writhe. See what sticks.

I caught a glimpse of Sam in the mirror, confusion and pity writ large on his face. That's when I gave up. I let my body crumple, and Sam let me go. When I spun away from him and looked down at my hands, they were shaking.

"Shana." He tried to put his hand on my shoulder, an innocent act meant to comfort. It made me flinch. "Look, you're not the first woman to come here. Not the first cop, either. I wish I could say my students did this as a precaution, but for a lot of them, it's about retaliation. Making sure there won't be a next time, because the first time around was real bad. You're stronger than most. But that's not going to help unless you can get this guy out of your head."

I pivoted away from him so he wouldn't see my mouth harden. *You don't understand,* I wanted to say. *I was held hostage by a serial killer who murdered three women and a rookie police officer.* But I knew that Sam was right. I had to get Blake Bram out of my head.

"Hey. You okay?"

"Fine." I held back tears of anger and shame. The room was uncomfortably quiet. I swiped my hands across my clammy forehead and turned to face him once more. Rolled out my wrists and stood tall. "Yes, Sensei," I said. "Let's do it again."

THREE

Some might say I was asking for trouble, driving aimlessly on the outskirts of town where the only sign of life was the tumbledown farmhouses that dotted the flat horizon. Walking alone for hours by the river's edge as the blustery wind buffeted my hair and stung my eyes. It had become a routine I enjoyed, a way to cope with my empty, endless days. I forced my muscles to relax as I studied the way the sky and river blended into a seamless canvas of pearly gray, and occupied my chattering mind by trying to name as many islands as I could.

Some eighteen hundred of them rose up from the water, many crowned with homes that dated back to the nineteenth century, when well-to-do gentlemen from cities like New York and Philadelphia traveled north by train to erect these grand weekend estates. In summer, the St. Lawrence hummed with boat traffic, and flags bearing the heritage of the islands' owners cracked in the breeze. Now, all was abandoned to winter. Aside from my own, there wasn't another beating heart for miles.

It was true that being out there in the open wasn't without its risks. The closest thing I could compare it to was immersion therapy; I feared the exposure yet craved the pain of seeing Bram again, the exquisite relief of finally confronting my most intimate fear. And so, turning into the November wind, I welcomed him with arms spread wide. *Come on, asshole. Here I am.*

It was late afternoon by the time I got back to Mac's, which meant it was dark as a grave. A sickle moon lolled in the sky, and as I walked from the car to the house, flakes of hard, dry snow bobbed in the air around me.

Mac had given me a key the same day she invited me to stay, and we'd joked about the enormity of this next step in our relationship. Now, I was happy to have it. McIntyre was visiting family up near Chippewa Bay tonight and wouldn't be home until late, so when I opened the door, it was me on the receiving end of her Maltipoo's unbridled euphoria. He exploded from his dog bed with a flurry of high-pitched barks and launched himself against my shins. "Hey there, Whiskey," I said as I scooped him up and latched the door behind me. Mac had left the heat on low, and the house was positively frigid. I gave the tiny dog—named not for the spirit, but one of the islands—a cuddle before dropping my bag and heading for the fireplace. Twenty minutes later, I was curled up on the sofa with a bowl of microwave mac and cheese, a glass of Cabernet, and a ball of fur in my lap.

The fire cast the room in a warm, golden glow. If every Saturday night panned out like this one, that would be okay by me. Somewhere in the village, Carson was partying. Right about now, he'd be charming some random girl with his carefully crafted story about a local boy who made it big as a police psychologist in the city before returning to the hometown he loved. He'd bring her back to the apartment we'd shared for two months and twenty-six days, just as if I had never existed. Word around town was that Carson was looking to buy a small island; Sam's sister was an agent at the local realtor's office, and she couldn't keep quiet about the exciting potential deal. So much for Carson saving up until his private practice was established. I was familiar with his real estate fantasy, and could easily imagine him tearing down a historic home to make way for some modern monstrosity. Maybe the girl he'd bed tonight would become the dutiful wife he needed to complete his storybook life. For her sake, I hoped she wouldn't. Carson's thirst for control was a long way from being slaked.

I'd just finished refilling my wineglass when the happy crackle of the fire was joined by the insistent droning of a mobile device. I hadn't looked at my phone in hours—one of the perks of being on leave—so it took me a second to remember I'd stored it in my gym bag. After rifling through my stuff, I found it buried in the folds of my gi pants. Glanced at the caller ID, and answered with a smile.

"Hi, Mom, what's up?" With the phone cradled against my ear, I crouched down to refold my uniform. The military-caliber New York State Police training I'd received at the police academy had stayed with me throughout the years. I no longer rose at 4:30 a.m. and went to bed at 10:00 p.m., but I'd sooner die than toss my laundry onto the floor.

"Shana." My mother exhaled as she said my name, almost as if she'd been holding her breath. "I'm glad I caught you. Do you have a minute to talk?"

There was something odd going on with her voice, a mien of formality typically reserved for when she delivered bad news. I leaned back on my haunches. "Everything okay?"

She must have picked up on my alarm, because when she spoke again her voice had returned to normal. "It's fine, we're all fine, nothing to worry about. You weren't worried, were you? Your father told me not to bother you with this, but—she's *fine*, Wally, for Pete's sake!" In the background I could hear my dad running a one-sided debate. He said something that sounded suspiciously like *The kid has enough on her mind*. As they bickered, I folded the rest of the clothing in my bag, but when I grabbed the T-shirt I'd worn to class, something slipped free and shot across the hardwood. Puzzled, I picked it up and turned it over in my hand. It was a playing card, the Three of Hearts. The reverse was emblazoned with a photograph of Heart Island, where Boldt Castle, built by the island's original owner, rose fairytale-like above the trees. I was sure the cards Mac and I had played with that morning were the standard Bicycle brand, but then, the deck we'd borrowed was from the bistro's game cupboard. This must have been a stray. How it got into my stuff, I had no idea.

"Listen," Mom said. "Something happened today. You know the Missisquoi Wildlife Refuge? That swampland over on Hog Island?"

"Sure." I stuffed the card back in my bag and resumed my position next to Whiskey. Della Merchant knew all there was to know about Swanton and made a point of checking in on the local rumor mill. I guessed her story was headed toward an affair. A roll in the marsh, as it were.

"I've got it on good authority the police found something out there. Human bones," she said.

I swallowed my mouthful of wine so fast my nostrils burned. "Seriously?"

"Now, Shay, before you—"

"Have they been ID'd? What's the cause of death? Were they—"

"Slow down. All I know is the police are investigating and don't have much to go on. They got an anonymous tip a few days ago, which is what led them to the area. Now, you tell me why a person who finds something like this can't be decent enough to leave their name?"

My mind whirred as I tried to imagine this news spreading throughout my hometown. Every mouth, set in a face bewitched by horror and bilious glee, would repeat this gossip tonight and wonder who, why, how. "I suppose they could have stumbled upon the site and been too freaked out to divulge their identity. You say the tip came in a few days ago? That takes us to midweek. Lots of people hike the refuge, even this time of year. It's got all those trails, and you can get there by canoe or kayak, either on the Missisquoi River or Lake Champlain. Could be an out-of-towner got turned around and injured. Those woods are pretty wild. Odds are good there's nothing nefarious going on—but keep me posted," I said, kneading the fur behind Whiskey's ears. The little dog groaned in ecstasy. "I bet Swanton hasn't seen this much excitement since Mickey Bellington painted his house black."

Mom laughed. "Will do. Mary Jo at the salon—she's the one who trims your father—has a brother who's with the police. He hears things at the station. And you know how people talk."

"That I do." When I was a kid, the names on the lips of those gossipmongers often belonged to members of my own family. *Bones.* I took another sip of wine. Truth be told, I was indebted to this news, which would be a welcome distraction tonight. My encounter with Tim and my psych exam still loomed in my mind. If I could push them aside, I might even manage a few solid hours of sleep.

"Before I go," my mother said, "I've been meaning to ask. How are things going with your therapist?"

McIntyre came home just before midnight, not long after I finished the dishes, took Whiskey out to pee, and put myself to bed. When I heard her bolt the door and shuffle off to her room, I pretended to be asleep. There was a disturbance in my bowels that had nothing to do with my pathetic supper or too much red wine, and I wanted to be alone with it. Figure out what it meant.

I used to sleep like a worn-out toddler, sprawled on my stomach and dead to the world. Lately, especially since ditching the pills Carson had prescribed to "nudge me into dreamland," I spend most nights like this one: coffin-stiff and staring at the ceiling. When Mac closed the door to her bedroom, my eyes snapped back open, and I watched the firelight turn specks of dust into spiders and sheetrock seams into canyons. Its trickery was a good metaphor for how I'd felt earlier when I told Mom the same thing I told Sam. *I'm good as new. I'll be reinstated soon.*

The claim wasn't entirely false. Aside from that unnerving moment with my sensei, I felt markedly better. I'd assured Sam the flashbacks I experienced on Tern Island had disappeared once I got back to the mainland, and they had. I'd left the panic attacks behind, too. I still had visions of Bram, but they felt more like grit the wind blew in my eye than a murderous fiend breathing down my neck. Again and again I forced myself into the open, unprotected, and found I could handle it. Take that, Carson Gates.

And yet, I knew I couldn't completely abolish my PTSD without facing the man who caused it. Gil Gasko, my counselor, said I had to accept the fact that my abductor was still free and learn not to live in fear. Fat chance. Blake Bram was the reason I'd been so detached during my game of Bullshit with Mac, my karate class with Sam, and everything in between. Bram had held me captive in a basement in New

York's East Village for eight days before shooting the cop who'd stumbled onto his chamber of horrors and seized his chance to escape. He may have left me behind, but he didn't let me go.

For months I'd turned this puzzle over in my head, trying to decode Bram's purpose. His three other victims were killed quickly, within days of their abduction, while he chose to keep me alive. He let me walk free—me, a police officer trained in suspect identification. A threat.

I'd gone back to Swanton again and again hoping to spot him. He was too clever to be flushed out so easily, but my instincts told me Bram was watching. I had no idea when he'd turn up again, or where, or what he'd look like when he did, but I had every intention of putting this fugitive behind bars. I'd find a way to lock him up. My need to contain him was innate. Sure, we shared the same hometown, but there was a deeper connection, one nobody was aware of but us.

And that's what scared me most of all.

FOUR

The morning dawned cloudy and cold. During the night the snow flurries had turned to drizzle, and the roads were black and shiny as I made the drive from Watertown back to A-Bay. With Thanksgiving approaching, a town employee was already hanging wreaths on the James Street lampposts. I considered stopping to inhale their piney scent. Swept my gaze over the street like a searchlight instead. With a flutter in my chest, I scanned every parked car and shop window. My life had become one long exercise in counter-surveillance. And that required copious amounts of coffee.

Over the three weeks I'd been seeing Gil Gasko, we'd been to every coffee shop in town. He didn't have an office like Carson used to; based in Syracuse, Gil went where the Employee Assistance Program said he was needed, and at the moment, he was needed at the Bean-In. Seated at a table for two, he blew steam off a cup of black tea while I ordered my own brew and joined him.

"Chilly out," Gil said. The way he eyed my insubstantial canvas jacket reminded me of Dad. *Dress for the weather, darling*, my father would trill, laying on his British accent extra-thick. Gil was younger than my dad by a decade, with dark hair, a wiry beard, and a pronounced widow's peak. Beneath his fleece and jacket, his body was shaped like a battering ram, and his fingers shared multiple qualities with hot dog rolls, but his gnome-like appearance belied a sweet and soothing disposition. The man oozed serenity. I'd come to think of this as a prerequisite for the job.

This was our routine, a few minutes of small talk before tackling the ugly stuff for which he'd come. "Got any plans for Thanksgiving?" Gil asked.

The question made me realize I didn't. Last year, I'd spent the holiday with Carson's family in Sackets Harbor, west of Watertown. We'd only been dating two months by then, but he insisted I get to know his parents. Rather than getting to know *me*, they'd spent all day spewing stories about their remarkable son.

As I considered Gil's question, I retrieved a hair tie from my pocket and pulled my unruly mop into a ponytail. A jolt of pain shot down both arms, the aftereffects of karate. "Guess I'll visit my folks," I said.

"In Swanton."

"Yeah."

Gil nodded. "It's been a while, right? Last time we talked you said you hadn't seen them in, what, three weeks?"

"Not since my suspension."

"Why is that?"

And we're back to business. Gil's job was to get me thinking about my feelings, my behavior, and how they were connected. His opinion of my condition mattered, because he'd be sharing his notes with my superiors prior to my psych evaluation, the evaluation I needed to pass in order to resume my role as BCI senior investigator. I had to show Gil I was the strong, stable detective the New York State Police expected me to be, so I'd done everything he'd asked, from the cliché (make a list of my fears) to the absurd (download a meditation app and listen to a guru murmur affirmations in my ear). I'd talked more over the last twenty-one days than I normally would in months, answering loaded questions like *Are you able to identify your core stressors?* and *Are you prepared to apply positive self-talk in your daily life?* I could only hope he liked what he heard.

"Why haven't I gone back to Swanton?" I asked, confirming his question. After so many previous trips, it was a valid one. "My parents know what happened on Tern. That was my first case up here, and it wasn't exactly smooth sailing. Couple that with my breakup and the situation in New York last year and . . . well, they're worried about me."

Gil used a napkin to dab tea from his mustache. "Sounds like the perfect time to visit. Bond a little. Talk it out."

"You'd think so," I said, "but sometimes seeing me isn't good for them."

"Why's that?"

I opened my mouth, then closed it again. Gil hadn't asked about the origins of my scar. As a rule I didn't tell that story, and I didn't plan to share it now. Instead, I lifted my hand. "They don't need a visual reminder of how dangerous my job can be," I said, showing Gil what remained of my burn. "This kind of work—it's my life. I'm a thirty-two-year-old woman who's wanted this since I was five. I'm not about to gin up a whole new career now. It'll be easier for them to accept that after my hand heals. Easier to forget the drawbacks of the job."

Gil set down his cup and gave me a look. "When you're recovering from acute psychological stress, having a good support system is crucial."

"It's not that they don't support me," I said. "But I'm their only daughter, and the baby of the family. I'm sure they'd prefer I had a nice, safe job in advertising like my brother, or did administrative work like half my old class-mates from high school. That's not me, though. My family gets that."

"That's good. And I know at least one other person who's supportive of your career."

I frowned. "You do?"

"Yes. Tim Wellington."

I hadn't mentioned bumping into Tim the previous morning. In fact, I rarely brought him up at all. "You talked to Tim?" I said.

"A few days ago. Lieutenant Henderson filled me in on Tim's involvement with the case, so I thought it might be good to touch base with him. I've gotta say, Shana, he's a fan."

"Of what?"

"Of *you*. He respects you as an investigator, and he values the contributions you've made to the troop since your arrival. He made that very clear."

Tim talked to Gasko and didn't tell me? We'd been alone at Nelly's, had even discussed the counseling I was receiving. Why wouldn't Tim mention he got a call from Gil?

"If it were up to Tim, you'd be reinstated already. There's just one thing bothering him." Gil twirled his stir stick between his stumpy fingers. "He wanted me to ask you about the connection between Blake Bram and your hometown."

Son of a bitch. The tips of my ears burned with anger. I choose not to divulge something personal, and Tim tries to force it out of me? It was a jerk move, but a smart one. Tim figured my counselor stood the best chance of bringing me to my senses. He didn't believe I was done with Bram, and he wasn't going to take my evasion lying down.

I shouldn't have expected anything less from a fellow investigator. On Tern Island I'd listened to the Sinclairs dismiss the local police force as blundering small-town cops, and watched as Tim purposefully lived up to their expectations. But it took skill to fool witnesses and suspects into seeing him as affable and benign. Initially, Tim hadn't struck me as the silent-but-deadly type, but I knew better now. He specialized in befriending witnesses and suspects, but wouldn't hesitate to use that against them for the sake of a case. Tim was a lot sharper than people gave him credit for.

"It's like this," I told Gil. "Based on data acquired through the dating app Bram used to attract his victims, and patterns in the similarities between witness accounts, my former colleagues with the NYPD believe Bram spent time in Swanton, same as me. Whether he was raised in the area or only lived there for a while, they don't know." *Don't, and won't.* Back in New York, the detectives in the Seventh Precinct had moved on from Blake Bram. They still hoped to apprehend him, but it had been a year and a half since the first murder, and fourteen months since my abduction. Without anything new to go on, the case was growing cold. "Does it bother me that Bram has history there? Of course it does. Swanton's my hometown, so I guess I see it as a violation. That's probably why Tim thinks I'm obsessed with Bram. Finding him, I mean."

Gil gave me a long, calculating look. "I'm impressed with the level of self-awareness I'm seeing from you, Shana," he said. "But are you? Obsessed?"

I turned my head toward the window. Across the street, a man exited his car and turned on his heel to look straight at me. *It's not him*, I chanted in my head as he crossed the street while holding my gaze, but I didn't look away until he disappeared into the restaurant next door. "I'd like to see him caught," I told Gil. "He's a violent, dangerous criminal. But it's not like I'm hunting him."

That released some of the tautness from my counselor's face. *Good*, I thought, but good wasn't what I felt. I hadn't lied to Tim or Gil, but I hadn't been wholly truthful, either.

"So," he said. "Thursday's the day."

Less than a week to go. "Yup. I'll be there."

Gil expressed his satisfaction with my progress once more before clearing our empty mugs. Outside, after we parted ways, I sank my hands into my pockets and pretended to search for my keys while the rain soaked my back. Again I scanned the street for signs that something was off. Short of sniffing the air for pheromones and tuning into the low-frequency vibrations traded between predator and prey, I was doing everything I could to identify threats. When I was satisfied that I was safe, I let my thoughts drift to Tim. He knew me better than I'd realized. But he didn't know everything.

It was me who tipped off the *Watertown Daily Times* about our appointment at headquarters. The story of Jasper Sinclair and his family was all over the news, and Jared Cunningham was hungry for new developments. A meeting with my supervisor was the perfect way to generate public exposure that would be hard to miss. *Tell your photographer to be stealthy*, I had said, knowing Tim would be by my side. *Make sure you get a clear shot of me, and use my full name.* I'd made it easy for the reporter to write a big feature for the paper, and slap my face above the fold.

No, boys, I thought as I walked to my car. *I'm not hunting Bram.*

Bram is hunting me.

FIVE

t's got a great view. See?"

The property manager leaned past me toward the window, and when she flipped her braid—gray and thin as a rat's tail—over her shoulder, it whacked me in the face. I forced myself to breathe through my mouth. The stench of stale cigarettes on the woman's clothes was unrelenting. "Chaumont Bay?" I said. "I don't see it."

She laughed, her voice like wet gravel. "You won't get a water view for what you're paying. But there are trees—and two churches, just a stone's throw from here. Location is everything, they say."

My gaze traveled over the living room. The vintage doorknobs were covered in layers of chipping paint, and there were so many stains on the wall-to-wall carpeting it looked like leopard print. *Damn*, I thought. It wasn't the woman who smelled, but the apartment itself.

"It's nine-fifty a month plus utilities." She studied me through unblinking eyes, attempting to assess whether I could afford her price. I must have passed the test, because at last she shrugged and said, "If you want it, you better be quick."

It was the fourth apartment I'd seen today, each more abysmal than the last and all at least forty minutes from work. Rentals in A-Bay, near the State Police station, were rare. This, too, was on account of the season. When I called McIntyre to get her opinion on the slim pickings in Evans Mills, Black River, La Fargeville, she assured me there'd be more on the market come spring. All I could think was too little, too late.

Rooming with Mac felt surprisingly natural, and I believed her when she said she'd love for me to stay, but at our age the arrangement couldn't be anything but temporary. There would come a day when the sheriff—a perpetual bachelorette married to her job, but smart and attractive— might realize the new guy in the County Clerk's office was worth a second look. As for me, I might meet someone at the Riverboat Pub and decide to bring him home. It could happen. Post-Carson, the idea of investing any amount of time in a romantic relationship was unthinkable, but seeing Tim with Kelsea made me realize I'd want that again someday. The morning-after breakfast with tousled hair and awkward glances. The lust that preceded it. The trust. For all of that, I'd need a place of my own.

Feeling drained and defeated, I thanked the property

manager and left in a hurry. Outside it was getting colder by the minute, and icy water seeped into my boots as I crossed the street to the used SUV I bought after the split. After locking the doors, I took out my phone. The only good thing about being on leave was the ample free time. I'd been using it to mend some fences.

There's often a lot of self-blame associated with PTSD, and this was definitely true for me. I was freighted with guilt, both over my abduction and my inability to detain Bram when I'd had the chance. My Gil-guided journey to self-awareness had brought up other sources of residual remorse as well, and if I hoped to recover, I figured I should address them. With that in mind, I'd logged onto my long-dormant Facebook account and reconnected with Suzuka Weppler.

I met my former best friend through a sixth-grade activity I'd been roped into by my art teacher. Suze was new to the school, having moved up from D.C., so for her, the pressure to participate came from her parents. For three weekends and a half dozen after-school sessions, Suze and I worked with a few other students painting colorful murals on the hallway walls of Swanton's combined middle and high school. Suze's outlook on the project was similar to mine—anything to get out of team sports—and it didn't take long for us to gel. Far as I know, our mural of Lake Champlain's legendary sea monster is still right where we left it.

Our friendship wasn't as enduring, and I thought of our time together with a mixture of fondness and shame. Suze was deep into her wild phase before the end of eighth grade, barely fourteen when she started ditching school and shoplifting in the village. That was also the year she began dabbling in soft drugs. Many a night I'd followed her into the woods to a bonfire party, the clearing filled with salvaged furniture, old mattresses, and—as the night wore on—empty beer cans. Led Zeppelin and Jamiroquai blasted on a portable CD boom box, kids chanted along with the Beastie Boys and Fatboy Slim, bits of ash spiraled up into the stripes of navy sky between the trees, and all the while Suze tried to indoctrinate me into her wayward ways.

I did some things I'm not proud of at those parties, while Suze sat on some randy boy's lap and cheered me on. Overall, I managed to keep my head, but the same couldn't be said of my friend. By freshman year of high school, the rumors circulating the cafeteria were cutting: *Suze was in a threesome. Suze once did a guy in his thirties. Suze can get you hash, mushrooms, whatever you want.* In our small community people often got restless, and drugs were a common distraction, but Suze's behavior grew increasingly dangerous. I was afraid she'd drag me down with her. Scared of getting hurt. After graduation, when I left for Albany and a career in law enforcement, Suze and the vestiges of our friendship stayed behind.

Over the years, my parents had briefed me on her life—her marriage, the birth of her daughter, the death of her dad. That news was a gut-punch. Mike Weppler was the best: funny and understanding even when his daughter went off the rails. He started teaching at the high school around the time my father took a job with the Board of Ed. Even the most jaded of students had liked Mr. Weppler. I'd sent a card, of course, but that was the extent of our contact. After fifteen years pretty much incommunicado, I'd reached out to my old friend with no illusions that she'd write back. Now, my mobile showed a new message waiting.

Suze's note was equal parts emojis and exclamation points. If she was upset that I hadn't approached her sooner, she didn't show it. Of course, the neglect went both ways. She gave me a rundown of her life before turning the mic over to me. I drew the map of my own recent past in cursory strokes: college, police academy, NYPD, Bureau of Criminal Investigation in Upstate New York. I opted not to mention the abduction and failed fiancé, though they'd probably interest her most of all.

As I typed my reply, I had the overwhelming sense that I was being watched. Pedestrians jogged along the sidewalk, shoulders shrugged against the rain. There were a half dozen men within a few yards of my car, their faces concealed by umbrellas and scarves. None gave me so much as a once-over.

I dropped my eyes to the screen.

It wasn't the knowledge Bram could be nearby that had me spooked this time, but what reconnecting with Suze was going to do to me. My past was treacherous, a quagmire of emotional states; step into it, and I risked sinking up to my neck. With the exception of my parents, I'd deliberately avoided all citizens of Swanton. The idea of conversing with a local outside my immediate family made my palms sweat. Everyone in town knew our history, and like the flashbacks I'd experienced about the East Village, talk of my mother's relatives sent me into a panic. If someone brought up the Skiltons—my aunt, uncle, or cousins—I wasn't sure I could control my nervous system. I'd probably hurl on their shoes.

Suze didn't mention my extended family in her Facebook message, and if I could keep our conversations surface-level, I might be okay. I hit send on a comparably cheerful response, stuck my phone back in my bag, and turned my thoughts toward lunch.

No sooner had I started the car than the ringer sounded on my phone. Mom's call the previous night had come as a surprise; seeing her name on the display again now left me dumbfounded. I'd been sitting in the cold SUV for fifteen minutes—what I wouldn't give for Gil's warm layers now—so while I loathed an idling engine, I turned it on and cranked the heat as I answered.

"We have you on speaker," my mother said. "Can you hear us?"

"Hi, love." My father's voice was strangely flat.

"Dad? You're not at work?"

"Ah," he said. "The school board insisted I take some personal days."

"Personal days?" I repeated, bewildered. "What for? What's going on? You guys are scaring me."

There was a beat of silence before Mom spoke. "I'm not

sure how to tell you this, hon. They've got it wrong, obviously. After all these years . . . and he *left*! It can't be him."

"*Della*," Dad said with uncharacteristic anger. I heard him sigh, a sound rife with frustration and regret. "The bones they found," he said. "That body. It's Brett."

The fans on my dashboard wrapped me in a dry heat, but I found I was shivering, my body tense and twitchy. I shut off the engine, plunging the car into silence. "What?"

"Brett," said my father. "He's . . . well, he's dead, darling. It seems he has been for a long time, they think about twenty years. Your aunt got the call this morning. She told your mum."

"But they're wrong," said Mom matter-of-factly. "The timing's all wrong."

"I don't understand." Uncle Brett, married to my mother's sister, was a ghost long before today. As a kid I rarely saw him, though his name came up a lot, usually in the context of behavior my parents tried and failed to sanitize for the sake of my brother and me. *Brett ran into some trouble with a fellow at work. Brett was misbehaving at the Franklin county fair.* Not long after he and Aunt Fee split up, Brett left Swanton and never returned. Dad had said his remains could be twenty years old. That took us to the late nineties. I would have been barely thirteen.

"They'll be doing some DNA testing to confirm it," he said, "but they found a pocketknife nearby. It was terribly rusted, but engraved with his first name. Felicia says she gave that knife to Brett on his twenty-fifth birthday, and that he never went anywhere without it. It could be that someone stole it, but since Brett's been gone as long as he has, and nobody's heard from him in years, well. There's a good chance it's him."

I shook my head and tried to make sense of what I was hearing. "But Mom's right," I said. "Brett left Swanton in the nineties. He moved away. Didn't he move away?"

"Well, that's a bit tricky."

"There's nothing tricky about it. He *did* move away," said Mom. "Snuck off like a thief in the night and abandoned his family for Philadelphia. You remember—Brett quit his job, told Felicia he was leaving, and was gone within forty-eight hours. He said he'd send money when he could, though of course he never did. So you see, Brett couldn't have died twenty years ago. He was in Pennsylvania."

"Here's the trouble with that," said Dad. "The police did some digging, and apparently when Brett buggered off, he positively vanished. They found no current ID, no tax returns. I don't believe your aunt's heard a peep from him since."

"So the last time you actually saw Brett was . . ."

"1998," said Dad.

"Late June," added Mom.

I tapped my finger against my forehead. No doubt someone was performing an autopsy on what was left of Brett's body, but if forensics had already called the crime two decades old, they must have been confident in their preliminary analysis. It was all so strange. "How did he die?" I asked. "Do they know?"

"That's just it," said my dad, and when he paused I heard Mom's breath catch in her throat. "They think he was murdered, love."

Hearing my father blurt that word in his chipper English accent hit me like a high-voltage jolt. I'd been sitting upright for the duration of the call, my spine hard as a crowbar, and when I leaned back against the driver's seat, my back spasmed painfully. I felt like I'd woken up to discover a nightmare I was desperate to escape was real. I thought of the message I'd sent to Suze minutes ago, my petty worry she'd bring up my family. Word of Brett Skilton's murder was about to descend on Swanton like a cold front, inexorable in its force. Before long we'd all be in the local news, rolling off a two-decade hiatus with a tale more sordid and sensational than ever before. A tectonic shift was taking place in our family, separating the *then* from the *now*.

A truck rumbled down the street and splashed my car with slop. The brown water on my windshield roused me from my trance. "Does Doug know?"

"We just told him," Dad said. "He insists on coming, but he can't get here for a couple of days."

So my brother was going to Swanton to see my folks through this tragedy. He lived just forty minutes away, and he was their eldest child, but this bulletin didn't sit right with me. I was the one who dealt in death and delinquents.

If anyone was going to hold their hands through this awful experience, shouldn't it be me?

"There's absolutely no need for Doug to come," said Mom. "If the police have questions, we can handle them ourselves."

Her veiled uneasiness only served to strengthen my resolve. I couldn't leave my parents to deal with a brutal discovery like this while I sat at Mac's pretending everything was fine.

I glanced at my watch and calculated the time it would take to pick up my overnight bag and shoot Mac a text letting her know about my plans.

"I'll be there in three hours," I said as I restarted the engine. "What's for dinner?"

SIX

A potluck gathering on the shores of Lake Champlain, where Felicia screamed at Brett across the picnic table.

Brett missing for days at a time while my aunt slammed cupboard doors in the kitchen.

Crissy flipping him the bird when he decided to play the responsible father and impose a curfew.

These visions plagued me as I made the familiar drive north along the St. Lawrence River, then east toward Swanton, Vermont.

When I thought about my uncle, it was mainly with indifference. Before he and Felicia separated, he sometimes brought us treats at odd hours, doling out warm cherry Cokes to the kids while he cracked open a beer from his ice-cold six-pack. He was also the dad who on more than one occasion had slept fully clothed on the porch swing, and who never missed a chance to chat up Crissy's friends. Wading through my memories of him was a slog, but I did recall snatches of the summer of 1998. Had I known it would lead to murder, I'd have paid more attention.

Despite my apathetic feelings toward Uncle Brett, the news of his demise made me feel ill. My cousins thought he'd abandoned them, and that was bad enough; the idea that Brett could have been in Swanton all along was torture. Decomposition is never pretty, but a death in the woods meant Brett's body had been picked apart by scavengers and insects. Exposed to the elements, his flesh would have burst open to purge its fluids in its haste to devolve into cartilage and bone. Nobody deserved to live with an image of their dad like that.

As I drove, sipping my afternoon coffee from a to-go cup, I evaluated what I knew so far. If the local forensic analyst was right about the age of the bones, Brett must have been killed shortly after he announced he was leaving Swanton. My mother's confusion about the timeline was understandable. We'd all believed Brett left of his own volition, no longer willing or able to deal with his estranged wife. The realization that he'd been in town all along, rotting in the Missisquoi Refuge just a few miles from our house, was incomprehensible.

The big question, of course, was who put him there.

Some towns announce themselves with fanfare, a gilded WELCOME sign boasting the date they were established. Sometimes there's even a slogan—gateway to this, home of the that. Swanton trickled into view like a rivulet of rainwater after a storm. A hodgepodge of bungalows and farm-houses came first, some with three different types of siding, others showing century-old colors through fissures of peeling paint. Weeks past Halloween, ghosts fashioned from white sheeting still hung on bare bushes, yet two houses already paraded inflatable Santas, one dressed in camo, the other riding a Harley. The farm equipment retailer, the maple candy store, the coin wash and pizza parlor behind dunes of grass gone brown . . . they were all right where I left them. This was no spit-and-polish New England village leaking charm from every orifice, but it was mine.

I rolled into the driveway of my childhood home when the sun hung low in the pale orange sky. The place was a manor by Swanton standards, a fifties-era colonial on a double lot. There was a Thanksgiving wreath strapped to the door, retrieved from a basement storage box where I knew it resided with its Christmas, Valentine's Day, Easter, and Halloween counterparts. Dad's car, freshly washed, sparkled in the asphalt driveway, which the hose had patterned in wavy fingers of ice.

They'd been busy, my parents. The innate need to distract themselves from the startling news of Brett's death was apparent in the meal they cooked as well. I'd given them little notice about my decision to visit, but they'd prepared a big Sunday dinner of lasagna in a creamy white sauce with Dad's famous Arctic roll, the sponge cake homemade, for dessert. When I looked at my parents and the feast they'd made so lovingly spread out before us, I felt my heart swell.

That joyful feeling was fleeting.

I inherited my father's face, triangular in shape with full cheeks and a nose as perky as a comic strip character's. Mom's looks had always struck me as more feminine than my own, but now the high cheekbones and delicate lips I'd coveted gave her a skeletal appearance that troubled me to my core. Dad didn't seem to be faring much better. Overall, his head—huge for his body and covered in bushy hair—looked whiter than usual. At some point he'd put on a paint-stained shirt to wash the car, and he hadn't bothered to change for dinner. There was a beleaguered ennui to their collective mood that went beyond standard-issue sadness.

"This is good, Mom," I said, reaching for a second helping. It was Carson who'd done the food prep in our relationship, and prior to that I'd lived on station pastries and white-bread PB&Js. My mother's home-cooked meals were the stuff of my dreams.

She smiled at me as I ate. "How's Tim?"

"He's fine. I bumped into him yesterday, actually." Though they had yet to meet him in person, my parents loved Tim. They conflated him with my survival on Tern Island, which was fine by me because that drew their attention away from the debacle with Carson. As I'd alluded to Gil, my parents weren't fans of my job. While they supported my decision to leave my fiancé, especially after learning how he'd manipulated my state of weakness, I knew they'd been hoping he could talk me out of my senior investigator gig in A-Bay.

Who could blame them? Within months of arriving in Up-state New York I'd been isolated on an island with a killer, had been attacked by a murder suspect, and had nearly drowned. Mom liked to joke she had to visit the hair salon weekly, so persistent was the gray I caused.

"How nice," she said now. "Tell him we say hello."

"Good Lord," said Dad. "When are we going to address the elephant in the room?"

I hadn't wanted to bring it up until I'd gotten my bearings and inhaled some calories to fuel my brain, but my parents' plates were already empty. It was time. I gave my mother a side-long glance. Slowly, she rose to retrieve something from the countertop. The latest edition of the *St. Albans Messenger*.

"Front page," she said, her expression grim. "Sounds like the police are getting nowhere fast." By which she meant *We're in this for the long haul, whether we like it or not.* She was eye-ing the *Messenger* as if it might attack, so I pushed the rest of my dinner aside and spread the newspaper on the table. There it was, a smiling picture of Brett under a blaring headline.

REMAINS OF LOCAL MAN FOUND IN MISSISQUOI REFUGE, POLICE CALL DEATH SUSPICIOUS

There was some new information, too. I felt a deeper kind of hunger as I pored over the inky words.

According to the article, which was leaner than I would

have liked, the Vermont State Police had received an anonymous call from a man who pointed them to the woods off VT-78, known in town as River Street. The body was found in the heart of the wildlife refuge. Thanks to the discovery of personal belongings at the scene, the local authorities managed to identify the victim in a matter of days. As for the cause of death, they must have had indisputable evidence related to how Brett Skilton was killed, because they had no qualms about calling his death a homicide. Anyone with information pertaining to the body, or about the case in general, was being directed to a police hotline. I didn't look up until I'd read the story twice, paying particular attention to the location of the crime scene.

"God," I said at last. "This is so surreal."

"It's terrible," said Mom. "But out of all the people I've ever known, I can't say I'm surprised this happened to Brett. He was always trouble. I told Felicia that from the get-go. Didn't I tell her, Wally?"

"It was thirty-some years ago," Dad said with a shrug. "But that does sound like something you'd say."

"My sister didn't need a man-child," Mom went on. "What she needed was help, and she got none of that from him. Instead, he left her with two kids she couldn't raise alone in her condition. She should never have married him. I shouldn't have let her."

The look my father and I exchanged was furtive and lightning quick. Mom's attitude about Brett's demise wasn't particularly strange. Family members who suffer a loss to homicide often experience misplaced anger, some even going so far as to blame the victim for the crime. It's hard when someone abandons you, regardless of who's at fault.

But her response to Brett's homicide felt different. Based on the loaded look in Dad's eyes, my mother was experiencing a classic case of self-reproach. Brett's death was a reminder of her sister's failed union. A marriage for which Mom appeared to feel responsible.

"They got married right after you did," I said. "Isn't that right?"

She nodded. "We were both in our twenties, but Fee seemed so young to me. She looked like a girl playing house when she walked down the aisle."

I'd seen Felicia and Brett's wedding picture, and now my brain dragged the image to the forefront of my mind. They'd looked like gussied-up teenagers to me, too.

"He was your typical charming rogue," said Mom. "I didn't approve, not in the least. I should have objected more than I did."

"Why didn't you?" I asked.

Her sigh was resigned, and a little shamefaced. "Frankly, I couldn't wait to leave home. Watching out for Fee was draining, and I'd been doing it ever since she was little."

This was a story I knew well. Felicia was a worrier, only hers weren't the niggling doubts the rest of us have learned to brush off but enormous fears that opened their gaping maws to swallow her whole. My grandparents tried everything from cognitive behavioral therapy to biofeedback, yoga, and deep breathing to get her emotions under control. Nothing worked.

"I thought it would be good for her, being on her own without me tending to her every need. I hoped it would desensitize her, you know? The year after your father and I were married, she was as bad as ever. Then she met Brett."

"I liked him, at first." Dad gave an unapologetic shrug. "Very sociable fellow. I thought he provided a nice counterbalance to Felicia's mercurial moods. Always good for a laugh, he was."

"That's what Fee liked about him, too," Mom said with a small frown. "He was always so positive, and he honestly thought he could singlehandedly conquer her disorder. I don't doubt that his intentions were good. Trouble was, he didn't follow through. Fee got pregnant with Crissy so quickly, and her condition got worse. Brett couldn't handle it. The more needy she got, the more disconnected he became. It was clear he missed the simple bachelor life he'd left behind. The situation didn't improve as Crissy got older. You know what that child was like."

Dad chuckled. "Whorls of golden hair and petulance to spare. Got that from her father, she did."

"As if Fee didn't have enough to contend with," Mom said.

"How's she doing?" I asked. "I know Felicia hadn't seen Brett in a long time, but this has to come as a shock."

My parents exchanged a look. "She's hanging in," said my mother. "A few years ago something like this would have crushed her, but she's healthier now, more in control. I left a message for Crissy yesterday. She hasn't returned my call."

"Brett's been out of their lives a long time, but they did love him once," said Dad.

As I reached for the newspaper and refolded it, watching the seam cut through the center of Brett's beaming face, I absorbed my parents' demeanor all over again. They looked depleted, utterly drained of life. Brett had his shortcomings, but he'd been a lot of things to a lot of people, including a brother-in-law to my mom and dad. We'd lost a member of the family in the most godless of ways. The whole town was talking about it. Doing the same thing now wasn't doing us any favors.

"Hey," I said. "The new Agatha Christie remake just came out. I bet it's playing in St. Albans."

Dad perked up. "I've been dying to see that. Smashing cast."

"Brett loved the movies." The way Mom cast a disapproving glance around the kitchen, I could almost picture Brett with his crooked smile and cold beer, trying to win my mother over with a dirty joke.

"Come on," I said. "My treat."

She closed her eyes. When she opened them, she said, "One condition. I want my own popcorn."

I smiled. "Done and done. We'll go to the movies," I said.

If only the solutions to all our family problems were as simple.

SEVEN

*H*ome. It should have wrapped around me like a hot towel from the dryer. Why couldn't I shake the feeling that the place was full of ghosts? Everywhere I looked I saw Brett's face, his fine, white-blond hair falling into pale Nordic eyes. It was hard to believe the chipper, crowing party boy had been reduced to dust.

By the time the anemic winter morning sunlight began to stream through my bedroom window, I was jittery and tense. I showered quickly, threw on some old jeans and a sweater, and pulled my hair into a dripping wet knob at the base of my neck. There was no one in the kitchen when I fixed my morning coffee, but my mother had left a note: she and Dad were running errands in St. Albans before dropping into a yoga class. I was glad they were trying to keep active. The movie had been a welcome diversion for all of us.

Distraction wasn't in the cards for me today.

The drive to Maquam Bay was shorter than I'd hoped, even with the stop I made along the way. I passed a school bus full of leering little faces as I turned onto Crissy's street. I passed Felicia's house, too. I'd made a point of distancing myself from the Skilton family, and Crissy had tried to do the same, but even though she didn't have much contact with her mother now, they lived steps from each other on the very same street.

Crissy's home was a converted trailer that overlooked the water. To the west, I could just make out North Hero State Park. To the north, my cousin had an unobstructed view of the outskirts of the wildlife refuge where Brett's body had turned from flesh, to jelly, to bone. If you took a boat across the water, like the one tied up to her dock, it would be a short trip to where the police found her father.

I hadn't called ahead, wasn't even sure I was going to make this trip until I found myself turning out of my parents' driveway. I could have gone to Felicia, and would have to, eventually. The need to talk to Brett's family was strong. My fear of what awaited me at my aunt's house was stronger.

When Crissy found me on her front steps, her face opened up in surprise. "Hey, cuz," she said. "Slumming?"

I managed a smile. "Hardly. This is some location." I gestured at the lake, visible through the windows behind her. "You made a great choice with this place. Got a sec?"

Crissy bit her lower lip and said, "I'm getting ready for work."

"I was hoping we could talk. Just for a minute."

Her eyes hardened as she looked me over, spending a smidge too long on my scar. "Okay," she said dispassionately, and I was in.

Crissy was the type of girl who'd always longed to become an adult. I'd heard Felicia warn her to be careful, but boys were Crissy's paper dolls, and she took pleasure in bending them to her whims. Crissy was cool, commanding, and pretty. I had a vague recollection of her confessing her goal in life was to be a model girlfriend, the kind that made men drool and brag to their friends. She would have been about twelve.

The woman who stood before me now was almost unrecognizable. Her pert nose and sharply arched eyebrows reigned eternal, but paired with pasty skin and a bouffant blond hairstyle, they made me think of Malibu Barbie on a bender. The weight she'd gained over the years had somehow settled in her chest, which verged on the obscene. She was dressed in a white T-shirt with a deep V-neck and donut-patterned pajama pants, and her living-room-slash-kitchen smelled of cheap perfume and instant coffee. Crissy held a mug but didn't offer one to me. Didn't offer me a seat, either.

"How are you?" Cold water from my wet hair trickled down my neck as I lingered by the door. "And the boys, they must be—what—seven and nine now?"

"Eight and ten."

"Time flies." Behind my cousin, I could see the makings of a school lunch on the kitchen counter. "I brought them something. Must have just missed them, huh?" I handed her the bag in my hand, heavy with the weight of two boxes of maple sugar candy. She dropped it on the coffee table without a second glance.

"Crissy," I said, "I'm so sorry about your dad."

There was no embrace between us. She didn't clasp my hands, and I didn't tip my forehead to meet hers. All Crissy did was open her mouth enough so I could see her tongue stud glinting silver, and rearrange her lips into a wry smirk. That mouth was what I'd dreaded most about seeing my cousin, the way it pitched upward on one side and made her look so sanctimonious. Brett had that same smile.

She walked to the couch and plopped down with a sigh. Her home was a mishmash of cheap furniture and frayed rugs, but the frames that held her boys' school photos looked new, maybe even pricey. There were no pictures of their father, I noticed, nor of her brother or Aunt Fee.

"This must be exciting for you," Crissy said. "A murder, right here in Swanton."

"Exciting?" I repeated, taken aback.

"Isn't that why you're here? You haven't bothered to visit in years, even though I know you come around to see Wally and Della, but you smell blood and you're back, circling my house like a fucking hyena."

Crissy and I were never close. It wasn't the age difference, though we were three years apart, but that we had little in common. I'd always been a tomboy, so I refused to let her do my makeup or show me how to shave my legs. If she paid attention to me at all, it was because she needed a scapegoat for her crimes. When we were young, she'd steal sugary cereal—our Saturday morning treat—from my parents' pantry and blame it on me. Later on, she began using sleepovers at my house as an opportunity to sneak out and meet friends.

If I'm being honest, Crissy had always made me a little nervous. At fifteen, she was missing for two full days before a search party, which included my father, found her in the woods on the outskirts of town. The story became a cautionary tale local parents recounted to their little ones at night. Crissy was wild and rebellious, with no regard for her health or well-being. Some people said she ran away from home; others insisted she'd been abducted. I always assumed she'd gone on an epic drinking binge, and if my parents knew otherwise, they weren't telling.

"That's fair," I said, though it wasn't. *A fucking hyena? Please.* I slipped out of my winter boots and crossed the room to sit down. She tucked her legs under her, and I saw I'd misconstrued the pattern on her pants. It wasn't donuts but pink and yellow diamond rings.

"So, what," she said, "you think the local cops can't hold a candle to a big-shot detective? They're not good enough, just like Swanton wasn't good enough for you?"

Now I tilted my head. My relationship with Crissy may have failed to thrive, but it wasn't inherently hostile. She was a woman in mourning, further soured by her shaky relationship with Felicia, but why the hell was she taking all of that out on me? I couldn't plumb the depths of her aggression.

"I'm sorry it's been so long. I should have kept in touch, stopped by when I was home." I showed her my bare palms, the blistering burn. I had nothing more to offer. Before today I'd no sooner have visited Crissy than skinny-dipped in Lake Champlain in January. Too many bad memories. Too much psychological baggage.

"The thing is, I don't want to know," Crissy said, as if I hadn't spoken at all. "What happened to him, who did it, whatever. It doesn't change anything. He's gone, and we got stuck with *her*." She slurped her coffee, deliberately loud. The *her* in question was Felicia.

"Have the police been by to see you?" I didn't like the way Crissy was talking. This blatant indifference to her father's murder wouldn't go over well with investigators.

That smile again, oily as an eel. "I can't believe it," she said with a hand on her heart, playing at affected. "Who would *do* something like this? *Why us*?" Just as quickly, the tender maiden act was history. "I'm not stupid, Shana. I bawled like a baby and told them what I know, which is pretty much nothing."

Jesus. Apart from her looks, my cousin hadn't changed a bit. "Crissy," I said, "this is serious. Don't think for a second the police will hesitate to slap you with an obstruction charge just because they see more jaywalkers around here than felons. They're treating Brett's death as suspicious.

There are plenty of good reasons to find his killer beyond giving your family some answers. Twenty years ago, someone was so angry and desperate to wipe him out they felt the only path forward was to take his life. The authorities are looking for that person now. Have you stopped to consider where that leaves you?"

My cousin stared at me, uncomprehending.

"You're Brett's daughter," I said, "and yes, you may in fact have no information of value to share. But Brett's killer doesn't know that. The discovery of Brett's body is all over the news. Any criminal with half a brain would be trying to gauge what the cops know. They'll be keeping an eye on the people who were close to Brett back then. Do you get what I'm saying? Whoever's responsible for his death could be back now—if they ever even left—and they're going to be watching. Are you comfortable with that person sharing the town where you work, where your kids go to school, now that you know what they've done?"

We were so close to each other I could see her cleavage, crinkly from years of tanning, pulse like a puppy's hairless belly. She looked away from me, her face shuttered tight, and for a second I saw what she did. Her boys, getting off the bus to find their front door ajar. A stranger greeting them instead of their mother, holding Crissy's favorite coffee mug while he coaxed the children inside.

"You want to know why I'm here?" I said. "I came to tell you to be careful. However you may feel about Brett, he suffered at the hands of someone whose motive we don't yet understand. Don't stray too far from home, okay? Keep those boys of yours close."

She cast me a dispassionate glance. "I've fought off plenty of men who've gotten handsy. I'm pretty sure I can handle this."

I wanted to tell her this wasn't like when some repellent high school boy had his mitt down her pants. What I said was, "Terrific. Don't let me make you late for work. Really great seeing you, Crissy. I'll show myself out."

EIGHT

The sun was high in the winter sky by the time I left Crissy's, and my stomach had started to growl. Knowing Mom, there'd be a pot of soup on soon, maybe even some freshly baked rolls, but moments after I got into my car and cranked the heat, my mobile phone chimed an alert. It was a new message from Suze. *OMG are you in town? I'm teaching all day at the dance studio on Merchants Row. Please come by, I would LOVE to see you!*

I stared at the message. How could Suze know I was back in Swanton? I looked up from her tiny profile picture to see a cloud of my own breath. Beyond the windshield, the bay water rippled and shimmered, but there was no motion whatsoever on Crissy and Felicia's street. Despite the sparse population, or maybe because of it, word traveled fast in this town.

After I'd worked for so long to keep my interactions with Swanton surface-level, this trip was quickly turning into a deep dive. Given what had happened to my uncle, I guess I shouldn't have expected anything less. I'd already visited my cousin after years of not seeing her. A chat with my ex–best friend couldn't hurt.

Be right over, I typed, and Suze replied with an emoji of a candy-apple-red lipstick kiss.

Suze hadn't bothered to give me an address because she knew I didn't need one. Merchants Row was an unassuming strip mall in the center of town, and above the door of the very last retail space, where the line of beige buildings came to an end, a white banner emblazoned with a silhouetted dancer flapped in the wind. I hurried in, desperate to warm up and certain the studio would deliver. Inside, the air was so humid the window to the street dripped with condensation. The coatroom was packed with women whose exultant faces shone with sweat, and they gabbed and laughed as they pulled on their heavy jackets and winter boots. In no time I spotted Suze emerging from the brightly lit studio.

She was the same age as most of the women heading outside—my age, that is—and had their same post-workout glow, yet there was no mistaking the girl I used to know. Half Japanese with a ready smile, coal-black eyes, and cappuccino-colored freckles on her glossy cheeks, she'd always been striking, especially in a strappy tank and snug jeans. The ends of her hair used to reach her lower back where, if senior year rumors were true, she'd gotten a butterfly tramp stamp. That hair was chin-length now, pushed back with a headband, and though her clothes were of the workout variety, I caught myself feeling self-conscious in my sweater and ratty jeans.

Suze noticed me hovering and bounced on her feet. "Shana," she gasped, pulling me into a hug. "Wow. It's really you."

"It's great to see you." The warmth coming off her body was intense. When she let me go, I wriggled out of my coat.

"Sorry. Hot as balls in here; these ladies work up a sweat." Her smile was wide in a way that felt wholesome, like Crissy's before she grew up.

"This place new?" I didn't remember seeing it. I could have missed it on my trips through town, though. I'd been looking for a serial killer, not a fitness class.

"Coming up on three years, if you can believe it. I sure can't. It's been going well, actually. Better than I hoped."

"You own it?"

She gave a modest single-shouldered shrug. "I always dreamed of doing this, figured I might as well put all that community college to good use. And you know I've always loved to dance. I actually think doing this was fate. I met Robbie when I started setting it up. He works for the Chamber of Commerce now—one day he was giving me some marketing advice, and a few months later he was down on one knee. How could I resist those baby blues?"

"Robbie, right," I said. Robbie Copely was in my brother's grade, and he and Crissy dated briefly in high school. Robbie's eyes, solid blue and framed by the dark, curly eyelashes of a beauty pageant contestant, were what made him stand out from the hoi polloi. "Sounds like you've got your dream job. That's great," I said, genuinely delighted. It was strange, standing next to Suze again. We'd been like sisters once, her clothes and the cloying scent of her drug store body wash as recognizable to me as my own. Through the edgy haircut I could see traces of the girl who had been my confidant. Had we not fallen out, I suspected we'd still be close. "Look, I'm sorry I didn't stay in touch," I said, and found that I meant it.

"Me too. I thought about calling, obviously, but I was pretty pissed at you for a while."

"*You* were pissed at *me*?" I couldn't help it: When I looked at her, I still saw Suze straddling one of the Boisselle twins and patting the empty space between her and the other brother. She'd spent an entire summer crawling through my bedroom window at two in the morning and threatening to jump to her death if I didn't accompany her to a party.

"Of course I was," she said with a slight frown. "You ditched me when I needed you most. I was a hot mess in high school. Middle school, too, actually. The drinking and drugs were a real problem for a while. Instead of sticking by me while I worked that shit out, you totally deserted me. I honestly couldn't believe it when you stopped returning my calls. You were always the sensible one, Shana. If you think I made bad choices when you were around, you should have seen me after you cut me off. And it's not like you were perfect. You had your faults."

I was speechless. What had I expected from Suze? Certainly not a lecture. But her dance studio, and her giddy customers, proved she was right. The behavior that drove me away was just a phase. Everyone had them. How could I have been so myopic? Instead of looking for ways to pull my friend out of her bad-girl stage, I'd put my own well-being first and written her off as a lost cause. All these years I'd been vilifying Suzuka Weppler in my mind, convinced she was to blame for my own far tamer indiscretions. She wasn't a heathen. I was never under her yoke, and yet I'd pushed her away. I'd seen myself as morally superior. In retrospect, it was disgraceful.

"I'm sorry," I stammered. "I didn't—"

"Hey." She put a hand on my arm. "It's okay. Seriously! We were kids. We didn't know what we were doing—if we did, I'd have been more particular about who I kissed. I can't tell you how awkward it is to run into all those boys in town now. The paunches on some of them, my *gawd*."

I laughed, and she joined in, our voices trilling in unison. For the first time in as long as I could remember, I was truly happy to be home.

"Listen, my next class isn't until three. Have you had lunch? I could eat a Clydesdale."

Before I knew it, Suze's arm was hooked through mine and we were girls again, the best of friends.

———

There weren't many places to eat in Swanton, and Suze didn't want to waste precious catch-up time driving into St. Albans, so we settled on the pizza place five blocks east.

Music was playing, a nineties indie anthem I'd liked as a kid, back when my life was simple, and the menu was a mixed bag of limp iceberg salads and deep-fried everything else. I ordered two slices of Hawaiian, Suze got a veggie calzone as big as a loaf of bread, and as we dug into our lunch, we dove into the past.

It was immediately clear to me that my friend's memories and my own didn't always converge. In fact, my recollection of events was often woefully skewed. Parties I remembered as ragers Suze recalled as totally lame. When she talked about Ben Bradley and Cody Brown, boys from our class we apparently thought were smoking hot, it was like I was hearing their names for the first time.

In some cases, my impression of our history appeared to be just plain wrong. I was sure Suze and I had almost gotten arrested for underage drinking in the park near the plaza that now housed her studio. My cousin Abe was there, too, that night, and thanks to his quick thinking he'd pulled us into the bushes moments before a police car drove by. Suze didn't perceive things this way at all. In her version of events, it wasn't a cop who showed up but one of her neighbors, the dad of a kid in our class. According to Suze, he feigned regret that we hadn't saved a bottle for him, and told us half-heartedly not to get into too much trouble.

Memory, I realized as we spoke, is a tenuous thing—the truth a filament thin as a spider's web—but I didn't like how much I'd forgotten. As she crunched her crust, Suze tried to put my mind at ease.

"I happen to specialize in storing useless information about ancient social events," she said. "We had a lot going on back then, and you had to make room in that brain of yours for more important things. None of that stuff is important anyway. It makes me tired just thinking about it—although that could just be the hormones." She patted her stomach. "I'm dancing for two."

"You're pregnant? Congratulations!"

Suze laughed, and the sound had the same warming effect on me as catching a whiff of my mom's butter pecan cookies after years of missing out. "Thanks. It happened a little quicker than planned, just like last time, but Erynn's super pumped about being a big sister. I'm due in late May."

"You lucked out. No huge belly in the summer heat."

Suze laughed, but I held my breath. Everything I knew about pregnancy I'd learned from my sister-in-law, but my niece was thirteen now. If Suze wanted to talk morning sickness and swollen feet, I'd have nothing to contribute, and inevitably the conversation would loop around to me. I could try to hide my failed engagement, but I wasn't confident I could evade her questions without inviting suspicion. With every passing minute I spent in Swanton, the less I felt like an investigator skilled at manipulating suspects and the more I felt like the insecure teenager I used to be with Suze.

She didn't ask about my personal life. The sense of relief I felt didn't last long. "Your scar," she said. "It looks good. Better, I mean. If I didn't know it was there, I would hardly have noticed."

I smiled and felt the mutilated, too-tight skin on my jaw hitch. "Time heals all wounds, right?"

"That was messed up. What he did to you."

Her gaze jumped all over the restaurant as she spoke. Suze was never one to shy away from sensitive subjects, so her discomposure startled me. By the time I got home from the hospital, stitches and bandages in place, I'd decided to shut her out for good. She hadn't been around to bring me stacks of *Seventeen* while I recovered at home, or to fill me in on the latest school gossip. But that was my choice, not hers.

I picked at a syrupy wedge of pineapple pizza and knit my brows. Pizza rigor mortis had set in, my cheese was congealed, and anyway, I'd lost my appetite. I set down the slice and wiped my hands.

"That kid always creeped me out," she said, staring down at her own plate. "It was the way he looked at you. He threatened me once, did I tell you?"

"No," I said quickly. "How? When?"

"Freshman year. I didn't even know who he was, but one day he came up to me and said it wasn't a good idea for you and me to be friends. He told me you had an overprotective brother who had a tendency to get violent."

"*Doug?*" My startled laugh sounded like a seal bark, embarrassingly loud. "That's ridiculous."

"I know that *now*, but I was super freaked out for a while. When I met Doug and he was totally sweet, I figured it was just a stupid rumor to keep us apart. Now I think he did it to hurt you."

All I could do was nod, because I knew she was probably right.

As soon as she took her last bite, I bused our table and reached for my coat. When Suze bent over for her purse, her shirt slid up her back and I caught sight of a colorful tattoo. The rumors were true. At the door, we paused.

"How are your folks doing?" she asked as we hugged again. This time I noticed the firm, shallow bump under her shirt.

"As well as you'd expect, considering the whole town is talking about my family. Any theories?"

"You're the detective." A microscopic wrinkle appeared between her eyes. "Isn't that why you're here?"

"What, to investigate?" Again I laughed. "Hell no. I just came to support my parents." I zipped up my coat, and we stepped into the wind. "According to local law enforcement, it's been almost twenty years since Brett died. We just didn't know about it until now. The case is stone-cold. I'm lucky I'm not the one responsible for warming it up."

"It's so crazy. I didn't know him well, obviously, but he was really nice to me." She lowered her eyes for a moment. "He was like an extra in my life, hanging out in the background. Remember that family picnic you invited me to? Brett showing up half in the bag? Felicia was livid."

Gobs of spilled potato salad embedded in the grass. Spittle on Felicia's chin. "There were a lot of days like that," I said. That event had been one of the tame ones. Brett made an appearance in the police blotter on more than one occasion for motor vehicle crashes, disturbing the peace, you name it.

"Poor Wally was so embarrassed, he kept apologizing when he drove me home," Suze said. "But the truth was that afternoon, before Felicia lost it, Brett spent ages listening to me complain about having a teacher for a father. My dad and I were in a bad place then—he was always harping on me to be an angel at school and make a good impression on his coworkers—and Brett was really understanding." With a shudder, she said, "You think whoever killed him is still around?"

"They could be, but I don't think you need to worry. The police are all over it."

"Think they'll find him, though? After all this time?"

I thought of Crissy, spitting mad in her trailer. My parents choosing to do their errands in a different town. "For everyone's sake, I damn well hope so."

NINE

Training to become an investigator is just like studying for anything else: facts and procedures are drilled into your head with such force that you're not likely to ever forget them. Eventually, putting them into practice becomes a matter of instinct. I suppose that's why, when I parted ways with Suze, I found myself puzzling over Brett's death.

No word of a lie, I wanted nothing to do with his case. I had no reason to believe the local authorities weren't perfectly capable of solving it. What I did have was a personal stake in seeing Brett's killer apprehended. Everything about his death made me uneasy. One thing I learned during my training is that about forty percent of homicide victims are killed by someone they know, and twelve percent of those are killed by family. With a crime like the one committed against my uncle, the involvement of a stranger was unlikely. Intimates are who we look at first. And most of the people close to Brett were members of my own family.

I didn't plan it, but instead of making the drive back to my parents' house, I found myself doubling back to First Street. Before I knew it, I was in front of my old school.

My gaze traveled over the large, low structure that housed both the middle and high school as I pulled adjacent to its windowed double doors. Had it always looked this much like a detention center? It certainly felt like one. I'd been about to start my senior year when I was injured. There were never any graduation photos of me in my parents' house. Even with some time to heal, the scar on my cheek was as pink and glossy as raw chicken when I donned my cap and gown.

By the time I pulled into a parking spot and put the SUV in park, I could think of nothing but Bram. Where was he now? All day long I'd felt a prickling sensation along my spine and the same cold trickle of disquiet I'd experienced at the bistro with McIntyre. Was he close? Could he be hiding among the dozens of staff and student cars around me, sneering at the institution he'd left behind? Spying on me?

And the bigger question: Could he have something to do with Brett's death?

I checked the car's mirrors and swiveled in my seat, probing my blind spot, but while the parking lot was jammed with vehicles and it was coming up on lunchtime, there was nobody around. I felt a little lighter. Being back at the school made my head spin with images from my time with Suze before we grew apart. We'd had fun together, we really had. I shouldn't have waited so long to reach out. It was becoming increasingly difficult to justify the decades-long cold shoulder she'd gotten from me.

I arrived home early that afternoon and found my parents had returned from their escapade du jour. The cheerful cooking sounds in the kitchen were accompanied by the mewl of sax-heavy smooth jazz. While she cooked, my mother swung her hips in an exaggerated fashion. After our movie night, Dad had bragged about mastering the lotus pose faster than her, an achievement that drove my stiff-hipped, yoga-obsessed mother mad. Her current swagger was a blatant F-you aimed at her limber husband, who was now rolling out pie dough at the kitchen table, but she delivered it with love.

"You're back!" she said when she spotted me. It was nice to see her smiling again. "And just in time to help me chop some mirepoix. I'm making chicken pot pie."

It was all I could do not to drool. She sashayed to the fridge, popped open a beer for me, and clinked her own against it with a conspiratorial grin.

"So I saw Crissy," I said.

Mom's face clouded. "How did she seem?"

"Honestly? Unsympathetic."

My parents locked eyes. They'd been together so long they shared thoughts like winter colds, trading them back and forth unconsciously. "Well," said Dad from the table, "they have a lot of history."

"I get why she'd be resentful," I said. "Brett left them. He wasn't very present on the best of days. But she just found out her dad was murdered. I kind of expected to see more grief."

As she minced carrots with uniform knife cuts, Mom said, "Crissy was old enough to have his number, that's all. I don't like to speak ill of the dead, but . . . well, the man made his bed. That's all I'll say about it."

Dad gave a nod. "I confess that when Brett left, I bid good riddance to both the man and his shortcomings. I suppose Crissy did the same. It wasn't just his parenting that was an issue, darling. You were young, probably too young to remember much. Brett hardly earned enough to support his wife and family, but more than that, he skimmed off the top of their shared bank account to feed a gambling habit and keep himself in Natty Light." Dad took a swig of his own beer and floured the dough. "After he and Felicia split—they never divorced, mind you, didn't have the savings for that—your aunt expected him to help support the kids. Brett gave her money when he could, but his contribution was minimal. Felicia's job as a shop clerk didn't earn her enough to manage on her own, and her health was an ever-present problem."

"She had trouble sleeping," added Mom. "She didn't always make it to work. And when she needed money, there was none, thanks to Brett. Those were painful years for your aunt. I often got calls from her in the middle of the night. She'd drop the kids here because she knew they'd be safe. It was the only way she could squeeze in a few hours of rest."

Snatches of giggles. Sleeping bags and fuzzy striped afghans strewn across the living room floor. "I remember," I said.

Dad scratched his chin, leaving behind a stripe of flour.

"Your mother was always helping out, and thank God for that. The only way to ensure the children got their baths and homework done was to bring them here. But Crissy made it difficult. She could be a right git sometimes, but later, after Brett moved out of the house and into his apartment, the girl went stark mad. The truancy, the drugs—and so young! We all knew what she was up to; she made little effort to hide it. We were concerned her behavior would send you and Doug off course as well."

"Your father did try to reason with her," said Mom.

"Not that it did much good. Eventually, your mother stopped asking Crissy over. What else could we do?"

My mother said, "Brett set a bad example, for what it's worth. While Crissy was out tearing up the town, her dad was doing the same thing. I'm surprised they didn't cross paths at a party somewhere. Who knows, maybe they did." She sighed deeply. "Crissy was furious with him for moving out, though. I do know that."

"At the time," Dad went on, lovingly shaping a second ball of dough, "we thought Brett buggering off to Philadelphia was for the best. If he had any hope of reforming himself, he wasn't going to manage with the likes of Russell Loming for a friend. Loming was more of a skiver than Brett."

"Russell Loming?" I said. The name wasn't familiar.

"His best mate. I ran into him at the hardware store, oh, last year it must have been. He's still working in manufacturing, at the maple-sugaring equipment plant now."

"Felicia was furious, too, when she got the news that

Brett was going away," said Mom. "God knows it wasn't easy living with Fee, and I can't blame him for wanting a normal life, but what kind of person leaves the state without telling his own children good-bye?"

"So Brett quit his job and left," I said. "That could have been when it happened. It's possible he planned to say good-bye but died before he could do it."

"I suppose," said Dad. I could tell he hoped it was true, that he was conflicted about how to treat the memory of his dead brother-in-law. My father liked to give people a fair shake, and Brett hadn't made that easy.

In my pocket, I felt my phone buzz.

The sight of McIntyre's name on the display was startling, an abrupt reminder of the life I'd momentarily forgotten in A-Bay. Wiping my hands on a dish towel and excusing myself, I hurried out into the hall.

"How would you like to spend a few days in Vermont?" I asked Mac, taking the stairs two at a time and ducking into my old bedroom. The walls were still yellow, the curtains Mom had sewed decades ago striped in ballet pink. "I could seriously use a distraction."

"I can help with that," said the sheriff in a tone I didn't like. "I'm calling on official police business. We've got a situation over here."

"Must be bad if I'm on your call list." McIntyre had kept me up to speed on the county's most recent crimes throughout my suspension, but only as dinner conversation or an aside as we passed each other in her hall. I was touched she'd gone out of her way to call about a new case. Touched and a little concerned.

"Tim's on it," Mac assured me, "but you're still my most senior investigator, so I want your take, too. Because you're right. It's bad. A kid's gone missing, nine-year-old boy by the name of Trey Hayes." She took a breath and rattled off the details. Local. African American. Brown hair and eyes. Small for his age. "Real cutie," she said sadly. "Last seen about two hours ago on a field trip to Boldt Castle."

"In November?" The castle, I knew, was on Heart Island, only accessible by water. School kids would have to take a ferry from A-Bay to reach it. It had already been chilly on the river back in October, when Tim and I worked the Tern Island case.

"The weather," Mac said by way of explanation. "Tours were supposed to end three weeks ago, but the winters here, they're long. Any place that can squeeze out a few extra days of tickets—"

"Or bear claw sales."

"Right." As she laid out the full story of Trey's disappearance, I grew just as despondent as she was.

At 9:00 a.m. that morning, thirty-nine fourth-grade students, two teachers, and four parent-chaperones had boarded a couple of district school buses bound for the Alexandria Bay Municipal Dock. A ferry owned by River Rat Boat Tours made two trips to transport its passengers to Heart Island. Although Boldt Castle was normally a self-guided experience, the school had arranged for a guide to take the group through the castle and around the grounds. Tim had confirmed Trey was on the tour, which kicked off at 10:00 a.m.

At 11:20 the group convened at the dock to reboard the tour boat bound for the mainland. That's when a head count came up short. Trey's parents, whom Tim had interviewed already, described their son as spirited but well behaved, not prone to fits of rebellion or likely to wander off. He liked school and had been looking forward to the trip. No signs of verbal or physical abuse, and both parents had alibis; they were at work when they got the school's call.

"Tim's still out there interviewing teachers and chaperones. Kids, too," Mac said. "I'm on my way to join him."

That many interviews would take some time. I drummed my fingers on the dresser, feeling the heat of the phone against my ear. Somehow, I seemed to attract missing persons cases. Pity, that, given the last two I worked ended in tragedy.

"The employees," I said. "Any progress with them?" I hadn't had a chance to visit Boldt Castle yet, though Tim kept telling me it was a must-see attraction. I did know it was a legitimate chateau: six stories with something like a hundred and twenty rooms, medieval-style turrets, an actual drawbridge. I thought back to my own school days and my father's complaints about field trip destinations that weren't sufficiently equipped for scores of visitors. As the man in charge of the field trip review and approval process for the district, Dad used to say unconventional sites were his undoing.

The Thousand Islands were tourist country, though. "There must have been staff around, even if it isn't peak season—which means there could have been a shift change," I said. "Someone might have seen something and left the island before Tim got there."

"I'll pass that thought along. Tim would call you himself, but he's deep in the weeds."

The weeds. My mind went to the river, crammed with kelp. "The water," I said. It would be glacial by now. "You don't think—"

"Don't know. At nine years old, a kid who grew up around here should be a proficient swimmer. But if he was injured somehow . . ." Her voice trailed off. "We've got the local media involved, and it sounds like a few calls have come in to the tip line already. But that water's deadly. Tim had better work fast."

As Maureen McIntyre spoke, I walked to the window and brought my face close to the glass. The cold had found its way inside and glazed the pane with frost. *Tim isn't alone*, I told myself as I used a fingernail to carve a line into the fragile layer of ice. There were other investigators at the A-Bay station who could help him search Heart Island, along with McIntyre herself. They'd be in full-on disaster mode already. Picturing the urgency of the chase, a kid gone and my team working as one to beat the clock, made the pizza I'd eaten earlier churn inside my stomach.

I'd only spent one night in Swanton, but I missed A-Bay terribly. I wanted to be back there with Mac and Tim, helping with this pressing case.

But the warning I'd issued to Crissy weighed heavily on

my mind. Whoever killed Brett might still be in town. *The locals are on it*, I reminded myself. *This isn't your job.* The closest thing I had to one of those was back in Upstate New York. In so many ways, Swanton was about the past; whereas, back at my new home in A-Bay there was a kid who needed help now. When I thought of it like that, staying in Vermont felt selfish. My parents seemed to be coping. They'd be okay without me for a few days, wouldn't they?

"Mac?" I said into the void.

"Yeah?"

"I'm coming back."

"What, already?"

"I know my eval isn't until Thursday and I'm not cleared to work. I know I can't lead the team. But I want to help in whatever way I can." I paused, and drew a breath. "Please let me help."

Mac didn't ask a lot of questions, not when I left Watertown for Swanton, and not now. I hoped she'd be glad to have me around, but when she spoke again I heard an intimation of uneasiness in her voice.

"I don't need to tell you how time-sensitive this case is."

"No," I said, "you don't."

"We can't wait to start the search until you get here."

"Of course not."

"Okay," Mac said. "It's your call."

I had to think it was the right one.

TEN

When I told them I was leaving, my parents didn't argue. "Work comes first," said Dad, though I knew my mother didn't share that philosophy. It was family first with her, always. She hadn't asked me to come, but I felt a twinge of guilt for leaving, and assured them I would be back soon.

Thoughts of Brett's irresponsible behavior and Felicia's struggle raising kids alone kept me company all the way to Chateaugay near the Canadian border. In Massena, New York, with an hour and twenty to go until A-Bay, I finally managed to put Swanton behind me and give my thoughts over to Trey Hayes. A boy, lost among the islands, just as the weather was starting to turn. A boy who, God willing, was still alive.

On Tern, while searching for Jasper Sinclair, picturing the man's unresponsive body galvanized me. Imagining him in physical peril sharpened my senses and turbocharged my legs. I couldn't take this same approach with Trey, though, couldn't bring myself to visualize a child left for dead in the brush. In the water. *In the weeds.*

What I did do was surrender to the ghastly thrill of the coming search. I urged my brain to fire up like a furnace. My heart thumped as I braced my palms against the wheel. It was all I could do to keep still.

The road unfurled before me, a russet landscape flitting past the windows of my speeding SUV, and before I knew it, I was back in A-Bay. I'd tried calling Tim via Bluetooth on the way, but got no answer. My efforts to contact McIntyre again had proved fruitless, too. There was no guarantee they had stayed at Boldt Castle. They'd need to interview people in the village, too, friends and family close to Trey, as well as search the shoreline. I was counting on meeting up with them on the mainland. No such luck. At the station I was told Jeremy Solomon and Don Bogle, the other two investigators from my team, had handled the interviews in town, and that Tim and Mac were still on Heart Island.

I'd ridden a wave of adrenaline back to the Thousand Islands, but without access to a boat, let alone the ability to drive one, I now found myself at a standstill. I wasn't supposed to be working, so I couldn't press Sol or Bogle to put my presence to good use. In the three weeks since my suspension, I hadn't felt as cowed by my ineffectiveness as I did standing in the station parking lot now.

There was only one way I could think of to release my nervous energy while I waited to hear back from Tim and Mac.

Making a U-turn in the station parking lot, I hit the highway once more.

I came to karate later in life, picking it up in my midtwenties because I thought it would prove useful for work. As it turns out, I rarely need to deliver a crescent kick to a criminal's face. By the time I arrive at the scene, the bad guys are usually long gone—but martial arts makes me more self-assured, and when I'm confident in my body's ability to react, I'm better able to focus my mind. There's solace in karate's rules and the precision of its movements. I find the lack of chaos soothing.

My private class with Sensei Sam was on Sundays, but he taught all week long, so I hoped to join as a walk-in. Really, I'd take any class I could get.

Back at the studio, I repeated the same routine of watching my back as I pushed through the door. The foyer was usually quiet, but this afternoon electronic dance music pumped through the speakers. No sooner had I walked in than four students filed out of the studio, bowing to their sensei and dropping to one knee to untie their belts. The teens were the after-school crowd, sporting smiles and a post-workout flush. Again I thought of Trey. These contented kids would get to go home to their parents, who'd steal a touch or swift embrace as they recounted the story of the poor boy's disappearance and warn their own children to be vigilant.

Sam's face brightened when he saw me. Today his gi was red, and the color suited him.

"Back so soon?" he said as his students collected their things. "You're really serious about this, huh?"

"Missed it more than I realized. Look, I don't have my gi or anything. I was just hoping to drop in. How's my timing?"

"Not great." He nodded at the kids. "This was my last class of the day."

"Ah," I said, trying to mask my disappointment. "That's okay. I'm really just killing time."

Sam laughed and said, "Ouch."

"I didn't mean it like *that*. I'll take any chance to see you that I can get."

"Yeah?" Sam's mouth twitched. "Tell you what, I'll help you kill time another way. Can I buy you three or four cups of coffee?"

I looked at the splash of color on Sam's high, apple-firm cheeks and the shine in his eyes and thought, *oh*. Strange, how the dynamic between two people can shift from innocent to complicated from one moment to the next. Had I done this? I replayed my last words in my mind and cursed myself. I'd never considered Sam in the context of a romantic relationship, not because I didn't know if he was single, but because I didn't see myself that way. My engagement was in the past, but only just. Was I even ready to consider dating again? With everything going on inside my head, my gut said *bad idea*.

The last of the teens pushed through the door just as a heavy man in a baseball hat entered.

"Hold that thought," Sam said merrily as he left to attend to his customer. He was expecting me to say yes. As he walked to the counter to dig up a class schedule, I racked my brain for an exit strategy. I didn't want to hurt Sam's feelings. I really had come to like the guy, and I needed this class with every brain cell and shred of muscle tissue in my body.

"This is all on the website, too," Sam said, "and if you want to leave your name and e-mail, I'll get you on the mailing list." The guy in the baseball cap got to scribbling, and Sam crossed the room to join me once more.

"So," he said, "ever been to the Bean-In? They make a killer—"

"Thanks for the offer, but—"

"Oh." Sam's expression hardened. "Hey, it's cool. No need to explain."

"No, it's just . . . I need to run some errands. A friend of mine turns fifty on Friday, and I have to find the perfect card." That much was true. Mac was milking the milestone for all it was worth, and I planned to take her out to a no-holds-barred fish dinner, but the occasion seemed to warrant a funny Hallmark message about senior discounts or entering the prehistoric age, too. "Rain check?" I asked.

Sam searched my face for a second before saying, "Sure. Of course. I've got your number from sign-up. I'll text you mine. FYI, Smuggler's Cargo has some great cards, and I'll be back here at 10:00 a.m. tomorrow if you're game."

"Thanks. Can't promise I'll make it," I said, contrite, "but I'll do my best." At the counter the man set down his pen, mumbled a word of thanks, and left.

"He won't be back," Sam said.

"How do you know?"

"I sensei it."

I groaned, but Sam knew he'd nailed the joke. We grinned at each other. He did have a great smile.

"Listen," I said, growing serious. "The other day, when I . . . you know."

"Clammed up? It happens, especially to people who've been through what you have."

"You seem to know a lot about PTSD."

Sam squared his shoulders. "My sister. It happened on a date."

Oh, God. "I'm so sorry. Is she okay?"

"She wasn't. She is now. Most of the time."

"Most of the time," I repeated, thinking of my sleepless nights on McIntyre's sofa. "So that's normal, then."

"It's a long road back from trauma like that."

"Yeah." I paused. "Here's the thing. The way I responded in class? That can't happen again."

"I've seen what you can do, Shana, and you're closer to your goal than you think. Keep coming in, and you'll get there. That's a promise."

I believed him, not because of his teaching skills, but

because of his sister. If I could trust anyone to train me the way I needed to be trained, it was Sam.

Back in my SUV, which had barely begun to cool, I checked my messages. Sam's number popped up on my screen, but there was nothing from Tim and Mac. Not knowing what they were doing, what they'd learned, whether they'd found some evidence of what happened to Trey, was driving me insane.

There were a disproportionate number of souvenir and gift shops in A-Bay, but I took Sam's advice and ten minutes later found myself at kitschy Smuggler's Cargo, where a huge rusted anchor welcomed visitors at the door. The place was a labyrinth of tight aisles crammed with merchandise that ranged from stuffed animals and shot glasses to mugs and sweatshirts. Much of it boasted a pirate theme. In the mid-1800s, famed smuggler Bill Johnston pillaged supply ships and the occasional passenger steamer on the St. Lawrence River, and he'd become an iconic figure in the village. As I'd discovered upon my arrival in A-Bay, the pirate was commemorated annually with a ten-day summer festival of family fun—breeches, waistcoats, and all.

There was nobody in the shop but the owner, an elegant older lady who said her name was Annette and looked ecstatic to see me. It was November in a town built for summer tourists; the poor woman had to be bored out of her mind. I let her show me to the birthday cards, even though they were displayed in plain sight not three paces from the door.

"It's terrible, isn't it?" Annette said while I browsed. "About that boy?"

If Mac had alerted the local news, reports about Trey's disappearance were being broadcast all over the county by now. No child would be walking the streets alone tonight.

"Horrible," I agreed. "I know everyone's hoping he'll be found soon."

It didn't take long for me to select a card from the rack. When I was ready to pay I decided to wander the aisles. Mac had forbidden me from buying her a gift, but maybe I could find a token item too trivial and silly for her to refuse. A jar of mermaid bath salts maybe, or a bag of locally made cheese curds. Everybody loved those.

I was just starting to plot my next move—pay a citizen with waterfront property to ferry me to Heart Island? Gnaw my nails down to the quick?—when I noticed the bulletin board near the register.

It was a community board, the kind papered with home-made posters for teen babysitters and dented cars for sale by owner. There were layers upon layers of them, but a new poster had recently been added to the mix. Crisp, bright white card stock, placed dead center to cover the others. It showed two photos, side-by-side.

"Everything okay, hon?"

Without realizing it I'd taken a step back, straight into a wall of Thousand Islands T-shirts. The hangers clattered as I disentangled myself from the rack. "This poster." My voice sounded weak. "Where did it come from?"

At the till, Annette craned her neck. "A man put that up, just before you came in. That's him, the missing boy." She shook her head. "What is this world coming to?"

I hadn't seen a picture of Trey, but I knew from Mac's description Annette had to be right. The kid was smiling, but barely, as if someone was forcing him to. The look in his eyes was pure terror. Next to him there was another face, another smile. This one belonged to my uncle Brett. Above them both, the word *MISSING* was written in dark ink.

With shaking hands, I pried the pushpins from the corners of the poster and peeled it off the wall.

Maybe I'm wrong, I thought as I clutched the stiff sheet of paper. *Maybe this is someone's sick idea of a joke.* But there was no denying what I saw. There was a message on the back of the poster, handwritten in pen, and the words echoed through my consciousness like a scream.

Wanna play?

No, I thought. *Please, not this.* "What did the man look like?" I blurted out. "Tell me everything."

The panic in my voice turned Annette's expression from courteous to concerned. She was guarded now, apprehensive, and I knew what she was thinking. One of us was crazy. Was it the person with the poster, or me? I said, "Listen, ma'am, I'm with the local police. I need to find the man who left this here."

That drew out a timid nod. Annette's description was

vague: he was tallish, blondish, youngish. *His face*, I implored, but she couldn't recall. All she really remembered was his hat, the words *Purple Pirates* across the front. It was the name shared by the local grade school's sports teams.

I ran past her and flung open the door.

Outside, every breath I took was like cold water rushing through my lungs. I scanned the street in both directions. The sidewalk in front of the variety store, fudge shop, and row of boutiques across the way was empty. It was the same story to the left, where James Street sloped down toward the river. I could see the water flowing black and smooth at the bottom of the road, and in the distance, Heart Island. This was A-Bay's downtown strip, and it was crammed with retail stores and well-concealed alleyways. Plenty of places to hide.

I went back inside and searched the walls and ceiling for a security camera, some sort of tangible evidence. Nothing.

The hat.

I took out my phone and called Sam.

"Change your mind about the coffee?" His tone was optimistic.

"Tell me you're still at the studio."

"I just left. Why?"

"Can you go back? I wouldn't ask if it wasn't important."

He only hesitated for a second before saying, "Sure, okay. Did you forget something?"

"Not exactly." I told him what I needed, and to text me as soon as he had it.

I dialed Tim next. When I left a message, heavy on the expletives, the shop owner looked nervously down at her hands. "Call me the second you get this," I said, and followed it up with a three-character text to show him I was serious. *911.*

At some point over the past two minutes, I'd started instinctively breathing through my nose. It was a coping mechanism Carson had drilled into me during therapy, and while I resented its origins, I had to admit it helped. My fitness for duty eval was three days away. I couldn't—wouldn't—lose my shit now.

At last, my cell phone rang.

"Shane, what the—"

"Tim, thank God. Trey Hayes. What was he wearing on the field trip?"

There was a pause. "Think you found him?" Tim's tone was cautious; he could hear the urgency in my own. Finding a missing kid isn't always a happy occasion, especially when you live by the water.

"It's not that," I said. "I just need to know."

"Last seen wearing jeans and a lightweight blue jacket. Black winter boots."

"What about—"

"And a baseball hat. Purple and black."

I drew a breath. "Purple Pirates."

"That's right." Tim sounded increasingly troubled. "What's going on?"

My phone buzzed. Sam was back at the studio.

So, yeah, his text message read. *The guy in the hat did leave a name. Abraham Skilton. Why do you ask?*

"Tim," I said, staring out at the street beyond the shop windows, my voice impossibly thin. "I think I know who took Trey."

ELEVEN

The cat was only the beginning.

We'll look for clues, Abe used to say. *Want to, Shay?* He'd bounce on his heels as he awaited my reply, even though it was always the same.

As a kid, my cousin poured all his energy into engineering mysteries where there were none. Swanton was small, and while it had its share of problems, real-world concerns like break-ins and unfaithful spouses weren't on our radar. There wasn't much material that appealed to a couple of kid detectives. And then, suddenly, there was.

When I was in fifth grade, forty-seven dollars disappeared from Mrs. Dooley's patent leather purse. Our teacher left the bag sitting under her desk like always, and at dismissal time, the money was gone. The whole class was questioned, but Abe and I ran our own investigation parallel to our principal's. I kept my ear to the ground and my eyes open, wholeheartedly believing I could solve the crime.

Weeks went by and the money still hadn't been found, but we'd been analyzing our classmates' behaviors, and felt confident a wayward boy named Will Thompson was to blame. Abe started calling him Willy the Weasel, and eventually that got him a punch in the nose. Only then did our principal find the stolen money. It was in Will Thompson's backpack.

Then there was the case of Laurie Calvo's brand-new tree house. It was the envy of every kid in town, lovingly built by her parents. In the middle of the night, mere weeks after the structure went up, the Calvos woke to find it aflame, the painted boards already blackened and charred. I theorized a jealous classmate had torched it. Though I never managed to prove it, I eventually discovered I was right.

Some of the mysteries hit closer to home. Like when someone scribbled *Abe + Shay = kissing cousins* on my locker door. I was never popular, but I wasn't a pariah, either. I occupied a comfortable middle ground where most of my classmates couldn't be bothered to tread, and I wanted things to stay that way—so when word of the message spread, I started avoiding Abe at school. Already belittled for his hair, his clothes, his crazy mother, he became more of an outcast than ever. At night, the guilt of shutting him out sat in my stomach like a lump of cold stew.

After several weeks of this, similar graffiti appeared on

other peoples' lockers. The focus shifted, and Abe and I were saved, but I found the whole event unsettling. Before the backlash started, Abe had declared that he didn't mind the message. *Kissing cousins.* It just implied we were close, he said, and we were. It took far longer than it should have for me to realize that aside from my parents and brother, Abe was the only one who called me Shay.

All the stories my kidnapper told me in the cellar beneath an apartment building in the East Village were about his childhood. They were also about mine. I didn't need to dust off old yearbooks to ID him. No rifling through the memory bank for me. The man who murdered three women and a young cop, the guy who drugged me at an Irish pub, was my equal. We shared the same hometown, the same childhood experiences, even the same DNA. With every bone in my body, I wished it wasn't so, but that didn't change the facts, and denial wouldn't erase the truth. He was the troubled kid on my mother's side who ran away at the age of sixteen. Blake Bram was Abe, my childhood companion.

My cousin.

My friend.

TWELVE

My plan had been simple: I would show Bram my cards. Make it easy for him to find me, and keep him focused on me alone. It went against both my principles as an investigator and my police training, but for more than a year I'd kept his identity a secret from everyone. I didn't do it for Abe. I was appalled and revolted and deeply ashamed, but more than that, I knew revealing what had become of him to my family would leave them with agonizing questions to which I had no answers yet. As for Mac and Tim, the more they knew about Bram, the less control I had over my pursuit. And I had to get to Bram first.

Back in the basement, he'd told me what to do: *You're going to have to figure this out, Shay. Why I did what I did to those girls. It's the only way to make me stop.* So, I recast myself as a diversion. I thought that if I could distract him, people would be safe.

But now a boy was missing, and there was a new game afoot.

The overhead lights in the interview room turned Tim's skin the color of ash. His face was wind-chapped, his dense eyebrows cinched tight as a drawstring above bloodshot eyes. He hadn't stopped wiping his nose since he walked through the station door. After nearly six hours on Heart Island conducting interviews and coordinating the search only to come back empty-handed, Tim didn't just look tired, but unwell.

"Bram," Tim said. The name altered his features as if he'd eaten something foul. "You think this has something to do with Bram."

After discovering the poster, I'd borrowed Annette's winter gloves to protect any prints left behind. Now it was tucked in an evidence bag and lay on the table between us. "McIntyre told you I was in Swanton?" I said.

Tim nodded. I tapped at the bag, the photo next to Trey's.

"This man is the reason why. His name is Brett Skilton, and his remains were just found in the woods out there. It looks like he's been dead for about twenty years. There's no doubt it was a homicide. He was my uncle."

"Shit. I'm sorry."

"Thanks. We weren't close. But as you know, Bram's from Swanton, too." I twined my hands. "He would have heard about the death on the news. He knew this poster would stop me in my tracks. It's his way of flagging me down."

Tim inclined his head. "The poster says missing. But your uncle's dead?"

"He left Swanton when I was thirteen—at least, that's what we all thought. As far as I know, nobody in my family had any contact with him after that. It's sounding like he didn't make it past the town limits alive."

"And you think Bram left this here for you?"

"Yes."

"But how did he know you were in A-Bay?"

This time I didn't reply at all, just waited as Tim found his way to the inevitable conclusion on his own. After a minute, his expression soured and he said, "It was that picture of you in the paper, wasn't it? Shit. Okay, let's say he does know you're living here. How could he be sure you'd find the poster?"

I saw the man with the hat clearly now, or at least the back of him, and rage bubbled up inside me. He'd been right there, that close, and I hadn't felt so much as a tingle. I was the only one who stood a chance of picking Bram out of a crowd, and I couldn't even get that right. After countless days of looking over my shoulder at gas station pumps and straining to see through the windshields of cars passing me in the Kinney Drugs parking lot, I'd allowed myself to become preoccupied with Sam, and I'd missed him.

I told Tim about karate, and my conversation with Sam about buying a card. "Bram must have gone straight to Smuggler's Cargo. Who else could have put up this poster? Who else would write a taunt like that on the back?"

Tim still looked unsure, but as he eyed the poster he said, "That's Trey, all right. I'll run this past the parents, see if they recognize the photograph."

"What did you find out there today?" I asked.

His sigh was heavy and rumbly with the mucus that coated his throat. "I was counting on there being surveillance footage. A historic house on an island, closed several months of the year, you'd think there'd be security cameras. The ones they've got point to the dock and main entrance, where we already had witnesses, so all that tells us is that Trey didn't leave on the ferry that brought him over."

"That's because he was taken. Think about it," I said. "Annette, the shop owner, is sure the guy who left the poster wore a Purple Pirates hat."

"Tons of folks around here have those hats."

"Including our missing boy. Trey didn't fall into the river while his classmates and teachers twiddled their thumbs. Somebody took him, Tim, someone who knew what they were doing. Who's abducted people before."

Leaning back in his chair, Tim rubbed his red eyes. "I should tell you, there's a possibility this is family-related. Turns out Trey's adopted, and the parents think this might have something to do with his birth mother. She lives in Syracuse, but apparently she tracked them down last spring and pressured them to let her spend time with Trey."

This was probably the outcome Tim was hoping for. He didn't like to believe his friends and neighbors had it in them to commit reprehensible crimes, and would defend his hometown to the bitter end. The biological mother was a viable lead. But that poster. The hat. "I don't think that's it."

"Less than one percent of missing kids are nonfamily abductions," Tim said. "Meanwhile, the last known sighting of Blake Bram was three hundred and fifty miles from here."

We'd only worked one case together so far, but we'd laid claim to our respective methods. When it came to investigating, Tim was organized and practical, while I tended to get creative. Take a different view.

"Explain the poster, then. The weird picture of Trey. The message on the back."

Tim chewed his lower lip. "I'll admit it's strange."

"Bram wants me to work this case," I said. "It's all a game to him, and he wants me to play it."

Two loud, deep voices boomed in the next room, and we turned in the direction of the sound. Through the window in the door I could see Sol and Bogle marking up the whiteboard with a timeline of Trey's disappearance and a list of potential suspects. The latter was woefully lacking.

"This is just so different," Tim went on. "Bram's crimes are against women."

"The crimes we know about."

"Right," he conceded, "but why would he take a kid? Why leave this?" He reached for the poster once more, and flipped it over to display the note on the back. "'Wanna play?' That could mean anything. It could have been written by anyone. If I run with this, and we're way off base, we've wasted valuable time. How can you be positive this is our guy?"

Tim was frustrated, and he had every right to be. He was the lead investigator on Trey's case, and I was asking him to take a wild presumption on faith. I hadn't given him enough information to support a theory that any halfway decent detective would see as ill conceived. But explaining the message would require me to explain a whole lot more, and I couldn't throw open the doors to that part of my life.

"Because," I said desperately. *That's how it is with us, how it's always been. Trey Hayes is another one of Bram's manufactured mysteries.* "He's trying to draw me out. You know what happened in New York. He wasn't ready to let me go."

I raked my hands across my scalp and said, "I don't know his end game, but this is his way of reengaging me. The note's an invitation. The opening bid. He took Trey, and I think I'm supposed to figure out why."

Another sigh. "Let's say you're right. Where do we go from here?"

"I know some things about Bram now, beyond the Swanton connection. All those stories he told me while holding me hostage? There might be something there. A clue."

Tim didn't answer right away. When he did, he dragged his body upright in his chair and reached for his iPhone. "Look," he said simply, placing the device in my hand. A sick feeling ballooned up inside me. He'd pulled up Trey's most recent school photograph, but in this picture, the kid's smile was real. "I was out there all day. Me and Mac, Sol and Bogle, the castle staff—we searched all over. We've talked to Trey's parents, grandparents, uncles, aunts, his best friend at school, and his worst enemy, a little jerk who torments Trey about his height. Nobody knows anything." Tim dropped his head back and closed his eyes as the cruel reality of the situation set in. "Trey's been missing close to eight hours. The temperature's gonna drop to twenty-five degrees tonight." When he lifted his head, he gave it a weary shake. "Just tell me what you think we should do."

This was one of the things that astonished me about Tim, a man I'd known only a few months. In spite of my secrets, and notwithstanding the shield I'd raised between us, he was always willing to give me the benefit of the doubt. It had surprised me when it happened before. It stunned me now.

I was ready with my answer, had thought about it all the way from the souvenir shop and felt good about my plan. "Basements," I said. "Search the one at Boldt Castle again, and the ones in town, too—apartment buildings, commercial businesses, places like that. In New York, he kept his victims in a basement. That might be his comfort zone."

Tim nodded as he jotted notes.

"In the meantime, who can we send to Smuggler's Cargo for a sketch?"

"We've got a forensic artist down in Albany. Part-timer, but she can usually fit us in, and she works remotely using illustration software to speed things up. I'll get her on a video chat with the shop owner."

"Perfect."

"What else?" he said.

My gaze traveled to his notebook. "I could look over what you've got so far, see if anything lights a spark."

Tim smiled a little. "Have at it."

I reached for the notebook in Tim's hand. He didn't let it go. "I shouldn't have complained about the cases we were getting," he said, and I recalled the work report he'd given me at Nelly's, the jokes we'd both cracked about Miss Betty and her stolen motorboat. "That little boy's still out there, scared. Maybe worse."

"Yeah, he is," I said, locking him in my gaze. "So let's go find him."

THIRTEEN

Tim left the room to call his contact, and I flipped through his notes, savoring the sensation of being back in action. It was a thrill to hold information in my hands that might help us save a life. If we solved this case, it wouldn't be my name on the report, but that was okay with me. As for my supervisor in Oneida, what he didn't know wouldn't hurt him.

While the majority of data these days is digital, Tim and I share a common love of paper. I'd never seen the inside of his notebook before, and at first poring over the facts as he perceived them, from verbal and nonverbal responses to stream-of-consciousness estimations he'd written in his tidy script, felt like an intrusion. I got over it quickly. There was no time for discomfiture now.

Half an hour passed this way before Tim reappeared with two bottles of water and the news that his forensic artist would be calling the shop owner shortly. "Anything?" he asked hopefully, nodding at the notebook. I'd scribbled a few notes of my own, but most of those were questions or comments about gaping holes in the case. I shook my head.

"The parents are pushing for a press conference," Tim said. "They want to make a plea to the public for help. I'd rather do a broader search first, send some divers into the water, but it'll be black as pitch in an hour, and I guess a conference couldn't hurt. I'm thinking first thing tomorrow."

I looked at my watch and was shocked to see it was almost 7:30 p.m. *A press conference.* I pictured Mr. and Mrs. Hayes huddled in front of the news cameras, begging for the safe return of their son, and sensed that Tim was doing the same. A look of understanding passed between us. Criminals can't resist keeping tabs on investigations into their misdeeds. I imagine it's like eavesdropping on a teacher-parent meeting after you've willfully broken a school rule: a preview of what's to come.

I bounced a pen off my teeth. "A press conference could help us flush him out, and I can help with surveillance."

"If you're right about this being an abduction, then yeah," Tim said. "That all sounds great. But if the guy we're trying to expose is the same man who imprisoned you for eight days in a filthy basement where he killed three other women, you can't be there, Shane."

It was weeks ago now, but I still remembered the fury in Tim's voice when I told him what Bram had done. That, and his appeal for me to let it lie. "I have to be there," I said. "If it's him, nobody stands a better chance of making a positive ID."

"What if he approaches you? What if he tries to—"

"He won't. Not in public. You don't know him, Tim."

"And you do? You were with him for a week, a couple hours a day, and you only heard what he wanted you to. It might be enough to get a sense of his personality, but you're not a criminal psychologist. You were drugged, traumatized, probably in a state of shock. You weren't in any position to psychoanalyze him. No one would expect you to be." Tim tugged a breath through his teeth. "You think you have some kind of connection with him, but all that bullshit Carson fed you about Stockholm syndrome messed with your head. I know you blame yourself for not detaining him when you had the chance, but here's the thing: you're right. Whatever sick act he planned to carry out down there was interrupted. That means there's a chance he wants to finish it. We don't need you in the open, in the middle of a crowd where this lunatic can make a move and slip away unseen. We've already got one missing person on our hands."

I couldn't blame Tim for seeing it that way, or for feeling the way he did. He didn't know Bram's message on the photo was decades in the making. "How about a compromise?" I said. "You hold the press conference tonight."

"Tonight? You're crazy. And how is that a compromise?"

"Just listen. It'll up the media coverage and expose the neighboring towns to Trey's photograph sooner, maybe even bring in more tips. It'll also show our guy how serious we are about getting Trey back. And it will be dark. Pitch-black, like you said. I can blend in."

But your scar. Tim was thinking it, I knew he was, and I didn't want to hear him say it aloud. "I'll cover my face," I said preemptively. "It's cold out; everyone will be bundled up. He won't even know I'm there, but I'll be scanning the crowd the whole time."

Accept my help on a case that was already stalled, or send me home and risk losing our target if I was right about Bram's involvement? From where I was sitting, the decision was easy. Tim must have known I wouldn't take no for an answer, because it wasn't long before his shoulders slumped forward in defeat. "See you back here at nine," he said.

While I inhaled a prepackaged sandwich from the Price Chopper up the road, chugged another bottle of water, and made the round trip to Mac's house for outdoor gear, Tim managed to pull a fully formed media event from his ass. I got back to the station to find a crowd of spectators had coalesced in the parking lot, where they looked expectantly at a flimsy plywood podium and a placard displaying an enlarged print of Trey's latest school photo, along with the phone number for our tip line. Night had long since descended on A-Bay, but the camera crews' equipment cut a swath of light through the inky darkness. The podium, and Trey's photo, shone like a beacon on a sea cliff. I hoped it would be enough to call the boy home.

The first person I ran into was Don Bogle, who, while speed-smoking a cigarette, told me he'd be videoing the event and streaming the footage to Twitter. At six-foot-six, he'd have a clear sightline to the podium over the heads of the civilians. When I praised him for the idea, he admitted it was Tim's. I was impressed.

Outfitted in McIntyre's old ski jacket and Cossack hat, with a flannel scarf wrapped around my face, I joined the mob of similarly dressed bystanders who'd come to watch. Like highway car crashes, these types of events always generated attention. I liked to think onlookers gathered out of sympathy for the family, but just as many were there to rap on the door to their humanity and make sure somebody was still home.

I hadn't been waiting long before Tim emerged from the station with Richard and Virginia Hayes. They arranged themselves behind the podium, where they were flanked by Jeremy Solomon, his gray hair oscillating like wheat in the wind, and Mac, who'd turned up as a show of police community support. With a solemn nod at the sheriff, Tim approached the mic.

It should have been me up there. This duty was right in my wheelhouse. But the crowd was where I belonged tonight. Peering out from between my hat and the scarf, I drew an icy breath and began to scan the dozens of faces that surrounded me.

"Good evening," Tim said into the microphone. "I'm BCI Investigator Tim Wellington with the New York State

Police, stationed here in Alexandria Bay. With the assistance of Investigators Solomon and Bogle, and support from Jefferson County Sheriff Maureen McIntyre and our local law enforcement partners, I am heading the investigation into the disappearance of nine-year-old local resident Trey Hayes."

My gaze slid to Trey's parents. This was usually the moment when family members snapped out of their daze and found themselves staring into the jaws of a real-life nightmare. Both Richard and Virginia Hayes were rigid but dry-eyed, staring blankly at the news cameras. Tim looked much the same. He was holding up well. Until I showed up in A-Bay, murders and kidnappings were practically unheard of, and that was the way Tim liked it. I knew how profoundly thoughts of this boy, cleaved from his family and out in the cold, must be affecting him.

They were affecting me, too. If I was right, and Bram was behind this, the blame was squarely on me. My history with my cousin was complicated, but there was no disputing the role I played in his departure from Swanton, and what leaving his family—leaving me—did to him.

"This is an active investigation," Tim went on. "We've received close to a hundred tips so far, and we encourage anyone who thinks they know something about Trey's disappearance or current whereabouts—no matter how seemingly inconsequential—to call. We're also asking those who were at or near the municipal dock here in Alexandria Bay this morning between the hours of nine and twelve to call in. If you think you've seen Trey"—Tim gestured at the placard—"whose photo is also available on the New York State Police Twitter and Facebook feeds, we urge you to contact us immediately."

After a beat, Tim cleared his throat. "I'd like to take this opportunity to thank the community for your support thus far. We're doing everything in our power to ensure that Trey is reunited with his family, and the assistance we get from individuals and local businesses here in town as well as the surrounding areas will be invaluable to our investigation. Now, I'll turn the microphone over to Richard and Virginia Hayes, Trey's parents, for a brief statement."

If the onset of a news conference is the moment when a criminal investigation is made real for the victim's family, then a statement from the parents is that moment for the community. Soft murmurs reverberated through the crowd as Tim traded places with Trey's mom and dad. To my left I could see Bogle, his iPhone held steady eight feet in the air. The mnemonic I'd created to distinguish between my two investigators when we first met—*Shaggy Solomon, Big Bogle*—flashed through my mind. Feeling my eyes on him, he dispatched a bleak smile. I hiked Mac's scarf up over my nose.

My eyes darted from one male onlooker to another. Too old, too young, too short, too tall. As Richard Hayes began to speak, reiterating Tim's plea to share any and all pertinent information, I noticed Tim watching me. It wasn't obvious. To anyone else it would look as though he was staring at the frozen horizon. Beneath his heavy brow, though, his eyes scavenged the area around me, ensuring nobody was coming too close, searching for signs of trouble. It wasn't until I realized he was monitoring my position that a cold frisson snaked up my spine.

What if this was a mistake?

As I stood among A-Bay's concerned citizens, listening to a mother beg for the safe return of her son, I suddenly remembered that Bram's games were easy to lose. Even in grade school, there'd always been a twist designed to throw me off-kilter just when I thought I had things figured out. Like that money stolen from my teacher. It was all I thought about for weeks, until a new scandal replaced it. Mrs. Dooley's original of our upcoming math test, complete with answers, was filched from the copy machine. Shortly after it began to make the rounds of the playground, I overheard my teacher talking to the principal about the strange timing of it all. The theft of her money was a smoke screen. The test was the target all along.

Tim had adopted a squint that told me he was having second thoughts about holding the event in the dark. At the podium, Virginia Hayes finally cracked. Tears coursed down her cheeks as she held up Trey's favorite stuffed animal and promised her son he'd be home soon. At my sides, my hands, red with cold, squeezed into fists. *How dare he.* Taking those women was bad enough, but this? This was deplorable.

Think, Shay. Where is he? What's next? If it were me Bram was ultimately after, he wouldn't leave me at a disadvantage. The game was no fun unless both players stood a fighting chance. I thought of that day in the fifth grade, how the other teachers helped Mrs. Dooley look for the money and the principal gave a speech about dishonesty while, one floor down, a cunning boy with dirty hair slipped unnoticed into the copy room. That's when it hit me. While the people of A-Bay were gathered in the cold, praying for little Trey Hayes, nobody was watching Bram.

The realization struck with the force of a falling branch. *He's not here, and he's not coming.* Wherever he'd been hiding Trey up until now, this was his chance to make a move.

"Thank you, Richard and Virginia, for sharing that with us." Tim was back at the podium to finish up. My hands were stiff and raw from the cold, the burn still too tender for gloves, but I fumbled for my phone and navigated to Google Maps. Seconds later I was looking at a map of A-Bay.

If Bram needed somewhere to hide a kid, this was the first thing he'd do. The second would be to find a place that meant something to me.

Heart Island was located in the middle of the St. Lawrence River. A-Bay sat on one side of it, while Wellesley Island and the Thousand Islands Country Club closed in from the north. On the mainland, Keewaydin State Park, Otter Creek Preserve, and the Cranberry Creek Wildlife Management Area made up the bulk of the woodland. *The cat in the forest.* The memory rippled through me like a shiver. We had no evidence to suggest Trey was in the woods, too, but such areas were attractive to criminals. The isolation and dense foliage made it easier to hide their victims. Brett was proof enough of that. The woods were a big part of our youth. I could see Bram incorporating them into his game plan.

I didn't notice it right away, but when I did it seemed absurdly obvious. There was a road that meandered straight into Alexandria Bay, and where it intersected Cranberry Creek, a patch of green denoted a thicket of trees. It assumed the form of a bird with its beak open. A forest, shaped like a swan. Those woods were six minutes from the center of town, just ten from any number of docks and rocky beaches along the river. The road was called Swan Hollow.

"No show?"

I looked up to see Tim standing in front of me, his scarf flapping in the wind.

"No," I said. "But I might have something." I showed him the map.

"Swan Hollow. Swanton." He lifted his eyes from the screen. Away from the lights the press had set up near the podium, his pupils were as dark and glossy as the feathers of a crow. "It's a stretch."

"Got a better idea?"

Tim was quiet for a moment before he said, "Looks like we can rule out the biological mother in Syracuse. Sol called around, and she's got an alibi for yesterday morning. She works at a nail salon, and the staff and customers all confirm she was on site."

It pained me to see Tim exploring other angles and working the case as if he had doubts about who took Trey, but had I left him any choice? By holding back my history with Bram, I was also holding back Tim. "I think we need to organize a search," I said.

"What, now?" He looked up at the cloudy sky, the lack of a visible moon. "A night search in below-freezing temps is going to look like a search for a body."

Fighting the urge to cringe, I said, "What we're looking for is a cabin, somewhere for Bram to hide Trey. If he took the kid as bait, as a way to get to me, Bram's going to need him alive." *But the girls.* I tried to ignore the voice in my head that had been chanting their names like a mantra for months. *Becca. Lanie. Jess.* Bram hadn't needed *them* alive. All I could do was hope this time was different.

Criminal investigations take baby steps. They totter, one foot in front of the other, always in danger of falling, failing, returning to the starting line. Whether because of Swan Hollow, or fifth grade, or some innate understanding of my lost cousin's mind, this felt like the right line to tread.

For the time being, precarious moves were the only kind we had.

FOURTEEN

It was late on Monday night when Troop D's investigators, a handful of other officials, and a few dozen volunteers set out across the Cranberry Creek Wildlife Management Area on the outskirts of town. Flashlight beams crisscrossed the terrain as voices shouted Trey's name through the woods. With its mix of wetland and marsh, the maple, birch, and beech trees straight as flagpoles, the environment reminded me so much of Swanton's own refuge I kept forgetting where I was. It was disorienting, like waking up in a different time zone and finding that whether it's the smell of the air or the color of the sky, something's off.

There had been a search like this in my town once, when I was a kid. That time it was Crissy who went missing. Searchers found her unconscious and injured. Something bad happened to her in those woods, though she never talked about what it was.

Come on, Trey, I thought. *Please be close.*

The ground had no give under the weight of my boots, the fallen leaves were tissue-thin, and the creeks were half-way frozen. If Trey was here, we'd see him straightaway. We searched the underbrush near the trails, looking for a lean-to or a snatch of color, any sign of life. For the most part the search party stayed together—Tim on one end of the line and me near the other—but an hour and a half into the hunt he slowed his pace, doubled back, and drew up beside me. Quietly, we veered away from the group until we had privacy enough to talk.

Leaves rustled and bounced lightly over the ground. The wind was picking up, and the cold made my teeth tingle. Tim coughed into his sleeve and wiped his nose on his glove. "How long do you want to keep this up?" he asked.

"By which you mean 'when the hell is your ESP gonna kick in?'"

"If this is what you think we need to do, we'll do it."

"Even though there's no evidence Trey has been, or ever will be, in these woods?"

"Even then."

While I appreciated the vote of confidence, part of me wished he'd second-guess my every move. What if I was dead wrong, and we were wasting time we didn't have? What if I was seeing connections where there were none?

I wanted to feel secure in the whispers that drifted in, the stirrings in my gut. I needed to be able to trust my intuition. There were plenty of things I remembered about Abe.

Just as many were as elusive as smoke slipping through my outstretched fingers. Lately, I felt like I was wandering the hinterland of my mind like a ghost. Thinking about my childhood in Swanton often turned up nothing but noise. It was as if someone cut the cable and the picture started twitching, a nightmarish phantasm of static and light. The only explanation I could come up with was that Bram reconditioned them somehow. His stories were my stories, too, but the retelling of my past made me doubt what I knew. I couldn't be sure my memories were still mine.

"If I could explain all this," I said to Tim, "I would."

"I trust you," he said. Then, "That message on the poster. Seems like it was personal to you. Have you gotten anywhere with figuring out who Bram is?"

Crap. "I think we went to school together," I said quietly. "It's not a big town."

In the faint moonlight, I saw Tim nod. "Do you think he was a friend?"

Damn it, Shay. Keeping things from Tim hadn't served me well before. The regret I felt—over Abe, and the people Bram killed, and the secret I was keeping from the man who was my partner—chewed at my insides like battery acid.

We've got to have trust, Shane. That's what Tim said to me on Tern Island. The first time I concealed Bram from him, it was because I feared he'd see me as weak. He knew me now, though, and respected my skills regardless of the mistakes I'd made.

I could tell him. Reveal Bram was Abe here and now and

stand aside while Tim and Mac took every shred of information I possessed to the NYPD and the neurocriminologists who specialized in the anatomy of violence. But that information was tangled up with my life, and my family's, too, and where would that leave them? Once Blake Bram's identity was made public, their connection to him would be trumpeted across the country. My parents, Felicia, Crissy, and Doug would be linked to Bram's sadistic crimes for all eternity.

Maybe that's exactly what Bram wanted. Maybe this was a test. I was a criminal investigator; Bram knew how ashamed I'd be of our bond. I was terrified of where honesty might lead. But enlisting the help of my peers might put me at an advantage, and didn't I need any leg up I could get if we were going to find Trey alive?

Yes, Tim, I thought. We were as close as two kids can be. I knew Abe Skilton loved Power Rangers and, later, grunge music, and that he'd sooner eat dirt than mayonnaise. I'd comforted him when he asked why his family couldn't be more like mine, encouraged him when he decided to convince his parents they should reconcile. Together, we'd walked all the way to the factory where Brett worked, hoping to talk Abe's dad into coming home. Good and bad, we shared everything.

Don't overthink it, I told myself. *Do what feels right.*

"Tim—"

"Sorry." He shook his capped head. "Christ, what a horrible thing to say. Of course you weren't friends. The guy's a goddamn monster, and probably always wa—"

Tim stopped walking. Stood stock-still, and stared straight ahead. As I stumbled to a halt and the crunch of dead leaves broke off, I heard the voices, too. They were coming from a few hundred yards up ahead. People were calling to one another. It was the sound of a commotion. Tim and I exchanged a glance and broke into a run.

Not far from where we'd been walking, the tree line came to an abrupt end at a small clearing. Low fence posts connected with chain encircled an informational sign similar to others we'd seen along the trails. "What is this place?" I asked, craning to see over the searchers' heads.

"It's a memorial for some of the soldiers who died during the War of 1812. The Battle of Cranberry Creek," Tim said. "It's a gravesite."

Bogle, his height an advantage once more, had elbowed his way to the sign and was urging the civilian searchers to step back. Tim and I pushed through the crowd, picking up Mac along the way. I felt my lips shape around commands I ached to utter—*out of the way, secure the area*. It was Tim who was in charge now, so I let him do the talking and hung back. Blood rushed through my ears as he rushed forward.

"Don," Tim said when he reached the rest of the team, "what have we got?"

Bogle's face was white as milk. His wide body blocked the sign, and as much as I tried, I couldn't see past him. I tilted my flashlight to expose the rest of the scene. The yellow beam gave the faces around me an unearthly glow. The searchers were shuffling forward now, straining to see over the investigators' heads, frenetic energy radiating from their bundled bodies. McIntyre spun away from the team to help manage the volunteers, and when she realized I was among them she gestured for me to come forward.

"Jesus," Sol said just as I reached the huddle. His deep-set eyes, perpetually ringed in tawny circles, seemed to retreat further into his skull. Bogle had finally stepped aside, exposing the sign in full. Behind him parents, grandparents, teachers, and friends grew quiet.

I shouldn't mind the sight of blood. Detectives are like surgeons that way; the frequent exposure is meant to make us immune. We can't allow ourselves to be diverted from the task at hand, so we ignore the visceral reaction that fills our mouths with bile, tune out the stench and ghoulish sheen inherent to the gore. It shouldn't bother me.

When I finally got a good look, I had to hold a finger to my lips to keep from vomiting into the grass.

"Get an evidence bag," said Tim, his voice cold as he reached for the blood-soaked Purple Pirates baseball hat, sticky and black in the half-light.

I couldn't go back to the station.

Believe me, I wanted to. In the next few hours, someone would deliver that bloody hat to our forensic analyst and confirm what we all suspected was true: the blood belonged to our lost boy, and there was lots of it. Tim would hold a debriefing tonight, and my colleagues would gather around a table cluttered with coffee cups and crumpled bags of chips from the vending machine to pool their collective knowledge and hatch a plan. I was already pushing my luck by being at the press conference and out in the woods with the team. I knew that if my supervisor got wind of my involvement with Trey's case, there was no way he'd green-light my return to the force. All I could do was reluctantly accept that while Tim, Mac, Sol, and Bogle headed back to A-Bay, I would be going home to Mac's place in Watertown, alone.

Minutes ago, when we'd disbanded the search party and the good people of A-Bay drifted stunned and silent back to their cars, I'd heard some of the searchers talking. Everyone believed they knew the lay of the land. The hat was a good sign, they'd said, much better than finding a body. Even bloodied, it meant Trey stood a chance. It took no time at all for Sol and Bogle to convince themselves a ransom note was imminent. I wasn't so sure. On the way back to the country road where we'd parked, Tim promised to feed me as much information as possible, but I couldn't help but feel a sense of dread as I watched him drive away.

When I unlocked my SUV and climbed into the driver's seat, that feeling was quickly replaced with a flash of alarm. Through the windshield, in the dark, a man's pale face stared back at me. Heart thumping, I got out and reached for the paper that was pinned down by a wiper. It was the article about Brett, the same front-page story from the *St. Albans Messenger* I'd seen in my parents' kitchen, Brett's smiling mug centered on the page. Now, a clipping of the article was here. In Alexandria Bay. Affixed to the front of my car.

I held it like a stick of dynamite as I slid back into the SUV and hit the locks on the doors. My hands shook as I flipped the newspaper over to see the message I knew would be there, scratched on the back of Brett's face in the same black ink that was used on the poster. Now, there was a second line for me to ponder.

Wanna play?
Go home.

Cold November darkness pressed in on me while I parsed the message in the context of two cases, one in Swanton and the other in A-Bay, and all at once I understood what Bram was playing at, where I fit into his scheme. This was a trade. Show me yours; I'll show you mine. One secret in exchange for another.

Nobody was going to find this lost boy.

Not until I could unravel the mystery of a murdered man.

FIFTEEN

The landscape was a blur of black and white, and through the window I'd cracked to help keep me awake, I smelled wood smoke and the clean, ozone scent that marked the threat of snow. I thought about Bram all the way to Vermont—because I did go back to Swanton, of course I did. It was days until my evaluation, the event that would determine my future with the New York State Police, and possibly the most important meeting of my life. But like the hat, the note on my windshield was a warning I couldn't ignore.

There was no ambiguity to this message. *Go home, or the next name on Bram's list will be Trey.* Weighted down by this warning, I'd tucked away the newspaper clipping, pocketed my apprehension, and texted Tim and Mac to let them know I was headed to my parents and would be in touch. I knew my shifty egress would baffle Tim, but there was no time to explain that. Actually, I'd be violating my suspension by investigating not one case but two.

As I drove, I went over everything I knew about Brett's death so far. After remaining hidden for two decades, his body was recovered for one reason alone: the police in Swanton had received an anonymous tip. The more I mulled it over, the more plausible it seemed that Bram was the one who alerted the police to the whereabouts of his father's remains. This would mean Bram knew his dad was dead, though, and something about that didn't prove out. Twenty years ago, my cousin and I were as close as two kids could be. If he knew, why hadn't he told me?

The only answer I could think of was so unspeakable that when I pulled onto my parents' street at 2:00 a.m., it was all I could do not to drive right by and leave this aberration of a life behind.

There was a car in the driveway that hadn't been there before, and through the living room window I saw a light on deep within the house. I'd called ahead to let them know I was coming back, and they'd hidden a key for me. That allowed me to creep inside without being heard. Even before I made it into the hall I knew what awaited me. Sure enough there was Doug, shoulders hunched at the kitchen table, a bright green bottle of Dad's J&B at his elbow.

My brother stirred at the sound of my footsteps creaking on the hardwood, and the corner of his mouth glided into a grin. The gravitational effects of age had drawn his weight toward his waist and his blond hair was graying around the ears, but to me Doug's face was etched with a lifetime of shared Christmases and family road trips. When he stood up, I rushed into his arms.

"It's late," he said into my hair.

"Sorry I broke curfew, swear to God it won't happen again." Doug's shirt had a chemical sweetness to it, that freshly laundered scent, and the realization of what I must smell like—sweat, rank marshland, Bogle's cigarettes—made me cringe.

"Not good enough," he replied gruffly, playing along. "You're grounded—and you can forget about that sleepover with Suze."

We laughed when we parted, equally amused. "I saw her, you know. Suze owns a dance studio on Merchant Row now, and she's married with a second kid on the way."

"Sounds like she got her shit together."

It was with fondness that I said, "Yeah, I think she did." I rubbed my eyes and felt exhaustion bear down on me from all sides. This day was a serious contender for the longest of my life. I'd seen Crissy and Suze and Sam and Tim, conducted a search for a missing kid, and driven for hours from Swanton to A-Bay and back again. I had watched my past and present converge, and the experience had left me dead on my feet. The soft, warm bed upstairs was persistent in its call, but I gave it the brush-off and slumped into a kitchen chair. "Josie asleep?"

"She stayed at home with Hen." Doug sat down next to me. "Work and school tomorrow."

"Ah." I hadn't seen Henrietta in ages, and feared that at thirteen my niece was on the verge of casting Auntie Shana aside. "No work for you?"

"Took a couple days off." He tipped back his head. "Don't act like you don't know why I'm here."

My brother and I haven't always been close. The three and a half years between us felt like ten when we were younger, when he had no desire to let a whiny tween shadow him wherever he went. That changed as we aged, and by the time Doug was off at college and I was plodding through my final year of high school, we'd cultivated a whole new relationship. It wasn't built on common interests or even sibling loyalty, but a mutual recognition that our family was screwed up, and a solid hunch that there might never be anyone else in our lives who understood that as well as we did.

Doug walked to the cupboard to retrieve an empty tumbler and poured me two fingers of scotch. "River Street, huh?" he said in a faraway voice. I knew he was thinking the same thing I was: Brett had been right under our noses for years. His expression darkened. "Well, sis, what do you say we have a chat about old Uncle Brett?"

"Why not," I said, and we raised our glasses to a dead man.

My brother has the best memory of anyone I know. Even now, in his midthirties, he can conjure the color of the tablecloth Mom used for his sixth birthday party and the names of every teacher, coach, and babysitter he ever had. When I don't trust my estimation of distant happenings, which lately is often, I've always counted on Doug to recount even the most infinitesimal details with total accuracy.

As with Suze, our conversation made me realize there were problems with my recollection of events. Some of the stories Doug told about Brett were familiar. The man used to make a great onion dip, and always looked the other way when we devoured half of it before the grown-ups could sink a single ruffled chip. Brett was also the one who introduced us to *The X-Files*. Unsolved cases involving supernatural forces were right up my alley, and I dressed as FBI agent Dana Scully three Halloweens in a row. But again, whenever Bram né Abe factored into the narrative, the likelihood that I'd retained all the particulars took a nose-dive. In spite of that, talking to Doug about our uncle felt cathartic, even comforting—until he asked why I was yo-yoing between my new home and my old one. "Please don't tell me you're thinking of getting involved in this," he said, his lips stretched over his teeth.

"I'm involved already. We all are. Brett's family."

"He *was* family, before he left Felicia and Crissy. Before he went and got himself killed."

Family is family for life. That's what Mom would say. What I said was, "Someone killed him, yes. That doesn't mean it's his fault."

"Look, Brett was fun, but he was no angel. Maybe you were too young to notice, but I saw him for what he was. For one thing, he was totally addicted to gambling. When that casino opened in Montreal in the early nineties, he drove an hour each way to hand over his paycheck every single week. Dad used to say the only French Brett knew how to say was 'hit me.'"

I thought about laughing and decided against it.

"Did you know," Doug went on, "that he defaulted on his mortgage? He spent every cent he made on gin and poker chips while his family lived on cheap hot dogs. A couple of times Felicia had to ask Mom and Dad for a loan, which she never paid back, of course. How could she, when he left her with nothing?"

"You don't have to convince me he was shitty at life, but it's not like the bank sent out a hit man."

"My point is, he was murdered—right here in town— and you shouldn't get mixed up in that. Anyway, aren't there rules about investigating family? As in, don't do it?"

Doug finished his drink, turning the glass in his freckled hand, and I wondered if this was his first or his fourth. His blinks were decelerating, and the booze would affect his concentration. I talked fast and prayed he'd do the same.

"What about Abe?"

"What about him?"

"You said Brett left Felicia and Crissy. But he left Abe, too."

"Yeah," Doug said with contempt, "and look what happened."

This was the last thing I wanted to discuss with my brother, but the drive over had planted a seed in my head, the same unspeakable idea that had almost compelled me to flee. Awful as it was, I had to lay the theory to rest, and I was hoping my brother's memory would prove useful.

"Doug," I said almost inaudibly, thinking of Mom and Dad in bed right upstairs, "do you think he could have something to do with this?"

Doug studied the empty glass in his hand. "You're asking if I think our cousin murdered his father."

Nausea rolled over me like a groundswell. If that was true, it meant Abe was a killer even then. That no version of the friend I thought I knew was pure.

I don't remember exactly when my mother told us Felicia had an anxiety disorder. Whether it was to shelter my brother and me, or to prime us for our family's deficiencies, she doled out the dark truths about Crissy and Abe's life over time. Every tidbit of information was a contribution to the arsenal of historical and psychological data Doug and I would need to navigate the craggy territory that was our kin.

When my cousins were kids, Aunt Fee wouldn't wash their clothes until they were stiff with dried food and sweat. She cut their hair at home with dull scissors, and berated them if they tried to minimize the damage. More than once I'd seen her break Abe's toys in some twisted attempt to acclimate them to her world, a place where faults made you undesirable, and being undesirable kept you safe.

There were more than a few flaws in her ideology. As a preteen, Abe had a terrible overbite, and as much as he begged, Felicia wouldn't take him to an orthodontist. His faults didn't keep him safe then. All they did was expose him to merciless mocking from his peers.

To everyone but her, Felicia's rules seemed illogical and cruel. Crissy's response was to fight off her mother's demands like a rabid opossum. For his part, Abe did as he was told, and suffered for his obedience. If it wasn't for me, I doubt he would have had a friend to his name.

"Abe's childhood was seriously fucked up, no question about that." Doug thought for a minute more before going on. "If Brett really was killed in 1998, that would have made Abe twelve. Almost the same age as Hen." He shook his head in a way that implied heartbreak, but in the warm walnut light of the lamp that hung over the kitchen table, his face held an angry flush.

"There are some kids in Hen's class who are awful," Doug told me. "This one girl? The lies come so easily to her, even when she's talking to adults, that she convinced us she had a brand-new baby sister, even made up a birth date and name. It was bullshit, every word. You can imagine what happened when Josie congratulated the girl's mom."

I gawked at him. Doug went on.

"As messed up as that girl is, Abe was worse. Something was missing with him. Innocence, maybe? I don't know. But after Brett left—or was killed, I guess—it only got worse."

I thought he was done with the booze for the night. When Doug's stare landed on my scar, he reached for the bottle again.

It happened at Abe's house, in the small garden shed at the back of the yard. That shed could have been lovely, a place to nurture seeds and trim away rot, but it overflowed with paint cans and rusted lawn furniture, piles of termite-ridden wood. Abe had asked me to meet him. He wanted to talk. It had been a while since we did that, and I knew he wasn't taking it well. Even Mom noticed the change, and chided me for my behavior. I told her it was nothing, hoping that by dismissing it, she'd do the same. In response, she reassured me that a friendship as strong as ours could survive anything.

When I approached Abe that day, there was a second when I wondered if Mom might be right. The spirit of our past bond seemed to hover expectantly between us. Maybe there was some way we could mend our broken ties. If anyone could change Abraham Skilton, I thought, it was me.

No, Shay. You can't change this.

For our little symposium he'd set up two old aluminum lawn chairs, the green-and-white-striped pattern of the seats black with mildew stains. Abe sat in one of them, his arms crossed over his chest. I lowered myself into the other and waited to hear what he had to say.

The questions came quickly. *Why don't you want to hang out anymore? What did I do wrong? You were always into it before. Why not now?* I tried to make him see he'd taken things too far. I needed him to understand I wasn't the dumb kid I'd been, that I knew about the cat now, the torched tree house and stolen money. I was seventeen by then, with my sights set on a career in law enforcement. I'd taken some psychology classes in school and was actively researching criminal behavior. Armed with the power of distance and retrospection, I'd looked at our childhood through fresh eyes and seen a lot of red flags. Abe deceived me. He'd done horrible, beastly things. Bottom line? I didn't trust him. And I was afraid.

For me, that meeting in the shed was a courtesy. I would be leaving for college soon, and in spite of everything, I wanted us to part on good terms. Abe thought we shouldn't part at all. He tried to convince me to stay in Swanton. *We can apply for jobs clerking at the police station right here*, he said. *You don't have to go away.* But I did have to go, because now when I looked at him, I saw a juvenile delinquent and felt a bone-deep sense of foreboding. Like Doug said, his childhood was fucked up, and with Brett gone and Crissy rarely at home, Abe had to contend with Aunt Fee himself. It wasn't right, but neither was the intensity in his eyes. I couldn't stand it. I had to get out.

There was no one around to see me jump up while my foot was stuck through the aluminum frame of that chair, and no one to witness the stumble that followed. Nobody but me saw the long, rusty nail my cousin had been hiding in his hand all along. That was the last day I ever spoke to Abe. In that moment, I piled thousands of late-night giggles and whispered confidences and words of solace onto a funeral pyre, struck the match, and watched the fire burn.

My brother finished what was left of his warm scotch in a single swallow. Finally, he set his glass down on the table and pushed it aside. "Abe was twelve," he said. "Twelve fucking years old. But he was a psychopath even then. So you tell me if you think our cousin could have attacked his father and left him for dead."

SIXTEEN

My conversation with Doug stayed with me long after we loaded our glasses into the dishwasher and parted ways in the carpeted upstairs hall. Outside, the moon painted the street silver, and the house sounds dwindled to radiator clinks and the wind whispering at my window. My overactive mind was compounded by a headache and a hint of wooziness from the scotch, but that didn't stop me from picking up my phone and scouring the Internet for mentions of Trey Hayes.

With the witness from the shop and Trey's hat as evidence, my station had issued an Amber Alert. It included Trey's picture, but until the sketch came back from Tim's forensic artist, we had no image of Bram to share. Most of the news outlets had published a paragraph or two about Trey's disappearance, along with phone numbers for Crime Stoppers and the New York State Police. It wasn't enough.

There was little chance Bram was going to parade the kid around town, and nobody but the shop owner and me knew what Trey's abductor looked like. If we were going to find either of them, it would be through a yet-untapped witness or by the grace of exhaustive legwork.

I kept seeing Trey's face alongside Abe's, the way Abe looked at age twelve. Could Bram's origin story really involve patricide? It wasn't unheard of for children to commit heinous acts. In Britain, a fourteen-year-old killed her mother and sister with the help of an accomplice her same age. More recently, two thirteen-year-olds murdered a schoolgirl in Dublin. The idea of delving into the psychology of these crimes made me burrow deeper into my blankets.

Drawing the comforter up to my chin, I texted Tim. I wanted him to look for garden sheds in and around A-Bay, another prominent place from our mutual past that Bram might try to replicate now. Was I forcing correlations that didn't exist? Maybe so. But I couldn't afford not to turn over every stone.

The temperature plummeted overnight, and I woke up to frost-covered grass that crackled beneath my feet as I walked to my SUV. The roads were black and dusty-dry today, and the drive to downtown Swanton took less than five minutes.

In my previous job with the NYPD, I'd seen quite a few detectives tackle cold cases. They'd ruffle through heaps of papers on their desks and pore over ancient data, hoping new eyes and fresh resolve would help them see something somebody hadn't. It was no easy feat. Aside from working with evidence no one else had managed to streamline into a solve, they often dealt with witnesses who'd long since died, taking their testimony with them.

In contrast, my cases were always handed to me. I was typically the one collecting the statements. So I wasn't sure what to make of the situation with Brett. There was no previous inquest into his death, which meant no files to reference or witnesses that I knew of. No missing persons report or predetermined timeline, either. Alibis would be hard to come by so many years after the fact, and anything else I did manage to rustle up would be tough to corroborate. I stood on the precipice of a crime so masterfully executed it took decades for anyone to realize it even existed.

How on earth was I going to do this? *By working the angles you alone can see.* I was here in Swanton, with direct access to Brett's family and friends. My mother hadn't been entirely surprised this happened to him. That suggested there might be something in the man's past that could point me to his killer. I may not have been assigned to find Brett's murderer, or even authorized to run an investigation in Vermont, but as far as I knew I was the only one who understood there was a link between Brett's death and the current missing persons case in A-Bay. I owed it to my uncle to pursue every line of inquiry.

That said, I didn't think the local authorities would take kindly to an outsider foraging for information, so I'd ignored the smell of marmalade toast and fried eggs crisp around the edges that wafted in from my parents' kitchen, and disregarded my yearning to join my family. I had work to do.

Swanton's police force shared a municipal building with numerous other government agencies, but it took no time at all for me to locate the guy I was looking for. That's the beauty of village life: the regal lady with the hooked nose at the DMV pointed me to Fire and Rescue, where I got the name I needed from a sinewy man with an earring and a red goatee. Swanton Police Chief Fraser Harmison had a cleft in his chin, a bushy white moustache, and thinning hair scraped back from his face. As he listened to me identify myself and explain that his victim was my uncle, he adopted a sideways squint.

"I'm not here in any official capacity," I assured him, "or to get in your way. I do plan on asking some questions, though, so I thought you should know who I am."

"So the stranger nosing around a homicide doesn't become our next suspect?" Harmison's jowls bobbed when he chuckled. "Probably a good idea."

"*Next* suspect? Got your eye on someone already?"

"We're looking at some of Skilton's past associates. Old friends and such. The boys in St. Albans are giving us a hand, but I'll be honest with you, this case is stone-cold."

I said, "I guess Felicia and Crissy Skilton already filled you in on the last time they saw Brett?"

"I interviewed them both yesterday morning. We know

he made plans to move to Philly in June of '98. We're working on a timeline of his final days here in town."

"Well, I'd be happy to share whatever I find out."

"I'd appreciate that." He paused. "I guess you're hoping I'll do the same."

I smiled at him. "If you're so inclined. The cause of death, perhaps?"

Harmison gave me an admiring nod. "Why not? It'll be in the paper soon enough. The bones are badly weathered, but we found a star-shaped fracture on the occipital lobe that suggests blunt force trauma."

The occipital lobe. Brett was attacked from behind. "Any thoughts on the murder weapon?"

"Best guess? A branch or log. So you can imagine what kind of success we had finding it at the gravesite."

"He was dumped in the woods, I hear. Anything about the whereabouts that wasn't in the news?"

"Let's see," he said, thinking. "You know Hook Road off Route 78? Runs parallel to the Missisquoi River?"

I nodded.

"There's a fishing access over there, a little boat launch with a parking area big enough for five, six cars. In the trees just off that lot is where we found him. Dumped might not be accurate, though. We're thinking the killer left him where he fell."

"So the gravesite's the murder site. Interesting. How far was he from the road?"

"Not very. About twenty-five yards."

"Jesus," I said, "that's a bold move. Those woods are dense in summer, but I bet the boat ramp gets a lot of use, and in winter the trees are pretty sparse. It's amazing his remains weren't found sooner." I had driven that road a hundred times since 1998. Passed my uncle's body without even knowing it. "What kind of grave are we talking about?"

"The half-assed kind. The killer threw some leaves and branches on his body and called it a day. Whoever left him there must have been in a hurry."

Or in a panic. "How much were you able to recover? If the grave was shallow, surely animals got to him eventually."

Harmison touched his nose. "Bingo. Bones were scattered, but we got lucky with that pocketknife. ID'ing him couldn't have been easier."

"Great for you, not so great for his killer. Any blood on the knife, his or someone else's?"

"Nope."

I chewed my lip. "Whoever did it must not have been aware Brett was carrying a weapon, which might mean they didn't know him very well." According to Mom, Felicia believed Brett carried the knife at all times. There was no telling whether he kept up the habit after their separation, but he did have it with him the night he was killed.

"At the same time," I continued, "Brett had a weapon and didn't use it. It's possible he didn't see the attack coming. It's also possible the perp was someone he knew. I know it's a long shot, but is there any evidence at this stage that might point us to the killer? Other lost objects at the site, maybe? I could drive over there, take a peek for my—"

"Look, Merchant, was it?" The expression on Harmison's lined face told me I'd crossed a line. "You seem nice enough, but I really can't have you stepping on my team's toes."

"I understand," I said. Then, "Can I ask about the anonymous caller?"

The police chief sighed. "Yeah, that was strange."

"How so?"

"Well, he didn't seem to know exactly where the victim was. First thing he said was there's a body in the woods off River Street, up in the refuge. He mentioned the fishing access, said we'd find the deceased nearby, but when my officer asked him to pace it out—those woods are huge, and without a precise location we'd be searching for ages—he got squirrely. So I'm wondering, if he couldn't pinpoint the location, how did he know the body was there?"

Good question. "I heard he asked to remain anonymous, but do you have anything to work with on that front?"

"Wish I did. We'd like to have a conversation with him, believe me. The officer who took the call thought he was on the younger side, late twenties or early thirties. No discernable accent, though my guy said he sounded local."

I tilted my head. "How could he tell that?" Some Vermonters do have an accent, but that folksy, lyrical cadence isn't as common among younger citizens.

"He called it River Street," Harmison said. "Out-of-towners usually say Route 78."

I gave a nod. "For what it's worth, I think Skilton's known associates are a good place to start. They might be able to help us put together that timeline of events."

"Us?" Another sigh. "Like I said, I can't have you—"

"No, of course," I said quickly. "But his family is my family. I'm coming at things from a different angle. You never know where that might lead."

Harmison agreed he couldn't do much to stop me from talking to my cousin and aunt. I didn't mention that I planned on questioning Brett's friends, too.

Before I left, we exchanged cards and a promise to keep in touch. All told, the visit served as confirmation that Mom was right. When it came to finding Brett's killer, the locals were getting nowhere.

When I lived in New York, the anonymity afforded by its massive population was one of the things I enjoyed most. Every morning I'd let myself be pulled into a writhing mass of humanity, just another herring in the school. Lying low in a small town is more of a challenge. That was unfortunate for Brett's former best friend. I drove straight over to the plant on Jonergin Drive and was face-to-face with Russell Loming in no time. The man was due for a break when I arrived in the front office, and his supervisor was kind enough to let us chat in the employee lounge, a cubicle-sized room that smelled of stale powdered donuts and sweaty feet.

It didn't surprise me that Loming was still working in manufacturing, trade jobs in Swanton being what they were. Like Brett, Loming was a local; I'd crossed paths with his youngest kid in school, a loudmouth named Max, but had no recollection of Loming himself. It took all of thirty seconds for me to see why he and Brett had been an inseparable pair. Even wearing faded blue coveralls, Loming had that same smirk and swagger, and while he might have passed for handsome once, his bulging middle now made him look considerably more pregnant than Suze.

Loming didn't waste any time with pleasantries, though he did shake my hand. "I already told that fat old cop I don't know anything about what happened to Brett, but I'm happy to repeat myself. Glad I wore my best suit," he said. There was something sexual about his grip. I snatched my hand away and resisted wiping it on my pants. I didn't bother to clarify that I wasn't with the local police, just flipped open my notebook and asked if I could take some notes. Loming gave me a withering look, but didn't debate my request.

"Why do you think I'm interested in interviewing you, Mr. Loming?"

Loming was balding, and had shaved his head down to quarter-inch gray bristles. He massaged the stubble as he spoke. "Brett and I used to be buddies. That was a long time ago."

"I'm sorry for your loss. What do you make of all this? Any ideas about what happened to your friend?"

"Ex-friend. Like I told you guys before, Brett must have rubbed someone the wrong way."

"Like how?"

"Like he owed someone money and didn't pay up."

Money. It was at the core of most crimes, the chewy black center you knew was there but had to crunch through layer after layer of lies to reach. Money—wanted, owed, distributed in a way deemed unjust—brought out the worst in people, from greed to desperation, jealousy to pride. Coming off a case where following the money had helped Tim and I catch a killer, I knew this for a fact. If Loming was right and Brett had owed someone money, this case might be more of the same.

"Any idea who he was in debt to?"

Without taking his eyes from mine, Loming said, "You seem awfully young to be a detective." Wetly, he snapped his tongue against his teeth. "Must be pretty dangerous work."

I can't explain it, but whenever my scar catches someone's attention, I feel their stare like a needle being dragged down the skin of my cheek. "Answer the question, Mr. Loming."

"Brett's stack of IOUs was taller than me."

"Did he owe *you* money?"

"He might have. Nothing major, though."

"Did you know Brett was planning on leaving town?"

"He told me, yeah. I didn't blame him. His wife was a

psycho bitch, pardon my French. They'd already split, but she wouldn't stop harping on him. I figured leaving Swanton was the only way he could cut ties with that woman for good."

"Did you keep in touch with him after he left?"

"Oh sure, we were pen pals. I was partial to scented paper and purple ink."

"Mr. Loming—"

"No," he said grudgingly, "we didn't keep in touch."

"Not even a phone call? Didn't you wonder where he ended up?"

"Brett's the one who convinced me to hand over my pay-checks to that goddamn casino up in Montreal. He was a bad influence."

I studied him. "You don't seem like the type to be easily influenced," I said, thinking, *You don't look that virtuous, either.*

Loming's shrug was loose. "Okay, so maybe it went both ways."

Something about Russell Loming's attitude reminded me of Crissy. This wasn't your average death, to be sure. Brett was gone long before we knew he was gone for good, and that made it difficult to gauge the nature of his relationship with others. How close had these men been, really? Loming knew about Brett's problems with Felicia, but that could have been due to idle talk. Half the town had heard about their squabbles. Were these men gambling buddies, plain and simple? I just couldn't be sure. "Do you remember what you were doing in June of 1998?"

"Do *you*?"

"Was there anyone else Brett was close to before he moved out of town?" I asked, plowing on.

"I was a married man by then, with two boys at home. I had better things to do than keep track of Brett's love life."

Wait, what? "I didn't say anything about his love life. Was Brett dating someone, Mr. Loming? You're under no obligation to answer my questions, but if you don't and I find out you know something, I'll wipe that grin right off your face."

"Ohh," Loming said, feigning an epiphany. "You're asking about Cheryl."

"Cheryl?"

"Brett's girlfriend."

My mind went into overdrive. As far as I knew, Brett hadn't left Felicia for another woman. It was possible, however, that he was in a new relationship before his death. "Got a last name for me?" I asked.

"Aw, hell, I can't remember that."

"When exactly were they dating?"

Lazily, he lifted his gaze to the room's low, dingy ceiling. "Don't know when it started. But I can tell you when it ended."

So can I, I thought, picturing Brett's lifeless body among the trees.

Loming's stare was distant. His mind was in overdrive, too. "Now that I think about it," he said, "if you really want to find out who did this, you should talk to Cheryl. They were hot and heavy for a while. I don't believe she was too thrilled when he took off."

"Thanks for your time, Mr. Loming," I said, tearing a piece of paper from my notebook. "I'll be needing your number and address, if you don't mind."

"Call me Russ." He scribbled down his number and forced his sweaty hand against mine. "And call me. Anytime."

SEVENTEEN

In the parking lot of the plant, I messaged Tim. He'd responded to my previous text with a thumbs-up emoji and no questions asked, but now he had bad news. *Got a land survey of the houses in town with standalone structures like garden sheds. Sol and Bogle searched the few we found. Nothing there, or in the basements.* I felt my shoulders slump. I never imagined thinking about my scar could give me comfort, but I'd been hopeful that Bram might incorporate parts of our shared past into his game. That maybe the reference to swans was only the beginning. At least then I'd stand a chance.

After my disappointing check-in with Tim, my attention returned to Brett. I spent ten minutes cleaning up my notes on Russell Loming and transcribing what I'd learned from Police Chief Harmison. If Loming wasn't lying, and assuming I could locate her, Cheryl might have some valuable insights to share. It was Harmison's report vis-à-vis Brett's autopsy that had me feeling cautiously optimistic. *Blunt force trauma. The killer left him where he fell.* Those factors deepened the pool of suspects. Anyone could attack somebody from behind. A man.

A woman.

A kid.

It felt good to puzzle over a case again. It was also a convenient avoidance tactic. The dread I'd felt about sinking helplessly into my past was back, but I could only delay it for so long. Today was about reconnecting with long-lost family, and that meant it was time to pay a visit to Aunt Fee.

The house stood less than a block from Crissy's, and I cruised up the road at a snail's pace, shocked all over again that this embittered mother and daughter shared the very same street. My memories of the Skilton family converged on a split-level from the sixties that wore its age like a curse—rotten siding on the outside, smelly carpets within, and a porch railing forever caked in dank green algae. Felicia's new place was nothing like that. Its white trim hadn't been left to yellow like Crissy's, and the driveway I turned into looked newly repaved.

After parking, I paused at the door, puffing out white plumes of breath and staring at the water. Felicia had the same spectacular bay view and easy access to the wildlife refuge as Crissy, and there was a motorboat tied to her dock. From what I could remember, neither my aunt nor my cousin had a history of boating. Despite living so close to Lake

Champlain, my family was always more comfortable with our feet on the ground.

"Shana, my God," Felicia said when she opened the door, her gaze alighting on my scar and flitting away just as quickly. "It's been too long."

As she ushered me inside, I got a timid hug and a chance to feel her ribs move under her loose skin. She was layered in scarves, a tunic, and a celery-green cardigan that made her pale blue eyes look yellow in a way that was unnerving. This was something else that distinguished mother from daughter: Felicia had shed a few pounds. Her fine, flowing hair was completely gray, and so long the ends tickled her elbows. I found her new look perplexing. Was she a mystic now? Had my aunt given herself heart and soul to Crock-Pot yogurt and transcendental meditation retreats? She was thin, but she looked healthy. More cheerful than I remembered, too.

Too cheerful to be grieving.

It was the strangest thing, seeing Felicia now that I knew the atrocities her son had committed, crimes to which she remained oblivious. So much of my job involves tracing bad people to their kin, not just because I'm following a lead, but because I need to know the life they came from, walk their path backward from criminal to harmless kid. I'd seen the volatility that surrounded Bram firsthand, and while I was determined to keep an open mind, facing Felicia now made me realize I took it as a given that my aunt shouldered some of the blame.

Felicia invited me to sit down in a living room that

matched her outfit and offered me a hot peppermint tea. She talked while she fixed it, her monologue distinctly devoid of substance. She told me the weather was unseasonably cold, as if I hadn't lived three-quarters of my life right around the corner, and explained about the Christmas light contest, to be judged by the Swanton Chamber of Commerce. Felicia had never entered before, but she'd always wanted to. This was going to be her year. By the time the tea had steeped and we were settled on the couch, she'd covered every topic imaginable, aside from her husband's death.

I sipped from a black-and-yellow-striped mug that read *Don't worry, bee happy* and said, "I'd like to talk to you about Brett."

Felicia warmed her hands on a mug of her own and sighed. "The man's never been so popular."

I gave her my condolences. Added, "This can't be easy."

"I still thought about him sometimes. Wondered where he ended up." Her laugh, a sharp *ha*, gave me a start.

The pastel room, the sinus-clearing tea, my smiling aunt—all of it made me feel ill, but I soldiered on. "As you know, the police are conducting a criminal investigation to determine exactly what happened. I'm not a part of that, but—"

"But you want to help." That last word—*help*—was delivered with a slightly disparaging look. I got the sense she didn't believe my presence in her house was totally selfless.

"Your mother called," she explained. "She told me you were in town. I worked the rest out myself."

So Crissy wasn't alone in thinking of me as a sicko obsessed with crime. Felicia's mint tea wasn't doing much to calm my nerves. "I know the police have already stopped by, so I'm sorry if these questions feel redundant. We're all just trying to track Brett's movements around the time of his departure, so we can figure out how and when he ended up back in Swanton."

"The departure part's easy," she said. "He quit his job on June 19th of 1998."

The same day we went to Brett's factory. That was when Abe and I stumbled upon his plan to clear out. The receptionist at the manufacturing plant took pity on Abe and divulged more than she should have. *Aw, honey, didn't your daddy tell you? He's moving to Philly. This was his last day.* Abe was shattered. From the moment Brett left Felicia, packing up his Levi's and his bottle cap collection—he used to let Abe organize them by color, challenge him to see how many he could stack—Abe imagined he'd eventually come home to his kids. He didn't.

If the day Brett quit was June 19th, then June 19th had been a Friday. I was sure about that because we had pizza for dinner that night. Friday was always pizza night at my house, my favorite. Abe's too. But Abe didn't join us for that particular meal. He was home, feeling betrayed and humiliated by both of his parents.

Was that true? Or was I remembering what Bram told me last year, in that godforsaken basement?

"You have a good memory," I told Felicia, unimpressed by the irony of that. I knew it was unreasonable, but it irked me that I wasn't the first investigator to speak with her. The date of her husband's departure was on the tip of her tongue, and I needed to know whether she'd clung to it all these years or dug it up for Harmison's sake.

I got my answer. "He left a week to the day before Crissy's sixteenth birthday," she said.

"And did you have any contact with Brett after that weekend?"

Felicia pursed her lips. "What was there to say? He made it clear he wasn't going to help us financially. He owed money to half the town by the time he left, and I didn't want to risk getting mixed up in that. I always hoped he'd get it together and come home—not to stay, but to be more involved with the kids, at least. Be a father to them. Abe was barely twelve when his dad took off, and Brett missed Crissy's Sweet Sixteen and didn't even call."

She hadn't answered my question, and her fencing act felt deliberate. "So no contact at all after the weekend? Not ever again?"

"Just the letter, and that was ages ago."

I frowned. "What letter?"

"The letter about Abe. It came a few years after Brett left, right after Abe . . ."

Cut you.

Ran away.

Felicia could have said any number of things. I felt my blood pressure nudge upward as she studied me, but she stayed silent.

I asked about the letter.

"It said Abe had arrived in Philadelphia. There was no phone number, and no return address. No way at all for me to reach them. It felt like a slap in the face, Brett's way of calling dibs on our son. I didn't even know they'd been in touch all those years, but they must have been or Abe wouldn't have known where to find him."

I jogged my knee as I recalled what Mom said about the age of the bones not adding up. The letter seemed to prove Brett had left Swanton as planned. I knew for a fact his son ran off in 2002. If Abe met up with Brett in Philly, Brett couldn't have died in Swanton years earlier. Did the forensic analyst get it wrong? It didn't make any sense.

"When was the last time you actually saw Brett?" I asked. "You, Crissy, and Abe?"

Felicia tucked a wisp of long silver hair behind her ear, and her pinky snagged on her hoop earring. "Lord, how am I supposed to remember that? He didn't visit regularly, as you know."

I nodded. I did know. "I don't suppose you still have that letter?"

I didn't expect her to say yes. Felicia had moved on from her last home and the bad memories there, but within moments she was walking to a linen closet down the hall. She returned with a shoebox in hand, and when she lifted the lid, I saw it was crammed with family photos. A single letter, folded in thirds, lay right on top.

She handed it to me, and I examined the writing in the

natural light from the living room window. The letter was dated September 4, 2002. Over all these years, the only communication my aunt had with her husband was a scant paragraph in length.

> *I'm sorry I left so suddenly. I hope you and*
> *Crissy are well. I want you to know Abe's safe in*
> *Philadelphia, and he'll be living with me from now*
> *on. I think you know that's for the best.*

"Did you show this to the police?"

"No," Felicia said, startled. "Should I have?"

The letter was crucial to establishing a timeline. Felicia had to know that. It didn't seem like she was going out of her way to help the local cops. On the contrary, if Felicia hadn't mentioned the letter to Harmison, that could qualify as obstruction.

I asked if I could hold on to the letter, and Felicia agreed that would be fine. When we sat back down, she lowered her eyes. "I wasn't a good mother to your cousins, Shana."

Oh, God. What to say? "I'm sure you did the best you could."

"All I ever wanted was to keep them safe, but I didn't know how, not without hurting them. I was so afraid."

"Of what?" I needed to understand. "What were you afraid of, Aunt Fee?"

She angled her head and said, "Losing them."

I never would have thought my aunt could be prophetic,

yet here she was describing a fear that ultimately came to pass. She'd lost them both, and much more.

Felicia said, "You must have heard some terrible stories about me."

My whole face burned. I'd heard stories, yes, but the worst thing I knew Felicia to have done I'd witnessed with my own eyes. Abe didn't want to tell her what we learned the day we walked to Brett's work. He knew how upset his mother would be. Felicia was still furious with Brett for leaving her the first time, but Abe was committed to changing his father's mind. That made it all the more heartbreaking when he failed.

By the time we got back to the house that Friday, Felicia was frantic with worry and demanded to know where we'd been. Abe made me wait out on the lawn while they talked, but I saw him through the kitchen window, its curtains flapping in the summer breeze off the bay.

When he got to the part about Brett moving out of state, Felicia grabbed a jug of milk from the counter and swung it straight at her son's head. The whole side of his face was purple for days. Afterward, Felicia cried harder than Abe did. But the damage was done.

"I needed help back then," Felicia went on, "but I was too overstrung to ask for it, and Brett's drinking and gambling made me even more paranoid. I used to be so worried any trouble he stirred up would find its way back to the kids. But the trouble, it came from me. When I think of what Abe did to you, I can hardly bear it. Can I tell you something,

Shana?" she said. "I *knew*. I didn't want to believe it, could never bring myself to tell Della, but I always knew it wasn't an accident."

Felicia's fingers unfolded themselves toward my face. I couldn't help it; I recoiled as if I'd been slapped. She snatched her hand back and stared hard at her lap. "It was the idea of you planning to go off to college that pushed Abe over the edge. He couldn't bear it, especially not after Brett abandoned him."

Abandoned. Was that how Bram felt?

"I wanted to do right by you," my aunt said. "I tried to set him straight. I told him he needed help. Therapy, maybe even medication. He called me a hypocrite. He called me all sorts of things. Everyone thinks he ran away, but we fought and fought that day, and in the end, I told him to go. I made him. But I never meant to drive him away for good, never imagined he wouldn't come back. He was only sixteen."

A chill shot through me. Only sixteen, and tossed out of the house. It was entirely possible Bram believed his mother had abandoned him, too. Despite what she said about their fight Felicia must have been relieved, in a way, to have him gone. After what he did to me, I didn't know how else she would be able to look her sister in the eye again.

I opened my mouth to question her some more, and found I had no idea what to say. This was what I'd been hoping for, straight-from-the-source insight into Bram's twisted mind, but Felicia wasn't the only one feeling repentant.

Back in the East Village, when I was face-to-face with

Bram and trying to identify the man who claimed to be from my hometown, I'd asked him why he left Swanton. *"I had to,"* he said. *"My mother wouldn't let me stay."* But if I hadn't been so quick to move on from Swanton, he wouldn't have attacked me. If he hadn't attacked me, Felicia wouldn't have kicked him out. And if she hadn't kicked him out, would he still have become Blake Bram?

Felicia collected our empty mugs and brought them to the kitchen, where the digital clock on the oven caught her eye.

"Oh," she said. "Hon, I'm sorry, I didn't realize it was so late. I've got a yoga class downtown in twenty minutes."

"No problem." I was happy to get going. The house and our history were suffocating. I was almost at the door before I remembered about Cheryl. "Felicia," I said. "I talked to Brett's friend Russell Loming, and he mentioned something about Brett having a girlfriend around the time he disappeared. A woman named Cheryl?"

I watched my aunt's face for a reaction. She hadn't alluded to a girlfriend, but now her mouth bent into a new shape. The haughty expression was reminiscent of Crissy's, but different. Darker. "The only Cheryl I know is Cheryl Copely."

"Cheryl Copely," I repeated miserably. "As in Robbie Copely's mother?"

She nodded. "Brett and I met her when Robbie and Crissy started dating."

Please God, don't let Brett's killer be Suze's mother-in-

law. "But you aren't aware of a relationship there?" I said, hopeful.

After a few seconds of silence, she pulled her cardigan across her chest as if she'd caught a chill. "No. Brett and I split in late '97. I didn't care to know what he did after that."

I didn't believe her; that *no* was bullshit through and through. On paper, Felicia and Brett were still married. She'd wanted him to be more involved with the kids. Surely she'd kept tabs on what was happening in his life.

"Brett didn't just leave you," I said. "He left his kids, his job, his friends, and a girlfriend, and it all happened very suddenly. Why would he do that, Felicia?"

That smile. She had the same thin lips as my mom, and now they were stretched straight across her small teeth. It wasn't really a smile at all, but a grimace.

"If I knew that," she said, "you wouldn't be here."

EIGHTEEN

My plan was to question Crissy about Cheryl Copely. Between Loming's insinuation that Cheryl was involved in Brett's murder, and Felicia's oblique reaction to the mention of a girlfriend, I needed another opinion. I had a feeling Loming was using Cheryl to deflect attention, but if she and Brett really had been an item, Cheryl merited an interview, and I wanted to get Crissy's take on her father's possible romance first.

The route to the office building where I knew Crissy worked required that I pass right by her house. What I saw there stopped me dead in my tracks.

It was nearly 11:00 a.m., but Crissy's car was still in her driveway—and it had a friend. I trundled to a stop across the street and saw the front door swing open and a small woman emerge. Her dark head was lowered, her features bunched together in distress. I felt my jaw fall open as I turned off the engine and got out of my SUV. "Suze?" I called into the icy air. "What are you doing here?"

"Shana! Hi!" My friend's eyes were huge with surprise, but she gave me a hug when I got close, her unzipped jacket flapping in the wind. "Sorry," she said, "I'm still not used to you being back. You startled me."

"Um, likewise. You're visiting Crissy?"

"Oh," she said. "Yeah. We do that sometimes. She's my go-to source for school questions."

"I didn't know you guys still talked." *Still* wasn't the right word, because as far as I knew, Crissy and Suze had never talked. We gave my cousin a wide berth when we were kids, though Suze had always been intrigued by Crissy's scandalous behavior. As the designated voice of reason, it was up to me to remind her how quickly sex and drugs could devolve from weekend fun to addiction, expulsion, prison time.

I couldn't imagine Suze and Crissy growing up to become friends, especially since Crissy used to date Robbie, who was now Suze's husband—but what did I know about their lives? In a town of sixty-five hundred people, there are only so many candidates for friendship to go around. As I pondered this, I suddenly understood how Suze found out I was in town. I'd visited Crissy on Monday morning. And Crissy had turned around and called Suze.

"How long have you been friends?" I asked.

"We reconnected a few years ago—thank God! Some of the other moms I know are straight-up bitches." The way

Suze tossed a glance down the street, I half expected to see legions of catty women in yoga pants, chubby toddlers propped against their hips. "I ran into Crissy at the nail salon a few months before I got married, and we just hit it off."

"But school questions already? Erynn's practically still a baby."

"She'll be three next month." Suze shifted her weight. "You have no idea how complicated it is to navigate this stuff."

Was there a hint of acrimony in her tone? "I'm sure you're right," I said. "Crissy's not working today?"

"She only works afternoons on Tuesdays and Thursdays. It's a small agency; they don't get that busy. Anyway, what are *you* doing here?"

"Same as you. Minus the grade school primer."

Suze shrugged. "Well, I better get going. I've got some errands to run before I pick up Erynn."

"Daycare?"

"She's with my mother-in-law."

"You mean Cheryl?" The words, my tone, it all felt disingenuous. Suze and I were trying to revive a friendship that had been on life support for years. And that was going to make what I had to do next very difficult.

Suze narrowed her eyes. "You know Cheryl?"

I took a breath. "Not really. But listen, do you know anything about Cheryl dating Brett way back when?"

Again with the surprised expression. "Seriously? Is that true?"

"I'm not sure," I said. "It's what I'm hearing, though."

Suze sank her chin into the folds of her fleece scarf. "I feel like Crissy would have told me that? But I guess we don't talk much about Robbie."

"Well, I'd like to talk to Cheryl about it. Just in case she can help with the case."

If this news alarmed Suze, she didn't show it. "Cheryl's a great lady, an amazing grandma to Erynn, and really supportive of me. I'm sure she'd be happy to answer your questions."

She took out her phone and AirDropped Cheryl's number and address. Then she said, "I've really got to go," and after one more fleeting hug, she was off.

As soon as Suze drove away, I knocked on Crissy's door.

No PJs for my cousin today. Her attire was business casual and fairly demure, apart from the hot pink button-down shirt popping open at her chest. Crissy oozed sarcasm when she said, "Perfect timing as always, cuz," but I wasn't taking no for an answer, and after I darkened her doorway for a moment, she let me in.

Today the miasma of perfume was even stronger, and I thought I detected an underlying stench of stale cigarettes.

"Cheryl Copely," I said as we sat down on the couch. "What do you know about her relationship with Brett?"

"Cheryl?" Crissy's tone was harsh. "You can't just waltz back into town and start messing with people's lives, Shana."

The time I spent with Felicia had thrown Crissy's long-simmering anger into sharp relief. Her mother might have accepted the true nature of my scar, but not Crissy. Those moments in the shed, when I stumbled, were unseen; it was my word against Abe's. In his version of events, I'd fallen on a box of old gardening tools. I shrieked and grasped at my blood-slippery face while Abe, loving cousin that he was, went for help. Crissy and I never talked about it, but if this was the story she gave credence to, if she blamed me for Abe running away, it was no wonder she was pissed.

"I'm trying to identify your father's killer," I said, tamping down my frustration. "Brett's girlfriend is the logical place to start."

"Do you even hear yourself? Why would his girlfriend want to hurt him?"

And just like that, I had confirmation Russell Loming was telling the truth. Brett and Cheryl had been an item. But the fact that Crissy knew this was troubling.

"What's going on here?" I said. "I just came from your mom's place, and she claims she had no idea Brett and Cheryl were dating. If you knew, why keep it a secret from Felicia?"

She laughed derisively. "If she found out about the two of them, she would have murdered Brett."

Her choice of words made me wince. Did Crissy ever call him Dad anymore? I wondered if this was her way of staying emotionally disconnected from the horror surrounding his death. If so, it didn't seem to be working.

"If Felicia didn't know about Cheryl," I said, "then how did you?" I had no recollection of Abe mentioning his father had a girlfriend, and he confided in me about everything. Crissy let my question hang in the air a long time before answering.

"They didn't exactly advertise it. I found out from Robbie."

I'd been steadily sinking into my cousin's too-soft couch since sitting down, and when I straightened my back in surprise, my knees almost touched my nose. It wasn't a professional pose, but I liked my proximity to Crissy, hoped she'd be easier to read up close. "Hold on," I said. In my mind, I sorted through the tangle of wending threads that linked Brett to Cheryl, Cheryl to Suze, Suze to Crissy, Crissy to Robbie. "That means your dad was dating your ex-boyfriend's mom? That's—"

"Gross," she supplied. "Believe me, I know. Thank God Robbie and I had broken up by then. We only dated freshman year, and they didn't get together until I was a sophomore."

"Was it serious?" I asked. If so, Cheryl couldn't have been too happy to learn Brett was leaving.

Crissy folded her arms. "I don't want to talk about this."

"The only way to figure out what happened to him is by learning as much as possible about his life back then. You and your mom deserve to know the truth."

Crissy's face went crimson. "My mom scared the living shit out of us as kids. She could have gotten help, but she didn't, and Abe and I were the ones who had to suffer. When I finally made it out of that house, all I asked was for her to leave me alone, and she went and bought a place on the same damn block. And now? Now I have to see her every day, standing on her lawn mooning over my boys like a stalker. My mother doesn't deserve a thing."

I cast about for something to say. I knew Crissy and Felicia weren't close, but I was shocked by the intensity of my cousin's loathing. After years of being imprisoned by her mother's senseless rules, Crissy hadn't just broken out: she'd set the jailhouse on fire.

A surge of resentment welled up inside me. If I had any hope of finding Trey, I had to figure this out. Yes, I'd made the choice to track down Brett's killer, but couldn't a girl get a break? The two women closest to him didn't seem the least bit interested in putting his case to bed. All I had to work with was my shared past with Bram and my family's accounts, all incomplete and unreliable. In a way, being back in Swanton under these conditions felt like being held captive all over again. But I'd be damned if I was going to let Bram trap me this time.

"Why can't you just be open with me?" I said, incensed. "Why does everything you say feel like evasion?"

"Why can't *you* understand it's killing me to think of him this way!" Crissy set her jaw and looked away. Her breaths were coming fast, but her body had grown still. "How would you feel if it was Wally out there? *Right there.*" With a trembling arm, she pointed in the direction of the window, the bay, the refuge beyond. Reflexively, I shook my head. *Dad, out there?* It was unimaginable.

Her voice was hushed when she said, "He would have loved my boys. I used to tell them about him, how they might get to meet him someday. Yesterday they came home from school and asked if it was true grandpa was dead. Don't you get it?" Crissy said, her voice breaking. "I don't care about being open. I don't want to help you find whoever did this. All I want is for it to be over."

But it's so far from over, I thought, trying not to let my pity for my cousin show. Crissy had a hard childhood. She'd cast her mother aside, and her father had suffered a horrible fate.

Bram would make it all so much worse.

NINETEEN

’d never seen Crissy cry. She would sooner hammer a sap spigot into her hand than show weakness, and I won’t lie: the sight of her wet, red face rattled me. I left shortly after that. My cousin and I may not have been close, but I knew her well enough to let her be.

Where did that leave me? All I’d succeeded in confirming was that Cheryl and Brett had dated. That made Cheryl’s house the next logical destination.

She lived a few blocks from my parents over on Jones Court, a tidy street that in the summer months was jungle-lush with old trees. Those trees were bare and colorless as skeletons now, and the way they lined the street gave the impression of ghostly sentinels stripped of their armor.

I hadn’t called ahead; over the years I’d had some success with getting the truth out of witnesses by catching them un-awares. I walked up the path to the narrow porch and peered into the sidelights as I rang the bell. Inside, the house was quiet. Didn't Suze say Cheryl was home taking care of Erynn? It hadn't been that long since Suze left to run those errands, but I supposed it was possible she'd already come and left. Maybe Cheryl was napping, or had gone out herself.

Or maybe she was lying low. Whether or not Fraser Harmison had already tracked her down, Cheryl might not be too keen on talking about her dead ex-boyfriend to a stranger. I rang a second time and knocked intermittently for several minutes before resorting to my phone. When Cheryl's number went to voicemail, I gave up and reached into my wallet for Harmison's card.

I owed the police chief an update, and managed to catch him at his desk. He was interested to hear about Cheryl and the letter from Brett, but it was immediately clear the top spot on his watch list was occupied by Russell Loming. Apparently Loming had a record that included domestic abuse. He'd beaten up his first wife on more than one occasion, and that history of violence, coupled with his allusion to an unpaid debt, made him a viable suspect.

Loming. He was little more than a blip on my radar. Had I been too focused on Bram and Felicia? Was I letting him off easy? By all accounts Loming and Brett had been friends, but I'd seen plenty of happy relationships turn toxic, especially when money was involved. Loming was one of the few people who knew Brett was leaving, and when. If Brett owed him some cash, Loming might not appreciate the man's hasty retreat.

Russell Loming had also made a point of trying to side-track me by bringing up Cheryl. Redirecting my attention would seem like a smart strategy to a guy who was guilty of murder.

I'd told Harmison my connection to Brett would be useful. *I'm coming at things from a different angle*, I'd said. But what if that angle was skewed, like so many moments from my past? Like that night Abe, Suze, and I went drinking. It was Abe who planted the idea in my head that he'd saved us all from a ride in the paddy wagon. If my obsession with the idea that the buck stopped at the Skiltons' front door was making me shortsighted, I might overlook critical evidence. What if that meant I couldn't find Brett's killer? What if it meant we would never find Trey?

Back at my parents' house, I parked next to Doug's car and turned off the ignition. I hadn't talked to Tim all morning, and while his silence didn't bode well for positive progress on Trey's case, I had to know what was going on. This time, he answered his cell on the first ring. That didn't bode well, either.

"Anything new?" I asked, sinking into the residual heat of the seat warmer. Through the big living room window I could see the back of my mother's head. She was sitting on the sofa.

"Let me put you on speaker," said Tim. "McIntyre's here, too." I heard a click, and the ambient sound of the station.

"Mac?" I said eagerly.

"I'm here. We just got the composite sketch from that forensic artist."

"Check your e-mail," said Tim.

In recent weeks I'd gotten used to the barren column of white that greeted me when I opened my mail app. Tim's message was a welcome sight. I clicked on the attached image and found myself looking at the man in the hat who had left the poster of Trey and Brett at Smuggler's Cargo.

To successfully evade New York investigators, Blake Bram had to excel at disguising his looks. I'd spent hours studying his face in that basement, committing every pore to memory while visualizing him behind bars. Since then I'd been living under the assumption I would recognize him if he passed me on the street. Sat down next to me at Nelly's. Walked into my karate studio. But the face on the screen bore only the faintest resemblance to the Bram I'd seen in New York. The nose was too broad, the eyebrows too arched. Bram had grown a goatee and cut his hair, and he'd gained weight, at least forty pounds. It smoothed the lines on his forehead and plumped the creases under his eyes.

He had worked hard to become invisible, but I knew beyond doubt it was him. He'd long since fixed his teeth, Abe's most distinguishing feature, but not the pointed ears that looked so much like my own. He hadn't managed to scrub away Abe completely. I doubted that he ever would.

"Is it him?" Tim's voice was strained.

When I didn't reply right away, Mac said, "Breathe, Shay. Is it him?"

"It's him."

"Jesus," said Tim, and I realized a part of him hadn't believed me, didn't want it to be true. "The analysis came back on that blood, too. It's definitely Trey's. The hat, along with your positive ID, is all we need to issue an APB. I'll connect with your old precinct in New York, let them know we've got a lead." After a second, he added, "We should put a man on you, Shana. Get you some protection."

"I'm fine."

"Are you?" asked Mac. "This guy trailed you all the way from Manhattan. What if he's still on your tail now?"

"There's no guarantee he stayed in A-Bay," said Tim. "He could have taken Trey anywhere, including Vermont. Swanton's his hometown, right? Same as you? If he's trying to bait you, that's exactly where he'd go."

Tim wasn't wrong, and that line of reasoning led me to another. It had already occurred to me that Bram could be monitoring Crissy and Felicia. What I hadn't considered was that he might be watching my parents, too. I glanced again at the picture window. My mother was still there, unmoving.

"I'm with my family," I said. "It's a tiny town, and I know what he looks like now. If he's here, I'll find him."

"That's the last thing I want you to do."

"I think what Tim means," McIntyre said, "is that you're in a vulnerable position out there. Unarmed, and miles from backup."

"Maybe you should come back," Tim said and paused. He seemed to be struggling with something. "I know you're there for your family. I know they need you. But Shane, Bram's got this kid, and you know more about him than anyone. We need you here, too."

Sometimes, I thought back to Tern Island and what it was like to work that first case with Tim. I hadn't wanted to tell him I'd been abducted, was mulish in my refusal to show any sign of weakness. The shame I felt over my failure to apprehend Blake Bram had been crippling. All of that was a piece of spinach stuck in my teeth compared to what I felt now.

With the identity of Trey's abductor confirmed, Tim, Mac, and everyone else in A-Bay would stop at nothing to track Bram down. What good would it do to tell them who he really was? I didn't see how that would increase their chances of finding him. All it would do is let the world know this heartless killer was my flesh and blood, and shine a spotlight on my family. Confessing days before my evaluation would also cast doubt on my character and abilities as an investigator. It might even destroy my chances of getting reinstated. It was best if I stayed the course.

"I'm here for my family," I said, "but I'm also working on Trey's case. There's a lot of information to be gleaned about Bram here."

"Okay," said Mac. "Let's back up. The fact is that you're still suspended, and it's against my better judgment to involve you in this at all. Maybe Swanton is the best place for you right now. Lay low and see what you can find out there. Did you tell her about the fisherman?"

She was talking to Tim. "What fisherman?" I asked.

"Bogle found a local angler who saw a man dumping something in Carnegie Bay, off Iroquois Point," Tim said.

I closed my eyes. "What kind of something?"

"Something wrapped in a tarp, about four feet in length." He drew a breath. "We did a sweep of the shoreline and the houses along the bay, but most are locked up tight for the season. We're sending in divers within the hour."

My eyes flew open. "There's no way Trey's in the water."

"We've got to follow every lead."

"Bram wouldn't dump him."

"The kid's blood is all over that hat," said Tim.

"That was an empty threat."

"Shane." I could picture him gritting his teeth. I drove him crazy sometimes. "The man killed three women and a cop and kept you in a cage for a week. What makes you think he has any sympathy for a child?"

"Without Trey, there's no game. Trust me, Bram won't hurt him, not until he gets what he wants."

"What the hell does he want?" said Tim.

To have me bear witness to the first kill he ever made? To find out who murdered his father? To torture me? "I don't know." I slapped the steering wheel with my splayed palm once, twice. Again and again until my burn crackled with pain. "I don't fucking know what he wants! I wish to God I did."

"I'm trying to understand," Tim said in a thick voice. "I'm trying to trust you. If there's a chance Trey's already gone, I have to think about his parents. If he's in that water, I can't let this drag on any longer than is necessary. I won't."

In my SUV, I hung my head. "It's your case," I said.

When I hung up, his final words stayed with me, sizzling black as a brand.

Is it?

TWENTY

I closed the front door behind me and sighed as I pried off my boots, heel to toe, one by one. Swanton was sucking the life out of me—too much family, too many bad memories—and now the situation in my new home was uncomfortable, too. Already there was a text on my phone from Mac. *You okay? Tim's just stressed. We all are.*

Of course. I understand, I typed back, but what I was thinking was, *I'm alone in this, and if I can't crack the code, we're all doomed.*

I found my parents drinking tea in the living room. My dad had enforced this tradition for as long as I could remember, and even now I often reached for a hot drink and a cookie in the late afternoon. It was barely twelve o'clock, though, and their heads swiveled when I walked in. They'd been waiting for me. The first words out of Mom's mouth were, "I talked to your aunt."

Oh, shit.

"Honey," she said once I was sitting down. "Your father and I don't think this is a good idea."

Play dumb. Feign ignorance. "What do you mean?"

"Come now," said Dad, "you're investigating Brett's death. It's obvious, love, you have that look, the same one you used to get when watching *Columbo*."

That made me smile. I did love *Columbo*. "I'm here," I said with a shrug. "Might as well see if I can help."

"You've only just recovered from not one, but two very traumatic experiences. The last thing you need is a relapse."

"I'm doing fine."

"And that's wonderful," said Mom. "But don't you think it might be too soon to jump back on the horse? Your evaluation is in two days. How does your counselor feel about your being here?"

I squirmed in my seat and let my gaze roam to the fireplace mantel, the bookshelves, anywhere but my mother's face. How would Gil feel? Not great. "He doesn't know I'm here *right now*, but I told him I was planning to come for Thanksgiving. He was fine with that. He said a good support system is crucial."

They leaned their heads toward each other and locked eyes. Another transmission only they could discern.

"This isn't an average case," said my mother. "Brett was your uncle. His passing is upsetting enough without you rooting through his dirty laundry."

"He didn't *pass*, he was *murdered*, and rooting is the only way to find out why. Don't any of you want to know who did this?" I dropped my elbows to my knees and sank my hands into my hair. "Felicia kept crucial evidence from the police. Crissy knew Brett had a girlfriend at the time he was killed and said nothing. He was dating Robbie Copely's mom, were you aware of that? Are you guys hiding things from me, too?"

Dad peered at me over his glasses and slung a sweatered arm across his leg. Mom set down her cup and moved her hands to her lap. "Cheryl Copely," she said. "Crissy's sure about that?"

"Russell Loming confirms it. I left a message for Cheryl, but she hasn't called back. When I asked Felicia about their relationship, she implied that it was news to her."

Mom reached for her tea again but didn't drink. She was trying to busy her hands. "If what you're saying is true, Brett was more of a cad than I thought. Cheryl and Fee were friendly. They had a few dinners together before Fee and Brett split up, back when Crissy and Robbie were dating. I don't know a thing about Cheryl seeing Brett. I ran into her at the grocery just last week. She was with Suze's little girl."

Suze and Crissy, Cheryl and Brett—everything about Swanton was different now. Connections existed where they hadn't before, and there were more secrets buried in this town than I could count. Tim liked to bore me with lengthy explanations about river bifurcation, how way up north the St. Lawrence River turns to salt water and splits into channels that head out to sea. That was what had happened here. Opposition and unification, divergent properties becoming one. I would never admit it to my parents, but it left me feeling anxious.

Mom kept talking—about protecting my mental health and giving myself enough time to heal. I nodded amiably to make her happy, but my mind wandered.

I hadn't ruled out the possibility that Bram was responsible for Brett's death. It was likely he was the one who'd called in the general location of Brett's body, and while something about that was fishy, it meant he already knew Brett was dead. I wouldn't put anything past him, not now that I knew what he was capable of.

And yet, I couldn't stop thinking about his mother. Crissy had implied Felicia would be furious if she knew Brett was dating Cheryl. On top of that, I'd witnessed Felicia's aggression firsthand. It seemed like my aunt had pulled her life together. She was aware of her condition now, mindful of her behavior. It was a different story twenty years ago.

"You were right about Crissy," I said abruptly. "She's really upset, not just about Brett, but Felicia."

"She knows how to hold a grudge," said Mom.

"Was Felicia angry?" I asked. "After they split?"

"You're darn right she was," Mom said. "As much as she hated to admit it, Brett was the more emotionally stable parent, and Fee knew the kids needed that in their lives. Was she sorry to see him leave the house? No. But when he left town, well. That was different."

I hesitated before asking, "Did things between Brett and Felicia ever get . . . er . . . physical?"

"They did have two children, love."

"Jesus, Dad, no. I mean did they fight."

My mom's thumb traced the floral pattern on her teacup. "Felicia and I have always been close. Even when things were at their worst, she talked to me about everything. Pop and Nana were so busy with the dental practice, driving back and forth from Colchester every day, that a lot of the time it was just the two of us. I think I understood Fee in a way my parents didn't, better than anyone. Brett was a lot of things," she said, "but he was never violent with my sister."

But that wasn't what I meant, not at all. I hadn't known Brett to threaten so much as a spanking, though Crissy gave him plenty of opportunities to lose his temper. I'd never seen Felicia black-eyed or bruised, either. What I did see was a jug of milk making a fast arc toward Abe's face.

I said, "The Friday of the weekend Brett was set to leave town, Abe and I went to his work to talk to him. Convince him to move back into the house."

"I remember," Mom said. "Poor Abe, he was still heartsick over Brett's decision to move out."

"Do you remember seeing Abe after that?" I asked.

My mother inclined her head and a strand of hair, blond streaked with silver, fell across her cheek. "I'm sure we did. It was a Friday, you say? He was always over here for pizza night on Fridays."

"Not that Friday," I said. "He had a bruise on the side of his face. He . . . didn't want to come."

"That, I remember," said Dad. "It was frightful."

"Oh," said my mom, "you're talking about when he fell down the front steps. He landed smack on the concrete. He was lucky he didn't have a concussion."

Felicia hadn't told her. There must have been a lot of things she hid from her sister in order to keep living the way she did. A chill spread over the backs of my arms. "He didn't fall, Mom. Aunt Fee hit him."

"What? No." Confusion. It rearranged her neat features. Her eyes were blank, then fierce. "Don't be ridiculous, Shana."

"Aunt Fee was angry," I said. "Abe had just told her Brett was leaving, and she reacted. She was sorry about it, but it happened. I was there. It was like she lost control." I swallowed. Said, "That's why I need to know if any of her arguments with Brett escalated to violence."

My mother anchored her gaze to mine. I couldn't help it; under her analytical stare, my cheeks burned.

"Oh my God," she said slowly. "You think Fee did this. You think she killed Brett."

"Mom, listen. There's no evidence of that yet, but—"

"Shana," said my father. His jowls were shaking. "That's quite enough."

"No." Mom sat up stiffly. I didn't like her color. I didn't like anything about this moment, and ached for it to end. "All Fee ever wanted was for Brett to take responsibility for his family. She wouldn't hurt him. She couldn't hurt anyone."

That wasn't true, and we all knew it. Plenty of people

who suffer from anxiety are excellent parents who would never resort to violence. I couldn't be sure Felicia was one of them.

"This is your *family*," my mother said, the lines on her face going taut. "Your flesh and blood. How could you even suggest your aunt is responsible for Brett's death? How could you be so *cruel*?"

How do you square wanton cruelty with family ties? *It isn't easy, Mom.* Her words stuck me like shards of glass, but they mobilized my mother. She got to her feet and didn't look back as she hurried from the room.

"Dad," I pleaded, but he waved me away.

"It's a difficult time," he muttered as he followed my mother upstairs. "You should try to be sensitive to that, Shana."

His tone left me cold.

When they were both gone, I sat in stunned silence. How had I expected this to go? It *was* cruel to suggest my aunt had a hand in Brett's murder. But this family wasn't immune to cruelty.

After a minute, Doug appeared in the doorway to the dining room. I took in his kind face and shook my head. *I don't know what to do. I don't know how to do this.* In response, my brother crossed the room, lifted my hand from my lap, and said, "Come with me."

TWENTY-ONE

Having fun, detective?"

Doug waited to say it until we were outside and halfway down the block. The street was as quiet as ever, apart from the feeble rustling of the few shriveled orange leaves left on the trees. My parents had chosen our house for the cul-de-sac, perfect for learning to ride bikes and playing street hockey. I used to feel safe here. Now, the thought of belonging to this place was like chronic pain, a torn muscle or a rock in my shoe.

"You were eavesdropping," I said as I kicked a pebble, sending it skittering across the asphalt.

"The house isn't that big. Do you really think Aunt Fee could have done this?"

Did I? "I don't know."

"For what it's worth," he said, "I agree with Mom and Dad."

185

"Great. Does nobody want to see Brett's killer found?"

"Of course we do, but you've been through a lot lately. You're supposed to be moving forward, not taking a step back."

"What does that mean?"

Doug shrugged and his thick tan field jacket, the kind with corduroy on the collar and soft plaid lining, shrugged with him. "Being around here has always been tough for you, hasn't it? Gotta be, after what Abe did. Maybe you're good at putting that out of your mind, but you're investigating his dad's death now. Abe is everywhere."

It was his turn to kick a stone. It tap-tapped its way down the road. "Now that I've got Hen, I can't imagine it," he said. "We have a few years still until she turns sixteen, but I can already tell you I'd rather die than let her walk out of our lives that young. Ever wonder what happened to Abe after he left home?"

All I did was wonder. Right up until the day I opened my eyes to find him staring down at me.

The cold was working its way through the pockets of my coat and into my hands. Their numbness reminded me of the press conference. A-Bay, Tim and Mac, and Trey. He'd been missing for more than twenty-four hours, and I was running out of time. I'd come to the conclusion that with a cold case like this, I'd have to work it like a missing persons. I had to figure out when Brett disappeared and identify the last people who saw him. I was still trying to connect the dots on Brett's last days in town, but I knew his departure had been rushed. He'd already quit the plant by the time Abe and I showed up, and he planned to be out of Swanton within forty-eight hours. Maybe Doug knew something about his need to hustle that I didn't.

Instead of answering my brother, I said, "Do you remember when Abe and I went looking for Brett at the factory?"

"That was a hell of a bruise," Doug said with a scowl. "You told me what happened the next day, at the movies."

"The St. Albans drive-in," I said, perking up.

"We all went on Saturday night. God, that place was the best."

It was and it wasn't. Doug was the only one of us with a license that summer, and he preferred to fill my parents' car with friends. Crissy had friends of her own with access to cars, so Abe and I had to get creative. Once we got there, it was up to us to find a vehicle to watch from or we'd be stuck sitting cross-legged in the Coke-sticky, ant-ridden grass.

"It was *The X-Files*," said Doug, and for once I wasn't quite as awed by his memory. I'd been obsessed with the series and dying to see the movie. I'd been talking about it for months.

I squeezed an eye closed, willing the memories to trickle in. "But I didn't get to watch it," I said. "Because of Abe."

We'd come to the end of the block. When Doug started heading back toward the house, I slowed my pace a little. I didn't want our conversation to end.

"You spent the whole night looking for Brett's car," Doug said.

"That's right. We couldn't find him on Friday, and Abe wanted another shot at convincing him to come home."

The image was clearer now. I saw a field crammed with cars and pickup trucks at dusk, the snack bar throbbing with parents and kids as the smell of burger grease and popcorn, gasoline and fresh-mowed grass filled the summer air. With a flare of sound the previews started up, and the colossal screen stuttered to life. I saw myself weaving between parked cars still hot to the touch with my head bowed low, circumventing sightlines, but the vehicles were in the hundreds, and many more patrons had set up camp in folding beach chairs, blocking my path. I searched as though my life depended on it while the movie I'd waited years to see played on. I did it for Abe.

"The place was packed," I said. "It felt like everyone in the county came out for that movie. Suze was there. I think she helped us search." She'd tried to, anyway, but Abe didn't want her help. He'd never trusted Suze.

"Dina Ledoux was there, too," said Doug.

"Redhead?"

"Goddess."

I laughed. "Was this the girl you were crushing on since your freshman year? The one you always wore that stinky bomber jacket for because she once said she liked it?"

"The very same. I was dying to talk to her, but Abe kept getting in my face."

"Getting in your face how?"

Again he shrugged. The high winter sun turned the gray

hairs behind his ears into tinsel. "He wanted me to look for Brett, too. Kept saying it was his last chance or his dad would be gone forever."

"He was right. The receptionist at the plant told us Brett planned on moving that Sunday. If I can reconstruct the timeline of that weekend," I said, "we might be able to figure out who killed him."

"Well, you know he was at the movies."

"Brett was? You saw him there?"

"Sure. You didn't?"

"We couldn't find him." I paused. Was that true? I knew that by the end of the night Abe was pretty upset. Wasn't that because we struck out? *Fucking Bram.* I couldn't tell which memories he'd contaminated. Would I have any fond ones of him at all if he hadn't drilled them into my head? "If you saw Brett there," I said, "he was still alive Saturday night."

That got a headshake. "He was alive a lot longer than that. He moved to Philly, remember? Abe went to live with him."

"See, I'm not so sure." It was certainly the story we'd been told by our parents: Abe ran away and ended up in Philadelphia with Brett. Severed ties with his mother and sister, choosing instead to live with his dad. But apart from the letter Felicia received, nobody had heard from Brett for years.

I pushed my hands deeper into my pockets and said, "What if Abe never actually reconnected with Brett after leaving Swanton? He was sixteen, a minor. Felicia would have had to report him as a runaway, but then she got a letter from Brett saying Abe had arrived. She could breathe easy knowing he was safe." *And Abe could dissolve into the ether.*

"Abe could have forged the letter," I said, spitballing. "He had lots of birthday cards from Brett to work with." It would explain the decades-old skeletal remains, and why Brett was never heard from again after his supposed move. "I don't think Brett left Swanton at all. I think June 20th, 1998—the day we went to the movies—could have been the day he died."

We stood cheek by jowl in front of my parents' house, both of us freezing, neither making a move for the door. "Let's say the killer knew about Brett's plan to take off," I said. "It's kind of genius, really. Nobody considered Brett missing because they knew he was going to be leaving the state."

Doug had grown quiet and seemed a little distant, but I didn't want to lose my train of thought, so I barreled on. "If I'm right about the timeline, I'd say we can rule out the possibility of the killer being a stranger. A murder like his isn't likely to be random. Too many major events converging. A man doesn't quit his job, leave his family, and immediately become the victim of an indiscriminate psychopath."

"Crissy," said Doug.

Had he been this pale five minutes ago? His freckles were strangely bright against his skin. "What about her?" I asked.

"You said major events around the time of Brett's disappearance. Brett quit the plant and planned to leave town, but that's also when Crissy disappeared."

"I thought she went missing when she was fif—"

A week to the day before Crissy's sixteenth birthday. That's when Felicia said Brett left.

"Mom was going to throw her a Sweet Sixteen party," Doug told me, "but she had to cancel because Crissy was still recovering."

"Holy shit." I pressed the heels of my palms into my eyes. "Does that mean she went missing the same weekend Brett did?"

"Yeah," Doug said. "I think it does."

It was like I'd suddenly discovered an unfamiliar mole on the back of my own hand. How did I miss it? It defied explanation. So much of what Doug was saying felt like moments in a story I'd been told, rather than memories pulled from my own life. Why had Bram talked so much about our past? What was it that he wanted me to see?

"Did you ever ask Crissy what happened to her?" I said. Doug had spent a lot more time with Crissy than I did. They'd even had some friends in common.

"Tried to. She didn't remember much. The blood tests showed meth in her system. Honestly, that was the most shocking thing about her disappearance for me. I didn't think she went in for hard drugs. Anyway," he said, "apparently she got in a big fight with Felicia and ran off, and somehow ended up unconscious in the woods with a nasty gash on her head and a mild concussion."

I didn't like the picture that put in my mind, or the visions of other women lying limp in the woods that flickered flipbook-style behind my eyes. "You don't think some guy—"

"No evidence of that."

"Where exactly was she found? I remember hearing about a creek."

"Charcoal Creek," said Doug.

"How far is that from the fishing access?"

"Fuck."

"How far, Doug?"

He'd dropped his head into his hands. When he looked back up, his eyes were ringed in red. "I don't know exactly where Crissy was found. Hook Road and that creek are close, though. A mile apart. Maybe less."

Father and daughter, both missing the same weekend, both in the area of the wildlife refuge, and only one found alive. What did it mean?

I pictured Crissy crying in her small house on the bay, still as furious with Felicia as she'd been two decades before. I saw the bruise Felicia left on Abe when she channeled her rage over Brett into that blow. I didn't know what to make of it all, but one thing was for sure. If Mom didn't like me casting doubt on Felicia, she sure as hell wasn't going to like this.

TWENTY-TWO

I declined to join my family for lunch. My mind was reeling, and I was racked with guilt over my suspicions about Felicia. I didn't think I could be in the same room as my mother without upsetting her again, so while my brother ate a late meal of grilled cheese and homemade tomato soup with Mom and Dad, I sent myself to my room.

As soon as I'd closed the door behind me, I took out my phone and dashed off an e-mail to Harmison. I didn't know if he'd be willing to do me a favor, but given we were both working toward the same goal, it couldn't hurt to ask. When I heard the telltale swish of the message sending, I looked up from my phone. An envelope lay in the middle of the bed, with a sticky note on top in my mom's handwriting. *Found this in the mailbox*, it read.

My name was on the front, but there was no postmark or return address. I thought of Suze, all those letters we'd passed to each other in class. Was this from her? There was no bulk to the envelope, although I could feel something inside. A bead from an old necklace, maybe? It had that shape. I slid a finger under the flap, tore it open, and shook. A human tooth fell onto the blanket.

I stared at it. It was a pretty tooth, not at all like Abe's had been. It was small, but it wasn't a baby tooth. The root, long and bloodied, was still intact. This was a child's molar, removed by extraction.

I bent over and braced my hands against my knees.

I'd promised Tim he could trust my instincts, that the kid would be okay. I felt sure I knew how this would go. Follow the clues and come out a winner, just like when we were kids.

Deep breaths. Keep it together. I channeled every technique Carson taught me and willed my pulse to slow as I lowered myself to the bed and reached for the envelope once more. There was a note inside, three lines this time.

Who killed Brett?
Stop wasting time.
The truth is out there.

We met at the entrance to the concession stand, where the poster for the featured movie shone glossy behind the glass. I was vibrating with excitement. *The X-Files*, at last. We'd watched every episode together, Abe and I, and the series tagline had become our maxim.

The truth is out there.

It was all about that night. But I was missing something, a key component of Brett's life that would explain his movements after he left the drive-in.

In my childhood bedroom, I wrapped the tooth in a tissue and thought about our decades-old evening at the movies until my head hurt. Hours passed that way, me sitting by the window watching the daylight fade, dusk plunging me into chilly darkness as I agonized over the newest message and scoured the street below for Bram.

Eventually, I called Mac. There was a piece of Trey in Swanton, part of the child's body inside my parents' house, and the fear of what that meant had me so tightly coiled my own teeth throbbed. When she didn't answer, I called Tim, but he wasn't picking up either. After our last conversation I didn't blame him, but I tried again two more times. Three. Who killed Brett? Not Abe, not if his note was to be believed. But he was a killer all the same.

You hear stories of cases messing with detectives' heads. Searches for serials can last for years as investigators work themselves to death looking for something, anything that will bring them closer to their man. Those cases can start to get personal. A suspect can become a detective's white whale. That was nothing compared to what was going on between me and Bram. Pulling Trey's tooth was psychotic behavior, a sadistic act meant to curdle my blood, but Bram's intent was also to leave me feeling sick with guilt.

Nobody knocked or called my name until almost six

o'clock, and only then did I realize some of the pain I'd been feeling was due to hunger. When I heard Doug's voice, my whole body relaxed. What I needed was a psychological escape. Obsessing over Bram wasn't good for me. I'd learned that the hard way on Tern Island. What's more, hiding from my mother in my room was childish. Everything would look brighter after dinner with my family, a good meal and some of my brother's stories to send us into fits of laughter and reboot my relationship with Mom. All of that would imbue me with the comfort and strength I needed to buck up and revisit my family's dark side.

When I got to the kitchen, I found my parents and Doug sitting at the table.

The chair that had been mine since childhood was occupied by Felicia.

"Hello, poppet," Dad said when he saw me, and reflexively, I cringed. I'd looked it up, that word, when I was younger, and found it described an object used in witchcraft, the British equivalent of a voodoo doll. It had bothered me ever since, but I couldn't find it in me to tell my father. I was a grown woman in my thirties, an accomplished criminal investigator, yet standing before my family with nowhere to sit and a pet name I hated, I felt like a child on the verge of tears. When Doug offered me his seat, I declined and crossed the room to pour a glass of wine. A big one.

"Fee stopped by," Mom said pointlessly as my aunt, picking up on my discontent, lowered her gaze to her glass of juice. Felicia was wearing lipstick and blush in warm shades that made her look like she'd spent the day sunning herself at a posh resort. My mother was a mess by comparison, hollow-eyed with her gray-blond hair hastily thrown into a ponytail. I found the contrast disquieting. It had always been Felicia who needed a hairbrush or to be talked off a ledge. When had that changed?

From the corner of my eye, I saw Dad nudge Doug with his toe. "We'll leave you ladies to it," he said. Once the men had replenished their beers and vacated the room, I finally took a seat and turned an inquisitive gaze on my aunt.

I still couldn't get over how different Felicia was now, nothing at all like the woman who'd terrorized Crissy and Abe. Her husband was a pile of bones, her daughter wouldn't speak to her, and her son was a violent runaway. How could she sip juice in my parents' kitchen as though she lived an untroubled life? Was it all an act? If she killed her husband all those years ago, reinventing herself might have seemed like a good defense. Anyone who came around asking questions would have a hard time imagining Felicia as anything but the level-headed woman she now was.

Anyone but me.

I expected Mom to be the first to speak, but it was Felicia who leaned forward. "I've been thinking about our talk. There are some things I want to make sure you understand."

"Okay," I said and waited.

She closed her eyes. When she opened them again, her yellow irises went a full shade darker. "I have an anxiety disorder," Felicia said.

I'd known this for so long the statement shouldn't have had an effect on me, but it was the first time I'd ever heard my aunt admit it.

"God," she said, "there were so many days when I thought your mother was going to ship me off to the psych ward. Maybe she should have. The first time she stopped by to see baby Abe, the day after Brett brought me home from the hospital, she found me cowering with the kids in the hallway like we were bracing for a hurricane. Crissy was petrified and Abe was wailing from hunger, but I'd convinced myself a stranger was prowling the neighborhood. The hall was the only part of the house without windows. The only place that felt safe."

This story was new to me, but not surprising. Many times I'd overheard Mom try to soothe Crissy and Abe when they were little. *Your mother loves you so much. She doesn't ever want to lose you.*

"It had complete control of me," Felicia went on. "Made me do things I'll regret until the day I die, things I could never have imagined myself doing. That's the nature of the disease."

"I wouldn't know," I said. That was a lie. A month ago, I'd shot a witness because I allowed residual feelings of fear to interfere with my work. PTSD was an anxiety disorder, too, and I wasn't myself when in its clutches.

And yet, a voice in my head said, *No. You saw the pain she inflicted on her kids. It isn't the same.* Felicia's struggle was undeniable, but the hurt it caused wasn't limited to outbursts of violence. Between the emotional neglect and her constant diatribes about the dangers of their world, she'd tinkered with their heads all their lives. There was no comparison between what Felicia had done and the inner conflict I called my own. Was there?

"I don't know what you see when you look at me," Felicia said, "and I'm not sure I want to. When you were young, your allegiance was always to Abe. You tried to protect him from me, but I hope you know I love him."

I pictured him in our kitchen. All those pizza nights with the cousins. He was desperate to get out of his house and into ours. It must have felt like escaping a battlefield and stumbling, stunned and blinking, into a meadow.

I love him, Felicia had said.

"I'm better now," she went on. "I've finally got the right cocktail of medications, and I'm seeing a good therapist. I'd give anything to go back in time and do those things sooner, be the mother I should have been, but I can't." Felicia turned her head to look at her sister, and Mom gave a nod. *Go on*, it seemed to say. *You can do it*. Felicia nodded back. "Please believe me, I wasn't right in the head back then, not at all. But I had nothing to do with what happened to Brett."

Loyalty among sisters. That's what I was witnessing. They'd die for each other, these women, do anything to defend one another against harm. My mother had clearly tipped Felicia off about my theory, and I knew she'd fight tooth and nail to prove Fee's innocence. Her devotion to her sister ran that deep.

Suppressing a chill, I held my aunt's gaze. "If you weren't involved, then help me. Tell me everything you know—the truth, this time. Were you really not aware Brett had a girlfriend? I talked to Crissy and Russell Loming, and I'm going to talk to Cheryl Copely. You're not doing yourself any favors by hiding the facts."

"Crissy," Felicia said sadly, glancing over at my mom. "I love my daughter, so I don't want to say this, but her memory . . . it isn't good. Drugs will do that to a person—don't bother," she said when I opened my mouth to, what, defend my cousin against an absolute truth? "I have personal experience with this subject," she said. "It's hard for Crissy to remember that time of her life. She's off the methamphetamine, thank God, and she's in a social support group now, but the damage is done. You have to take what she says with a whole handful of salt."

It was a curious statement, coming from a woman who imagined baby stealers skulking in her backyard. It also seemed like a patent attempt to derail my questioning about Cheryl. For the moment, I let her think she'd succeeded. "When did that start?" I asked, thinking of Doug's comment about the meth. "The hard drug use?"

"Crissy started smoking marijuana when she was around fifteen. It took me longer than it should have to realize it, but she wouldn't have listened to my warnings anyway. It was her abduction that hooked her on meth. Whoever took her forced her into it, and after that . . ." With a desolate expression, Felicia shook her head.

I did, too, but not for the same reason. Crissy had been young and stupid, yes, but her home life was a nightmare. Though I didn't condone it, I could understand why she took the path she did. "Her disappearance," I said, taking note of that word *abduction* and pressing onward. "What happened there?"

"We don't know," Felicia said. "She snuck out, but something went wrong."

"Did it have anything to do with Brett and Cheryl?"

"What?"

I was grasping at straws, but I needed to pivot the conversation. "I think you knew about Brett's girlfriend," I said, "and I'm trying to understand why you didn't tell me. The only thing I can come up with is that she was more involved in your family's life than you're letting on."

Felicia and my mother quirked their eyebrows at each other. So it wasn't just my dad who had a secret language with Mom.

"I wasn't lying about Cheryl," Felicia said. "But I do remember the last time I saw Brett. It was that Saturday night. I didn't know he was seeing Cheryl"—another glance at my mother—"but there was someone else."

"What do you mean?" I said. "Another woman?"

"No. A girl."

The room tilted. Next to Felicia, my mother's face was stony.

Felicia said, "The weekend Brett was moving, the kids went to the movies." She narrowed her eyes. "You were there. Abe and Crissy, too. Abe had just told me Brett quit his job and was moving away. I was very angry. Against my better judgment, I went looking for him.

"Russ Loming was always my first call," she went on. "He told me he was meeting Brett at the drive-in. So after I dropped off the kids, I stayed. The place was crawling with people. It took half the movie for me to find him. He was parked back at the tree line near the picnic tables, as far away from the other cars as you could get. I was ready to give him hell, but when I got closer, I saw he wasn't alone." Felicia wrinkled her nose. "She was a high school girl, if I had to guess."

"Christ," I said. "What were they doing?"

"Talking. The girl looked upset. Brett put his hand on her shoulder. I think they kissed."

What the hell? A second girlfriend meant another motive for Felicia to kill Brett. If this mystery girl knew her beau was headed out of Swanton, it might even mean another suspect. "What did the girl look like?" I asked. "Did you recognize her?"

Felicia shook her head. "She had dark hair, but I only got a glimpse of her face. If it was Cheryl, I'd have known it."

"What happened next?"

"Nothing," she said. "I left. He was with a girl who was clearly underage, and she didn't seem displeased about it. What was I supposed to do? Seeing him with her, someone who might have been the same age as his own daughter, made me realize we were better off without him. So I went home. And that was the last time I saw him."

"That's all she knows," Mom said. "Isn't it, Fee?"

"That's all."

"You should have told me this sooner," I said.

"I didn't think it mattered."

"So what changed?"

Felicia twined her fingers with Mom's and held on tight. "Your mother told me what you do. I knew you were an investigator, but I didn't really understand what that meant. I didn't consider how hard it must be to solve a crime nineteen years after it was committed. I hated him sometimes," she said, "but I do want to know who did this. Crissy and Abe were deprived of so much as children. The least I can do is help them get some closure about their dad."

Closure, I thought. *Is that what Bram wants?*

It was what I wanted, but I had a feeling closure was a long way off yet.

TWENTY-THREE

Dinner was an hour of awkward pauses and forced chuckles—in other words, sheer anguish. Afterward, I took another walk down the block, alone this time. I tried to channel the feeling I'd gotten so good at embracing in A-Bay—*Come on, asshole, here I am*—but the familiar sense that Bram was watching was ill-defined. He might well be close, but his focus was on Trey. And that terrified me.

During the Tern Island case, Mac had been on the mainland, but we'd remained in close contact via phone. Being that it was my first case after New York, she was concerned about my mental state, and rightly so. As much as she needed to check in on my frame of mind, I'd needed her more. When I got to the corner of my street, I took out my phone and called her. I felt my limbs loosen when she picked up.

"Nothing new, I'm afraid," she said when she answered. "We're still searching."

"Yeah, I heard the same from Tim. Got a sec anyway?"

Mac whistled, and the wet sound of happy panting filled my ears. I felt a pang of longing for little Whiskey. "There's a beer in my hand and a dog in my lap. I've got all night," she said.

"I found something. A tooth. I think it's Trey's." I explained about the envelope on my bed, and the message within.

"Holy hell."

"I know. I think it's time to consider the possibility that Bram's here in Swanton, and that he brought Trey."

I gave her Harmison's name and number. Mac promised to call him first thing in the morning. Then she asked after me.

"I'll be honest," I said. "Things aren't great. I don't mean I'm relapsing"—*let's be clear*—"but I'm struggling."

"You just lost your uncle; that's hard on anyone. And I know how much you wish you could be back on the job."

"Sure," I said, "but Mac, a kid is missing, another innocent life thrown into the mix. Bram was supposed to come after *me*."

"You wanted him to, maybe even convinced yourself he would. But you can't fathom what goes on inside a lunatic's head."

"But that's exactly what I need to do. I spent all that time with him: I should be able to figure this out. It doesn't help that I'm following a million different lines of inquiry on Brett."

The second I said it, I cursed myself and hung my head. I knew what was coming.

"Shana, are you investigating your uncle's death?"

She was going to talk to Harmison. Mac would have found out anyway.

"Swear to God, you're impossible," she said when I made a hangdog confession. "That's a conflict of interest, and you know it."

"I'm helping. Nothing official."

"That seems to be your MO these days."

My face was hot. My body, too. I wriggled clumsily out of my jacket and folded it over my arm as I walked. "I'm sorry, okay? I'm fucking sorry. I'm doing the best I can."

"Oh, Shana."

She waited for me to recover. I did my breathing, and closed my eyes. "When we were on Tern, Philip Norton told me he once found a deer on the island. It swam across the channel, all the way from the mainland. That's me, Mac. I'm that deer in the river."

"Don't get all existential on me now."

"No, listen. I'm paddling like crazy, but—"

"The currents."

"Right. I'm not completely in control, but I have to keep going. I have to trust I'll make it to shore. The thing is, I'm scared of what I'll find when I get there."

"That's okay," she said. "Just don't let go of that trust." Her words were like a gentle hand on my shoulder. "And let me give you some advice. Whatever happens from here on out, don't make any decisions out of fear."

"But that's how I make all my decisions."

Mac laughed. "Now," she said, "what is it you want to ask me about your uncle's murder?"

I smiled. There was no getting anything past Mac. "Have you ever worked a cold case?"

"Once or twice. It's not easy, primarily because it puts investigators at a huge disadvantage against the offender."

"How do you mean?"

"Well," she said, "the information you're working with is decades old. But it's not just that. Whoever did this has had years to plan what they'd say if someone came around asking questions. They're bound to be prepared."

She was right. Motives and timelines were relevant, but I was used to watching for nervous tics and suspicious behavior when I conducted interviews. I'd been trained to sniff out anger that never abated—but what I should be looking for was the opposite of that. Composure. Utter calm.

Those were the characteristics that would point me to Brett's killer.

TWENTY-FOUR

I woke up the next morning to find Swanton had gotten its first snowfall of the season. It had let up, leaving the sky a cloudless blue, but the trees wore fur capes, and everything sparkled in the magical way that makes you forget winter's flaws.

Verifying the address he'd provided, I drove to Russell Loming's place and parked across the street. Given his appearance and oily demeanor at the plant, I wouldn't have been surprised if he lived in one of the tumbledown farmhouses I'd seen on my way into town. I found none of that. Loming's home was well maintained, and I arrived just in time to see a woman in her midsixties usher three small children into a car while a jolly Loming, dressed in a blue bathrobe, waved at them from the living room window. When he saw me emerge from my SUV, the smile melted from his face.

"Looks like you had a wild night," I said when he opened the front door.

"Russ Jr.'s got the stomach bug. Gran and Pop to the rescue."

"Mind if I come in?"

"Jesus." He wasn't subtle about weighing his options, but in the end he drew the robe across his chest and waved me inside. He seemed shorter to me than when I'd seen him at the factory, the result of poor posture. I suspected that had something to do with his embarrassing attire. "Look," he said once I was in the front hall, "can we make this quick? I'm running late." His hair was damp and there were several nicks on his neck that suggested he'd shaved in a hurry.

"The faster you answer my questions, the faster we'll be done."

With a sigh, Loming led me to the kitchen and reached for the coffeepot, filling a mug for each of us. Colorful cereal bowls and sturdy plastic spoons were strewn across the table, the detritus of a kid-friendly breakfast. Loming reached for the belt on his robe. He'd been a slimeball during our first meeting, and I half expected to be writing him up for indecent exposure once our meeting was through, but he only drew the belt tighter, slouched in place, and said, "Fire away."

"My theory," I explained, "is that Brett disappeared the weekend of June 20th. I have some new information about that Saturday. He went to the St. Albans drive-in. *X-Files* was playing. Sound familiar?"

"Ma'am, I can't remember what movie I watched last week."

"It was a long time ago. I get it. Just do your best."

He furrowed his brow. "Yeah. I saw it."

"With Brett?"

"Oh sure, we held hands across the console." He rolled his eyes. "He was there. So was I. That was it."

But Felicia had specifically said Loming had plans to meet Brett. It was because she was so sure Loming had been at the movie with my uncle that I'd decided to pay him another visit. *That, and his status as the Swanton Police Department's prime suspect.* "So you went alone?" I asked.

"Yeah."

"There was a lot of hype about that movie. I, for one, was dying to watch it. Were you a fan of the TV series?"

"Not especially."

"So why'd you go to the drive-in that night?" My gaze was drawn to the table once more. I thought of the son with the stomach bug, and the other one I knew from school. I set down the coffee Loming had handed me. "How old are your children, Mr. Loming?"

He ran his fingers across his burnished jaw. "Russ Jr.'s thirty-four and Max is two years younger. Why?"

I did the math and said, "That would make them, what, fifteen and thirteen that summer? Prime drive-in age. That movie was big with teenagers." Just about everyone I knew had planned to be there for its release. "You didn't bring them with you?"

Looking baffled, Loming said, "I guess they didn't want to come."

Or you didn't want them around. "Did you talk to Brett while you were there?"

"Sure. We always parked in the same place, way off by the picnic tables."

"What did you talk about?"

"Baseball. Politics. The weather."

Asshole. "And money?"

Next to his history of assault, money was the reason the police chief was keeping a close eye on Loming. Loming sighed before he answered.

"Like I said, he owed me. Maybe two hundred. Not a lot."

"Did you threaten him?"

"No!" The flesh on Loming's healthy, freshly scrubbed cheeks dulled. With his buzz cut and his face bunched up with apprehension, he looked like an overgrown kid.

"Did you kill him because he didn't have the money?" I said.

"What?" Loming gave a start, and his coffee splashed onto his robe. "God, no."

"Brett was perpetually broke, always gambling away his earnings. Must have made you furious to know you'd never get that debt back."

He cinched the belt on his bathrobe even tighter. "I knew he was leaving, so I went over to his car and I asked for the money. He promised he'd mail it to me once he got to Philly. It never came, but I really didn't care."

"So you didn't argue or fight that night. Any witnesses to confirm what you're telling me?"

"Witnesses! How am I supposed to know? It was dark out there, and I was talking to Brett." Loming was starting to come apart. "I'm telling you the truth. I had nothing to do with Brett's death."

I studied him. The man wouldn't quite meet my eye. I tried another angle. "Did you bump into anyone else that night? Anyone Brett knew?"

Whether it was the truth or not, I expected him to name Cheryl. If he was trying to protect himself by throwing me off track, staying consistent with his claim that Cheryl wasn't happy about Brett's intention to leave town would be the smart move.

Realizing he hadn't taken a single sip of his coffee, Loming set down his cup and sank his hands into the pockets of his robe. "It was crowded. That movie was new, and people came from all over to see it. But I did recognize a few faces." He rubbed his chin. "After I left Brett's car, I saw Felicia."

I felt my spine go taut as a wire. "What was she doing?"

"Just walking. Searching for someone, looked like. I didn't wait around to find out."

"Anyone else?"

"Crissy was there, talking to another kid." Loming shook his head, as if trying to dislodge the memory. "They were arguing. I didn't envy Brett, thanked God every day I had sons and not daughters. With her looks and sass, the girl was a handful."

That, too, was interesting. From what I could recall, Crissy had kept to her own friend group that night. I hadn't seen much of her at all. If her disappearance and her father's death were connected, her movements might matter just as much as Brett's. I asked, "This kid she was talking to. Boy or girl?"

"It was a guy."

"Did you recognize him?"

"I don't know. It was dark."

"Could you guess his age?"

"Same as Crissy, more or less."

"How was Crissy acting?"

"What do you mean?"

"Did you get the impression that she was on drugs?" I was thinking about my conversation with Felicia. She seemed to believe Crissy was given meth by her abductor, but methamphetamine can stay in your system for several days. Crissy was smoking pot by then, so while Felicia hadn't mentioned her daughter was acting strange that night, it didn't seem like a long shot to imagine Crissy could have taken the meth herself. That she'd been seen with a guy in the most remote part of the drive-in bothered me, too. I'd heard rumors—we all had—about the older kids going over there for drugs. A dark, quiet corner of a public place was usually a good place to score some dope.

"I don't think she was high—she'd be crazy to do that with her dad around," Loming said, "but she was definitely worked up. Whatever they were talking about, neither of them was happy."

In the quadrant of my brain that churns out theories, a raw but meaty idea started to form. "I need you to be honest with me, Mr. Loming." I softened my gaze as I said it, and hoped he'd interpret the act as assurance that I was on his side; I was looking for intel, nothing else. "You and Brett both arrived at the drive-in alone. You both made a habit of parking away from the crowd. I already know Brett met a woman at the movie. What I'm trying to understand is what brought *you* there."

Loming said nothing.

"You had two kids at home and a shift job at the factory, yet you're telling me you didn't care about recouping two hundred dollars. That just doesn't sound plausible to me. Everyone has their vices, Mr. Loming," I said. "For Brett, it was gambling. I'd like to know yours. If you're holding something back that's pertinent to this homicide investigation, I should warn you that I'll have to charge you with obstruction of justice."

"Brett didn't gamble."

"What?"

Loming's shoulders sank again, and this time the belly I now realized he'd been trying to play down strained against the belt of his robe. "We didn't go to Montreal to gamble. Well, we did at first," he said, "but that didn't pan out too well. Brett was in the hole to a bunch of fellas he worked with here in town. He couldn't even pay his mortgage for a while. Then we met some people up there."

"What kind of people?"

"Two guys—guys just like us, with wives and kids. They started telling us they made thousands in extra cash a month. So they invite us to this booze can," he said. "Brett talks to them for a couple of hours, and next thing I know our trips across the border don't have anything to do with playing cards anymore."

Cards. The word set off alarm bells, but I was too preoccupied with Loming's admission to pay it any mind. He and Brett had frequented illegal after-hours clubs in Montreal, smuggled their drugs across the border, and sold them to Swanton teens. "You ran an international drug operation?"

Loming blanched. "No! No, it was nothing like that. We sold a little pot and hash to college kids in Burlington, and we were lucky if we split a grand a month between us. I don't know how anyone around here got wind of it, but one day a local kid from the high school came up to Brett wearing this big grin, and next thing we're setting up shop at the drive-in. We were nervous—it's a small town, and we both had kids at the school—but some people were dumb enough to pay double what the stuff was worth." He gave a helpless shrug as if to suggest anyone would have done the same thing.

"But Brett was broke." Always. It was one of the things that drove Brett and Felicia apart.

"Bullshit," said Loming. "That's just what he told his wife. After we got the business going, he started saving the money he used to blow at the casino, and his take from those sales, too. How else could he afford to leave Swanton for Philly?"

My mind was racing. I had so many questions, but we both heard the soft crunch of tires on snow signaling the return of Mrs. Loming. My witness's eyes went wide.

"Shit. Don't tell my wife. Please."

"Don't tell her what? That you were dealing to minors the same age as your own sons? Jesus. Is that how Crissy got into drugs? Did Brett send her to school with hash brownies in her lunch?"

"Hell, no! He wasn't even living with the kids anymore. He didn't want them anywhere near that shit."

"Then where did Crissy get her supply? Her mother says she started taking drugs when she was fifteen. That means it happened the same year you and Brett started your operation."

"Ma'am, I don't know, she sure didn't get 'em from me."

The slam of a car door. Loming's muscles seized. As soon as his wife was in the house, he would shut down, and I might never get this close to cracking him again. I had a minute, maybe less. "So what you told me about Brett owing you money was a lie?"

"No! That's all true. About a month before he bolted he started talking about wanting out of the business. But we'd pooled our money to buy the stash from Montreal. He took it from Felicia, out of the bank account they used to share." He was talking fast now. Getting desperate. "When we went to split the stash, I realized our supply was crazy low. Brett said he had nothing to do with that, tried to convince me it must have been stolen. I thought he was trying to screw me."

"What happened to the rest of the stash? Did Brett give it to you?"

"No. He took it all with him."

No wonder he'd called Brett an ex-friend. "Why did Brett want out of the business?"

"Because of Crissy. He found out she'd been using and he freaked."

"Hang on," I said, "Brett found out Crissy was using after a chunk of his stash disappeared?"

"That's what I remember."

"Did it ever occur to you that she could have taken it?"

"No. I don't know!"

"So you were selling drugs with Brett at the drive-in that night."

"Yes, okay? Yes!"

"You say Brett didn't give any to Crissy, and you claim you didn't either. You sure about that? Last chance, Mr. Loming."

The front door opened with a creak, and Loming's wife singsonged his name from the front hall.

"Not her," he said. "I never sold to Crissy, just that kid she was with. He came around a lot."

I could picture it: Darkness, punctuated by flashes of blinding light. Hundreds of cars carefully maneuvered into place, and on the outskirts of it all, two men. Russell Loming and Brett Skilton, lurking in the shadows of the trees where abandoned picnic tables sticky with dried ketchup attracted flies, and the goods they concealed attracted kids in search of a rush.

Kids like Crissy.

TWENTY-FIVE

I paused on the threshold and took stock of the street before leaving Russell Loming's. I was feeling significantly more optimistic than when I went in. After our initial conversation I hadn't expected to find much meat on the bones of his account, yet here I stood with the knowledge that the small-town drug dealers my parents always warned me about included none other than Uncle Brett.

Loming's statement, assuming it was unvarnished, had flipped my investigation on its head. Despite his insistence that Brett never furnished his daughter with drugs, the tally on Brett's supply had mysteriously come up short. It was possible—likely, even—Crissy had her hand in Daddy's cookie jar. The missing drugs, the money owed, all added up to motive. Not only was Brett indebted to Loming, but my uncle had become a liability; his decision to quit dealing put Loming at risk of exposure and threatened the future of his side hustle. Could Crissy's abduction have been Loming's idea of a shot across the bow? I recalled Tim's report about the drug case he'd been working in A-Bay, the husband-and-wife operation that fell apart when the relationship soured. I could easily imagine Loming and Brett coming to the same end.

There were other possibilities, too. I was happy to consider the prospect of an entirely new suspect, a Canadian drug lord come to clean up loose ends, but that didn't quite fit. After everything I'd learned, I refused to believe there was no connection between Crissy's disappearance and her father's death, and if a kingpin from Montreal heard Brett planned on going straight and Crissy somehow got caught in the cross fire, Brett's killer would never have let her live. I still had a strong suspicion the person I was hunting was a close acquaintance of them both. Loming fit the bill. I couldn't be sure if I was right, however, without first eliminating another potential suspect from the mix.

For the second time, I drove to Cheryl Copely's. I took my time walking to her front door, noting the absence of snowy tire marks leading out of her garage, and wondered if she'd left the house at all since the news broke about Brett.

The first time I rang the bell, I got no answer. I rang again. Still nothing. "Mrs. Copely," I called, pounding my uninjured fist on the door. "I'm a senior investigator with the police. I need to speak with you about Brett Skilton."

After another few whacks loud enough to alert the neighbors, the door swung open to reveal a petite blond in her midfifties. She wore a plum-colored cardigan and matching lipstick, and her penciled eyebrows hovered in a way that made it clear she was pissed. But her *eyes.* They were the blue of a lake in summer when the sun breaks through the water. Robbie had inherited his best feature from his mom.

"Can I help you?" she said tartly, as those blue eyes darted around the street.

"I've been trying to reach you. I left several messages." I smiled at her. "I'm an old friend of Suze's. May I come in?"

Taking a final glance at the neighborhood—*was she expecting to see a news van? A couple of suits in an undercover vehicle?*—she reluctantly stepped aside.

Cheryl's living room was furnished with two enormous beige couches. I let my gaze drift around the space. There were pictures of her son and granddaughter all over the place, at all stages of life. Little Erynn had Suze's coloring and a long mane of dark hair, but the eyes were pure Copely, jewel-toned and bright. "She's gorgeous," I said.

"I know who you are." Cheryl's expression was smug. "People talk, you know. Brett was your uncle. You interviewed Crissy and Russell Loming. But you're not the investigator on his case."

The local grapevine covered even more ground than I'd realized. "Not officially," I admitted, though that was putting it mildly. "I have a personal interest in knowing what happened to Brett. I'm sure you do as well."

"What are you implying?"

Cheryl lowered herself onto the sofa, and I did the same.

There was a basket of toys on the floor, and a half dozen minuscule figurines lined up along the edge of the coffee table. "Just that I'd appreciate your help," I said. "I know you two used to date." I slipped out my notebook. "How long were you in a relationship with Brett Skilton, Mrs. Copely?"

"About eight months," she said.

Eight months. Based on what I knew about Brett and Felicia's marriage, that meant the affair started before they split. "Would you say it was serious?"

"I was a single mother working my you-know-what off to support my son. I wouldn't have bothered unless I believed Brett and I could have a future." That last word caught in her throat. "He'd already left Felicia. He was going to ask for a divorce. I just don't understand it: one day we were talking about renting a place in St. Albans to get a fresh start, and the next he was gone."

"How did you feel when he told you he was moving?"

Cheryl wrung her hands in her lap. "He didn't tell me. He just disappeared."

"He didn't tell you in advance?"

"No."

"Huh," I said, scribbling furiously. "Did you have an argument?"

A crease appeared between her eyebrows. "No. Everything was fine."

"Did he seem unhappy? Unstable in any way?"

"He was perfectly normal." Those hands. They couldn't

be stilled. Plucking one of the tiny figurines off the table, she rolled the colorful knob of plastic between her palms.

"Can you think of any other reasons why he'd want—or need—to leave? I know he had a gambling problem—"

"You're wrong," she said. "He quit gambling as soon as we started seeing each other. I insisted. Brett promised he was done with that."

Only because he was onto bigger and better things. "It seems like he was under pressure to leave quickly, though. Could he have been mixed up in something?" I looked up from my notes. "It's been suggested that he was trafficking drugs."

"*Drugs?*" Cheryl's mouth dropped open, but there was a canny look to her eyes. "No. That's impossible."

"I've been told Brett fell in with some dealers in Montreal. He and Russell Loming were smuggling small quantities of drugs across the border and selling them in Burlington. Right here in Swanton, too."

"Well, I don't know where you get your information," Cheryl snapped, "but you're absolutely wrong about that."

"Did Brett ever talk to you about Crissy? How things were for her and Abe at home?"

"All the time," she said, relaxing slightly. "He worried about them constantly. I knew about Felicia and her . . . condition. Brett said it was getting worse. I floated the notion of having Crissy and Abe come live with us."

"Did you really?" That wouldn't have gone over well with Aunt Fee. I'd have thought that if anyone was going to broach the idea of relocating the kids, it would be my mother, but Felicia had made it clear she had no intention of parting with them. Still, it had always struck me as strange that Brett didn't work harder to get custody, considering Felicia's mental state and the disaster that was their home life.

Then again, he wasn't exactly a model citizen, either.

"His plan was to file a petition for custody," Cheryl said. "That was another reason why he quit gambling. He wanted to clean himself up, so when the time came he was clearly the more dependable parent."

"Uh-huh." The skepticism I felt was like a tickle in the middle of my back, insistent but too far out of reach to scratch. *Clean himself up?* Brett was dealing drugs to minors. He'd decided to quit, yes, but he planned to move immediately afterward, and he wasn't taking Cheryl with him.

Something else about her claim bothered me. "Two more kids in the house in addition to Robbie. Wouldn't that have put a damper on your romance?"

Cheryl said, "I'm not saying it would have been easy. Crissy was a wild one. But I thought it would be nice for Robbie to have some company."

I almost laughed. Two hot-blooded teen kids who'd already hooked up, living under the same roof as pseudo brother and sister? It was like something out of a dirty movie. "I'll be honest, Mrs. Copely, I'm surprised to hear you say that. Crissy and Robbie were an item once, weren't they? Wouldn't making them live together be asking for—"

"Robbie wasn't interested in Crissy." Cheryl said it

through tightly drawn lips. "Whatever happened between them was in the past, nothing but a silly freshman fling. If he still had feelings for her, I never would have started seeing Brett."

"Mind if I ask how you and Brett got together?"

"Robbie introduced us, when he started dating Crissy. He was quite taken with Brett—that's not unusual for boys who grow up without fathers. We didn't get together until long after they'd broken up. Robbie was very supportive. Crissy was not."

I always knew Crissy's reputation in town wasn't stellar, but I hadn't appreciated the extent to which parents wanted to keep her away from their own offspring. "I get the sense you weren't Crissy's biggest fan."

The skin around Cheryl's mouth tightened. "I wasn't disappointed when they split up. She wasn't a good influence on him."

It was always the same old story. Crissy was brazen, licentious, out of control.

"She was wild, like I said," Cheryl told me. "Alcohol, drugs—and all at such a young age. Getting her out of that house would have been the best thing for her."

"It would have cemented your relationship with Brett, too."

"I wasn't trying to trap him, if that's what you mean," Cheryl huffed, and the sagging skin under her tiny chin wobbled. "Everyone says being a single mother is hard, but they don't know the half of it. The one income, the need to parent constantly with no relief or support, all of that's easy compared with trying to make up for what your child is missing. My husband died when Robbie was six years old. We did okay, just the two of us, but I was soft on him. I felt sorry for him, I guess, growing up without a father, so I didn't always discipline him the way I should have. Maybe I spoiled him a little too much. When he got older he took advantage of that, even talked me into buying him his own car at sixteen. As cliché as it may sound, he needed some discipline in his life. A father figure. I thought Brett could be that for him."

"Once he cleaned up his act, of course."

"Of course."

"Mrs. Copely," I said, "Brett was seen at the St. Albans drive-in on Saturday, June 20th. That was the day before he planned to move out of Swanton. Were you at the movies that night?"

"No."

"Are you sure? It was a long time ago."

"I never went to the drive-in. I didn't want to encroach on Robbie's time with his friends. You know how easily embarrassed boys are at that age."

I also knew that if Cheryl avoided the movies, Brett could be sure she wouldn't be around. That made the drive-in the perfect place to deal drugs and meet up with a pretty schoolgirl. The girl from Brett's car that I still hadn't identified.

"The reason I ask," I said, "is that I've got a witness who

saw Brett there with a woman. A girl, actually, possibly in her teens. The witness saw them talking in Brett's car during the movie. She thinks they were kissing."

Cheryl brought a hand to her mouth. Did Brett, and the promise of what could have been, still upset her so much that she was hurt by the idea of him canoodling with an underage girl almost two decades ago? Her shock over this news could have been an act. In a town the size of Swanton, it was feasible Cheryl might have been well aware of Brett's indiscretion. I didn't think so, though. In that moment, in that living room, Cheryl's pain seemed real.

"There are a few things I haven't managed to figure out," I said. "One of them is why Brett left. You're telling me you two were happy, and that he wanted to improve his life and bring the kids to live with him. But none of that happened. Could this explain why Brett left you? If he was seeing someone else?"

She was talking again before I got the sentence out. "Brett was a very social person, very loving. That's what made him so attractive—to me, and to everyone else. Brett was loyal." Cheryl gave a brisk nod. "I know that in my heart. Whatever your witness saw, they got it wrong."

"With all due respect, if he was that loyal, why did he plan to leave town without letting you know?"

"I've had almost twenty years to wonder about that, and I still don't have the answer."

She looked down at the toy she'd been holding, and slowly placed it on the table. Glanced up at the photos of

Erynn that hung on the walls, and drew a shaky breath. "We think she's autistic," Cheryl said. "Did Suze tell you? Robbie's been looking into early intervention programs, driving all over the area to find the best one. Not that he has time for that, but he does it anyway. We all struggle to get through to Erynn. I'm with her for hours, almost every day, and sometimes it's like I'm not here at all. It's not fair."

She wasn't just referring to her granddaughter. "No," I said, "it isn't."

"He left before we had a chance to be a family. He didn't even say good-bye."

I looked on as tears formed and spilled onto her cheeks. She wasn't the only woman Brett left behind in Swanton, but Cheryl believed she'd had top billing in his life. Even now, she still felt the need to defend him. Play the role of devoted partner. Had she told herself she was everything Brett wanted? Promised him she'd heap affection onto his family and give them a life that was orderly and calm? Cheryl might have had a plan for their future, but Brett hadn't invited her to be a part of his.

"Ma?"

Behind us, the front door had opened and Robbie Copely stepped inside, stomping his snowy feet on the mat. He was dressed for work in khakis and a button-down shirt under a puffy jacket. Aside from filling out a bit and growing a tidy beard that was two shades darker than his blond hair, he looked just the same. In his arms was little Erynn.

Robbie stopped short when he saw me, and a smile

spread across his face. "Well, I'll be damned," he said with delight. "Suze told me you were back, but I almost didn't believe it. Shana Merchant, in the flesh. How the hell are you?"

I'd barely managed to get to my feet before he had me in a bear hug, the child squeezed and squirming between us. He smelled of aftershave and mint gum, and when he let me go, I felt myself blush. Up close his eyes were even more striking, with lashes galore.

"I hear congratulations are in order. Another baby. That's great."

Robbie said, "Hey, thanks," but his attention had already transferred to his daughter. "Boots by the door," he told her as he set her down. When Erynn went straight for her grandmother and the toys, he only laughed. "You've made Suze pretty happy, you know, with this visit of yours. She never got over losing you as a friend. She talks about it sometimes. I get the sense she was kind of devastated about the way you left her."

"Oh." Hearing it put that way was devastating in and of itself. "I do have some regrets about that."

"Bah, you were kids. What can you do?"

"Right," I said, all too happy to have an excuse.

I hadn't thought much about Robbie since my conversation with Crissy, but now that he was here, I wasn't going to let the opportunity to question him slip by. His relationship with Crissy hadn't lasted long, but a lot can happen in a few months when you're a teenager. A lot had.

"Not sure if Suze told you," I said, "but I've been talking to Crissy about Brett."

He nodded. "Man, that news came as a blow."

"Yeah. I had no idea she and Suze were friends, by the way."

"Oh, *that*. Not gonna lie," he said, "it was a little weird at first, but Crissy and I dated for like five minutes when we were fourteen. In a small town like this, everyone's paths cross eventually."

"Come on, sweetie," Cheryl said, taking Erynn's hand. "Let's get you a snack."

As soon as they were gone, Robbie sat down. "It's hard for her," he said, nodding after his mother. "She doesn't like to talk about Crissy, and she definitely doesn't like Suze spending time at Crissy's place. She reminds her too much of Brett, I think. Let's face it, she was no angel, and when her dad left out of the blue . . . Ma needed someone to blame, I guess."

I'm not in the habit of putting words in people's mouths. When I'm interviewing a witness, I keep my questions dead simple to flesh out the situation and look for discrepancies. To try to catch them in a lie. Leading questions aren't just unproductive; they can muddy the waters of an investigation. So while I was dying to ask whether there might be another reason Cheryl couldn't stand to look at Crissy— *lingering guilt over offing her father, perhaps?*—I held my tongue. "Can I ask you something?" I said instead. "When

Crissy was fifteen, she went missing for a while. Do you remember that?"

Robbie's expression softened. "'Course I do. Let me tell you, now that I've got Erynn not a day goes by that I'm not cursing all the psychos out there waiting to prey on an innocent girl."

"Tell me about it," I said, and Robbie, as if he'd only just remembered my profession, gave a knowing nod. "I'm trying to piece that whole thing together, but my memory's a little fuzzy."

"The police thought someone took her after she snuck out," Robbie said. "They talked to everyone Crissy knew, and a lot of folks she didn't. In the end, they figured it had to be a stranger who was passing through. A drifter or a transient worker. Lots of those around here in the summer months."

"There was a search party. My dad was part of it."

He nodded. Said, "I was there, too. I wasn't supposed to be, but a bunch of kids from school showed up wanting to help." When he registered my surprise, he added, "Big place, that refuge. The cops couldn't really stop us."

"Wait," I said. "How did they know to search the refuge?"

"Someone spotted a girl along River Street not long after she went missing, but when the police got there, she was gone. They thought it might have been her, so they searched the woods. I wasn't around when they found her, but I heard she was in bad shape." Robbie puffed out a breath. "I guess she was lucky. Could have been a lot worse."

"Meaning?"

"Well, Crissy was banged up and high as a kite, but okay in the end. It wasn't exactly a no-harm-done situation, but close to it. Maybe that's why the cops gave up so fast."

"That was Felicia's doing." Cheryl was back, holding Erynn by the hand and carrying a platter of sliced coffee cake. She offered a slab to Robbie, who immediately took a crumbly bite. "As soon as they found her," Cheryl said, "Felicia asked the police to drop the investigation. I had a friend who worked as a clerk at the station back then. She told me."

When I was abducted, and my NCO supervisor informed my parents, they harassed him for updates day and night. I know this because Doug drove them six hours to the city, where all three of them loitered on the sidewalk outside of the precinct waiting for news. "Why would Felicia ask the police to stop looking for her daughter's abductor?" I asked.

"Because she's heartless," said Cheryl.

"Ma," Robbie mumbled through his full mouth.

"No, honey, I'll say what I like. The whole town thinks it anyway. Felicia hurt those children; I know that for a fact. That boy of hers ran off before he even finished high school, and what did she do about it? Not a thing. She didn't try to find out who took Crissy because she couldn't be bothered to care, not about her daughter, her son, her husband, or anyone else."

It was only after she said it that Cheryl remembered who

Felicia was to me. Her color high, she opened her mouth, but then Erynn made a dash for the kitchen and both Cheryl and Robbie's heads whipped around in alarm.

"Whoa there," he said, scooping her into his arms. "Give Daddy a good-bye kiss. *Oof.*" When he set his plate down and tried to lift her, his free hand shot to his lower back. Robbie was only a few years older than me, but when our eyes met, tacit knowledge passed between us. *Aging is for the birds.* "I'm sorry," he said, "I've only got a few minutes to get Erynn settled. On my way to work."

"It's fine. I have to get going. It was good seeing you."

"Likewise. Any more questions, you know where to find me. It's terrible what happened to Brett. I liked the guy, I really did. If we can help in any way," he said, "please let me know."

As Cheryl showed me to the door, I heard Erynn's voice for the first time. A squeal of joy tripping across the room, sparked by her father's love.

TWENTY-SIX

When I stepped back out onto the welcome mat, it was snowing lightly once more. Across the street, one of Cheryl's neighbors was stringing Christmas lights onto a leafless apple tree in his front yard. Aside from that, there wasn't another person in sight.

With my back to her door, I pulled out my phone to check my e-mail. There was a message from Harmison in response to my inquiry, along with the item I'd been after: the report from Crissy's disappearance. I opened it and scanned the words on the screen with interest before sending him an update on my talk with Russell Loming, which included what I'd learned about the drug dealing and the possible second girlfriend. There was plenty there to keep him busy; as far as my contributions to his investigation were concerned, I hoped I was being more of a help than a hindrance.

On my way back to my car, I noticed a sedan parked

halfway up the block. Like my SUV, it was covered with a light layer of snow, just enough that I couldn't be sure if it was white or silver, a Honda or Toyota. Based on that snow, it must have arrived after I'd gone inside. That wasn't especially unusual. What I found odd was the person in the driver's seat. It was a man, that much I could tell. The span of his shoulders gave the impression of brute strength. He sat perfectly still. Watching me.

My karate training, first in the city and more recently in Watertown with Sam, was about putting some power behind my punches. To defend myself effectively, I needed to leverage my size and use an attacker's moves against him. I did it to sharpen my reflexes, too—which is why I was so angry when, during my private lesson, Sam got the better of me. I'd spent innumerable hours visualizing the moment when Bram and I would meet again: where it might be, what he would do, how I'd retaliate when it mattered most. I can honestly say our imagined encounter was never on a Wednesday morning while snow turned a quiet residential Vermont street into a Christmas card.

"Hey," I said.

The word sounded puny at first, but when I spoke it again—"*Hey!*"—I found my voice. I started toward the car. It was very foolish, pretending this counterfeit courage could take me to war, but the violence embodied by Trey's tooth was rapidly bleeding into me, a transfusion of pure, hot rage. In the car, the figure shifted his weight toward the door. In my chest my heart stuttered, but I kept coming. The door swung open and the man's foot met the curb. When his head ducked down to clear the roof and he emerged into the snow-bright light, I jolted to a stop. My shock was quickly replaced with relief, the relief with confusion.

"Hey, stranger," said Tim.

"What are you doing here?" I blew out a frosty breath and shook my head. Tim Wellington in Swanton? It was inexplicable. The most horrible thoughts eddied through my mind, about Trey and Mac and everything in between.

"It's a valid question," Tim acknowledged. A fisherman's sweater peeked out from his charcoal-colored winter coat, and he tugged at the neck as though it was itchy. "I grappled with it myself on the drive over."

"How did you even know where to find me?"

"There aren't too many Merchants in town. I pulled up to your parents' place just as you were leaving. Been shadowing you ever since."

"Nice," I said with derision. "You're my protection, is that it?"

"Actually, I was hoping you could protect me. I couldn't karate-chop a cube of Jell-O."

From the corner of my eye, I saw Cheryl's living room drapes twitch. "Get back in the car and follow me."

To his credit, Tim did as he was told.

The drive to John R. Raleigh Memorial Field was a short one, but it was far enough from Cheryl and other inquisitive locals to satisfy my urge to flee. Cheryl's remark about town gossip had reminded me to be careful. If Brett's killer was still in town, I didn't want to make it any easier for him—or her—to monitor my investigation.

I'd been to the baseball field a couple of times in recent months, secret trips to look for Bram, and had yet to come to terms with what he did in those woods. After he and I happened upon the cat, I'd betrayed his confidence by telling my dad. I didn't like the idea of the animal out there alone all night, its eyes dull in the gloaming, or the possibility that someone else could find it. Dad went to the spot I described that evening and dug the cat a grave. Bram never asked what became of it, and I pretended to lose interest in the mystery. There would be many more to come. I parked in the lot next to the field, Tim pulled up beside my car, and I motioned for him to join me.

"Nice digs," he said as he slipped into the passenger seat beside me. "This is quite an operation you're running here." He lifted a half-empty takeout cup from the console. "I especially like the artisan coffee bar."

"Make do with what you've got, I always say." I couldn't help but grin. "I know it's not the sophisticated mechanics of my investigation that brought you out here."

"I do have some news," he said. "We found the guy with the tarp."

His tone was too cheerful to be announcing a bad break. I asked what they'd found.

"Local guy was dumping leaves in the water. He had

them rolled up tight as a cigar. I can see why the fisherman was suspicious."

"Does that mean the divers didn't find anything?"

"That's what it means."

I exhaled. "And you came all this way to tell me that?"

Of course he didn't. McIntyre had told him about the tooth, and the strong possibility Bram was in Swanton.

Tim looked away. "Our conversation yesterday. I didn't like it."

"Me either," I said. "I know you're worried, but you have to trust me."

His eyes traveled over the houses on the outskirts of the field while snow fell on the roof of my car. "Any leads on your uncle?"

"A few. He had a friend who's definitely a person of interest. It sounds like he and Brett were involved in a drug-trafficking operation out of Montreal, and Brett may have been dating two different women—one of them underage, according to my aunt." I didn't mention that Felicia was also a suspect. "There's something else," I said. "Around the time Brett disappeared, my cousin Crissy did, too. My aunt had a pretty serious anxiety disorder back then, and I gather the two of them got in a fight. For two days nobody could find her, and when they did she was in the woods not far from where Brett's remains were just found."

Tim's eyes widened. "I never realized how boring my family is until now."

"Consider yourself lucky."

"What does Crissy say about all that?"

"Not much. She was my first stop, even before I made the connection about her disappearance, but I think she knows more than she's told me so far. I need to talk to her again. Dig deeper."

"So what are we waiting for?"

"We?"

Tim averted his eyes. "I've tried everything back home. We searched everywhere, exhausted every lead. You know the stats: more than seventy percent of child victims are dead within three hours of being abducted. Trey's been gone forty-eight."

Christ, I thought. Two days gone was way too long.

"If you're right about Bram wanting you to solve this murder," he said, looking at me again, "I should be here helping. Think of me as your secret weapon." He waggled his dense eyebrows. "I'll charm the truth out of her."

I laughed at that. "You stand a better chance than I do." I tipped my head toward the road. "Let's go meet my cousin."

The insurance agency where Crissy worked as an office manager was located in a brick house next to Village Green Park. I tried to imagine her walking its winding paths on her lunch break, throwing bits of her sandwich to the swans that paddle in the park's scenic fenced-in pond, but the image was at odds with Crissy's X-rated cleavage, and it was too cold for a stroll anyway. We found her at her desk, and Tim managed to sweet-talk her into an empty office for a chat. She was decidedly less excited to find out I'd be coming with them.

"I already told you everything I know," Crissy said as she began fixing coffee in an ancient-looking machine. "Not my fault you don't know what to do with it."

"I appreciate your help," I said with an affected smile. "I just want Tim to hear it from you directly. I'm not sure I trust myself to get the details right."

As Crissy turned her back on us to fiddle with the coffee maker's on-switch, Tim winked at me. Playing the ingénue with witnesses was his specialty, not mine, but it was an effective method for gaining trust. I took his visible pride in me as a compliment.

"Shit," Crissy hissed, glaring at the machine. "This thing is total crap; it's always hit or miss."

"Here," Tim said, "let me try."

Crissy's expression was dubious, but she stepped aside. Before long Tim had drained the water, removed the back panel, and fished a hunk of debris from a clogged valve using one of Crissy's fake jewel-encrusted bobby pins. "I like to watch those shows about how stuff is made," he explained sheepishly as he worked. "These are pretty simple contraptions; only a couple of things ever go wrong. There. Try it now."

Crissy refilled the reservoir, and moments later the room smelled of freshly brewed dark roast.

"I won't make you talk about Brett if you don't want

to," Tim said. "What I'd actually like to ask about is your disappearance."

This seemed to surprise her. "Well, then, you're out of luck because in case you hadn't heard, I was unconscious."

"You were unconscious when you were found. What about before that?"

"You snuck out of the house, right?" I said.

"So?"

"So what happened to you that night might be connected to what happened to Brett. Crissy," I said, "you and your dad went missing the same weekend, and you were found in the woods close to where the police found him. That has to mean something."

My cousin looked away.

"Did Brett have something to do with what happened to you?"

She hit me with a titanium stare. "You mean, did my own father leave me in the woods to die?"

"That was a poor choice of words. Shana didn't mean to imply that," said Tim. "We just need to rule it out."

We hadn't discussed how we were going to work the interview, but when Tim undermined me to mollify my cousin, I felt us slip seamlessly into a routine that felt right for the situation. Crissy nodded. *Fine. Go on.*

Tim said, "How were things at home back then? I understand your mom had some problems."

"Still does."

"Was it worse that summer? For her?" He paused. "For you?"

We were sitting around a desk now. It must have belonged to a sales agent once, but its sole purpose at the moment seemed to be collecting dust. Tim laid a hand on its gritty surface and waited. He would never touch a female witness, not even to comfort someone in pain. Small-town officers weren't immune to sexual assault charges, and Tim had been well trained, but the act of physically reaching out to Crissy was enough to eke out some trust. She drew a breath, released it with a shudder, and met his patient gaze.

"You have no idea what it was like," Crissy said. "The things she tried to convince us of. The stuff she had me believing. There was this time when the AC guy came to repair our system, and she told us she was scared he'd set it up to pump toxic air into the house. It made no sense—what possible reason could he have for wanting to hurt us?—but she refused to turn it on. Temps were in the 90s for weeks that fall. I thought we were all going to suffocate."

I felt a jolt of recognition. This was one of the childhood memories Bram subjected me to in the cellar. Another strip of his past, snaking around mine.

"She checked closets and stove knobs constantly, until we were so late we had to skip whatever we had planned and stay locked in the house. She would wake up in the night screaming her head off about intruders, but there was never anyone there. It was all in her head, but it was real to her, and that made it real to us. I was so afraid I'd become like her.

That's why I started using," she said, and for a split second my stubborn and cynical cousin let her mask slip, exposing the frailty underneath. "It was a way to escape her, the only way I could think of at the time."

"Why didn't she take medication to manage it?" I asked, remembering that Abe had called her a hypocrite for suggesting he do the same. If Felicia's mental state was yo-yoing more than usual, I couldn't imagine my mother choosing not to intervene. Surely she insisted Felicia get help? But then I remembered the conversation I'd had with my parents, and Mom's impression that Abe's bruise was the result of a fall. When it came to her sister, Felicia was good at downplaying her disease.

"She didn't like the way the pills made her feel," Crissy said. "Sometimes she'd take them, sometimes not. By the time I was fifteen, she was off them completely, and refused to go back on. You wouldn't know that," she said, sounding sullen. "Not even Della did."

She paused to pinch the bridge of her nose. Tim gave her a nod of encouragement, and she continued.

"Abe never talked about it. He thought if your parents found out how bad things were for us, they wouldn't let him spend time with you anymore. He said if he couldn't see you, he'd die. So I didn't tell Della, either."

I tried to swallow, and realized I'd been holding my breath.

"It was hard on him," Crissy said. "He was always on edge. When she had one of her episodes, Abe would cry for hours. The littlest thing would set her off, and then it would happen all over again."

In all the years I'd known Crissy, I'd never seen her give a damn about her brother. Or was it that I'd convinced myself she didn't care? I was starting to wonder just how badly I'd misjudged my cousin.

"So you didn't tell your aunt," Tim said. "Did you talk to anyone else? Shana's dad? A teacher? Your father?"

Crissy gave a small nod. "Just before the end of the school year, I told Brett. I couldn't stand the thought of being alone with her all summer, and I was worried about Abe. Brett confronted her about it. I'm sure the whole block heard the yelling. Felicia wouldn't go back on her medication, and he couldn't change her mind."

"So he decided to leave?" I said, confused. Why would Brett try to help his children, only to ditch them a few weeks later?

Behind us, the coffee maker gurgled, and with a spluttering release its cycle came to an end. Crissy startled and tried to cover up her nerves by brushing her bleached hair off her shoulder. "No," she said. "He decided *we* should leave. All three of us."

It was the last thing I expected her to say. Brett had always seemed so selfish. That was the footing on which my perception of my uncle was built. In the past couple of hours, I'd come to find out the man I thought I had pegged had quit gambling, started dealing drugs to build a nest egg, and launched a mission to rescue his children from his ex.

"It didn't happen right away," Crissy explained. "Brett had just started seeing Cheryl, and she wanted him to hire a lawyer, try to get sole custody. He was looking into that, but it was taking too long. He tried to threaten her. Everyone saw us, our clothes, those haircuts." Crissy's expression was etched with fury. "Everyone knew she had problems, so Brett told Felicia he'd go to child services. She just laughed. He didn't have a leg to stand on. Everyone knew about his gambling and drinking, too. After a while, he realized the only way to get us out of there was to take off."

"What about Cheryl?" I said. "She thought they were in a serious relationship."

"He liked Cheryl," Crissy acknowledged. "He was sad about having to leave her. A couple of times he even said he'd try to convince her to move after we got settled—if he could get her to forgive him, that is. Cheryl had it in her head that she was going to reform me." Crissy snorted. "Anyway, the main thing was that we had to get out of town, and Brett didn't tell Cheryl anything about that. He said he had a whole plan—he was going to quit his job and collect his final paycheck, and then a few days later we'd clear out. We were going to do it when Felicia was at work. We kept it from Abe. The only way we could pull it off was if Felicia didn't find out."

"But she did find out," Tim guessed, reading the grief in Crissy's eyes.

Again, she nodded. "Abe picked that Friday to try to corner Brett at work. You were with him," she said, shooting daggers my way. "When he found out Brett had quit the plant and was planning on leaving, he flipped out and ran straight to her. If he'd just kept his mouth shut, she wouldn't have had a clue. God, was she furious—not with Abe, with Brett. Abe just happened to be the one standing in front of her."

Again Crissy's gaze flicked to me, sharp as the tongue of a snake. As if I needed reminding about what happened next. For Tim's benefit, she said, "Felicia hit him."

Heavily, Tim rose from his chair and lumbered to the coffee machine. As Crissy reached for the full mug he set down before her, a new emotion brewed behind her eyes, but I couldn't surmise what it was.

When he sat back down, Tim asked about Brett. Crissy explained she'd called her father and told him what happened.

"He wanted to leave right away after that. We had plans to go to the movies the next night and didn't want to look suspicious, so he said we should take off afterward. Get away before she knew what hit her. So we went to the drive-in," she said, "but as soon as Felicia dropped us off, Abe started looking for Brett. All he knew was that his dad was leaving town, and he was scared he'd never see Brett again. I panicked. I didn't want him making a scene, so I decided to tell him the plan. Abe got real quiet. He didn't argue, though, and I thought, *Okay, we're good.* After the movie, Felicia drove us home and we went to our rooms. I packed a bag and told Abe to do the same. Then I sat down and counted the minutes until it was time."

Crissy took a sip of coffee and licked her lips. Some of her sticky pink lip gloss came off on her tongue. "At one in the morning, I went to get Abe. That was the plan—I'd get him, and we'd sneak out. When I opened the door, he was sitting on his bed and his eyes were like saucers. Felicia was right next to him. She looked ready to skin me alive."

"He told her," I said.

"Yeah. We were supposed to meet Brett in less than an hour, and Felicia had a death grip on Abe. She said she'd never let him take us, that she'd report him to the police and we'd never see him again, and then she propped a chair under my door handle so I couldn't get out. She literally locked me in my room." Crissy turned to me, and for the first time I felt the full weight of her wrath. "It's your fault," she said. "All of it."

"*Me?*"

"Don't you get it? Abe told Felicia everything because of you. He was obsessed with you, Shana, and you lapped it up. You're the reason we couldn't get out of there."

Obsessed? Lapped it up? My legs turned to jelly. "We were friends."

"Some friend," she said. "He was a damaged little kid with some pretty sick hobbies, and you encouraged him. You *loved it.*"

What? No. I could feel Tim's puzzled gaze bore into me.

"They were just games," I said and almost choked on the words. I felt sick.

"*Games*," she repeated with disgust. "We had a chance to start over, to get away from Swanton and live a normal life with Brett, and Abe refused to leave you. He picked you over his own father, and look what happened. I hope you're fucking happy."

"Hey." Tim lifted his hands. "There's a lot to unpack here, a lot of history between you two. I know this isn't easy, Crissy, but we need to know exactly what happened that night. If Felicia locked you in your room, how'd you end up high on meth in the woods?"

Crissy's eyes shot to the right, and I thought, *My God. Had Bram been abandoned by his sister, too?*

"I *had* to go," she said weakly. "I couldn't stay in that house one more fucking minute. I snuck out the window and went to meet Brett on Hook Road."

"That's gotta be three or four miles," I said. "And you walked it?"

She nodded.

"What happened when you got there?" asked Tim.

"He never came. I waited and waited for him, but he never showed up. Next thing I know, I'm in a hospital room."

Tim leaned forward. "Do you remember anything else? About what happened out there, or the drugs that were found in your system?"

She shook her head.

My eyes grazed Tim's. "Crissy," he said. "All these years, what did you think happened to your father?"

She flexed her fingers around her mug. "I thought he left without us. That's what I believed, and that's what I told Abe later on. I thought Brett was a selfish bastard who left us both behind, and sometimes?" She swallowed hard. "Sometimes I think he deserved to die."

TWENTY-SEVEN

S he's lying."

"You think?" said Tim.

I wanted to give Crissy the benefit of the doubt. Like Uncle Brett, she was a lot more nuanced than I'd realized, but Mac's comment about the killer having years to hone their act had made an impression on me. "I don't buy that she can't remember what happened that night. She resisted talking about it for all this time when she could have given everyone more information. I think she's still covering something up."

I felt punchy and on edge, would have given a kidney for a strong drink, but it was early afternoon and I was having a hard enough time unraveling these two cases sober. What I needed more than anything was to debrief with Tim, so I drove to the field again. Leaned back in the driver's seat, and watched the tree line like a hawk.

"If Crissy really wasn't involved in Brett's death," I said, "why not tell us everything right now?"

"Could she be trying to protect someone?"

"Not Brett. It's too late for that."

I took out my phone, pulled up the e-mail that came in after I left Cheryl's, and passed the device to Tim. "The chief of police up here, guy by the name of Fraser Harmison, let me sneak a peek at Crissy's file. The officer who filed the report confirmed she sustained a blow to the head and said her short-term memory appeared to be compromised. What Crissy's describing isn't temporary memory loss, though; it's full-blown amnesia. A meth high can last twelve to twenty-four hours, more if you binge, but I don't see how it could wipe out her memory."

"Know anyone who might have wanted to mess with her head?"

"Russell Loming," I said at once. "Brett owed him money. He could have tried to use Crissy to barter. There's also Cheryl, Brett's girlfriend at the time. She claims her relationship with Brett was serious, but he left her without looking back, plus I don't think she liked Crissy very much, despite the fact that she was supposedly willing to take the kids in."

"Could she really attack a teenager, though?" Tim asked, his disgust plain in his voice. "Or kill the man she claims to have loved?"

"It might have been unintentional. If Cheryl accidently killed Brett in a fit of rage over his decision to leave, and

Crissy saw it happen, Cheryl might have felt trapped. But if Cheryl wanted to impair Crissy's memory, there are better drugs than meth for causing confusion and amnesia. Rohypnol, for one." Just saying the word numbed my tongue and sucked the moisture from the insides of my mouth. My intimate experience with such drugs might come in handy for my job, but it wasn't something I liked to revisit.

"How does Crissy feel about Cheryl now?"

"Actually," I said, "she indirectly discouraged me from investigating Cheryl. That could be because of her relationship with Suze, though—she's an old friend of mine, and Cheryl's daughter-in-law. So where does that leave us?"

"Maybe what we need is a fresh angle," said Tim. "Should we look at this from Felicia's point of view?"

I didn't want Tim thinking my aunt could be a killer, for many of the same reasons I didn't want him knowing about Bram. Tim was perceptive, though, and he'd heard more than enough from Crissy to realize Felicia warranted examination.

"I know it's not what you want to hear," he said tenderly, "but is there any way Felicia could have had a hand in Brett's death? Brett was trying to take her kids away, right? Her only alibi witness is her son, who was a child at the time. Are we absolutely sure about her movements that night?"

"You mean could she have driven to the refuge and offed her ex?"

Looking uncomfortable, Tim said, "Well, yeah."

"Honestly, there was a time when I thought that was

possible. But what about Crissy's head injury? Felicia did hit her son once, but I'm not sure I can see her staging a violent attack against Crissy, no matter how hard it was for them to get along."

I stared out the window at the baseball diamond, which was covered in snow. Beyond it, I could see the place where the trees parted and a path snaked into the woods. The sight of it made me feel numb.

"Is this what you do?" Tim said. "Drive out to the most remote spots you can find and hope for a face-off mano a mano?"

"Sometimes."

"Jesus. You're not in some cheap action movie."

I ignored that and said, "Can I ask you something? Did you talk to Gil Gasko about me?"

Tim went quiet. I wasn't going to bring it up, but the past few days had left me feeling brittle. The confidence I'd had in my recovery was cracking at the seams.

Tim said, "I may have, yeah."

"You told him you think I'm ready to go back to work."

"Right."

"Do you still?"

Tim's dark eyebrows, his most notable feature, came together. "What I think is that this case is too personal for you. If there's any chance Felicia and Crissy are mixed up in Brett's death, you've got to defer to Harmison. You're in no position to conduct an objective investigation, not even an unofficial one."

"I disagree. I'm perfectly positioned to get this solved. There's a lot about the Merchants and the Skiltons you don't know—that nobody knows but me. We're not your average family."

"Does that even exist? I was raised by two moms. I've got a sister and two stepbrothers, one of them adopted from Haiti, and more cousins than I can count. I kissed one of them by accident once." His cheeks flushed. "There were so many around town I didn't even know we were related."

"But there was love there. Loyalty. Trust."

"Of course," he said. "Was it not like that for you?"

"In my house, definitely. But you heard Crissy. Things were different for her."

The car windows were fogging up. I wiped a circle with the side of my fist. In my mind's eye, I saw my ten-year-old self burst from the deep green shade of the trees around Raleigh Field and cross the grass. It was hot as a furnace that day, the sun a searing blanket on my back and my skin shrink-wrapped to my bones. I remember realizing, with a pang of regret, that I was sunburned. I knew I'd get a lecture from my dad, whom I had to thank for my English complexion, but in the moment there was no reversing the damage, and I had a job to do. So I put my head down, looked for clues, and ignored the impression that my ears were being singed to black.

I only felt his eyes on me when I reached the parking lot. After finding the cat, we'd decided to go our separate ways: I would search the field, while Abe explored the woods. But he wasn't doing that at all. I sensed his eyes mapping my movements as if through a rifle scope. I spun around, and my gaze raked the distant forest. I couldn't see him, but I knew he was there.

"Family," I said again, my voice crisp. "I wonder what it's like to have one you really know. This whole thing has made me realize I don't know the Skiltons at all—and that makes me wonder how well I know myself. All that stuff about nature versus nurture? You can't tell me genes don't play a big part in who we become. Are killers born, or are they made? It has to be both. That means it's in your blood."

"Where is he, Shana?"

"Who?"

"Abe."

The question felt like a guillotine, the blade raised above my neck. "He ran away," I said. "Right before our senior year."

"Crissy said he was obsessed. That he didn't want to leave Swanton because he couldn't stand to be away from you."

I couldn't breathe. I couldn't let him draw this conclusion. It was a burden too heavy for my family to bear. Felicia, Crissy, my mother, they didn't have it in them to face a media circus. There would be questions: *Did you suspect? See the signs?* They'd have to acknowledge, as I had, that Abe was never right in the head. We'd have no choice but to admit to the world we turned our backs on him, and that whether we admitted it to ourselves or not, we'd sighed with relief when he was gone.

"I've been trying to understand," Tim said. "Even before you saw the composite sketch, you were so sure Bram was behind Trey's disappearance."

"Because of the poster. He knew Brett's face would get my attention."

"That message on the back you said Bram wrote. It sounded like an inside joke. It made no sense to anyone but you."

Across the field, at the entrance to the woods, an army of trees swayed in the winter wind. I hadn't seen him muss it, but Tim's hair stood on end. It was bushier than usual, and I realized he hadn't cut it since before the Sinclair case. The last month had felt like one of the longest of my life.

As I looked at him, it occurred to me that maybe this was what I'd wanted—or needed—all along. Tim's job was to flip through conversations and burrow into witness accounts. Did I really think I could keep him in the dark forever? Did I honestly believe he could talk to Bram's sister and not arrive at this place? There was no hiding it now, not anymore. "His name is Abraham," I said. "Abe, for short. Or, if you shorten it another way—"

"Bram."

We were silent. I felt like I'd just exposed a close friend's sordid secret, except the secret was my own. Tim hated silence, will say anything to fill the void. This time, he let it stretch on for miles.

"Who else knows? Your parents? Felicia?"

I shook my head. *No one. Just me. Now us.* "They can't find out, Tim. They just can't."

His cheeks were a mottled blend of scarlet and white. I waited for him to admonish me all over again. This secret spoke to our lack of professional trust. All he'd asked was that I remain truthful.

"This is why you blamed yourself for your abduction," he said, "and for letting him get away in New York."

"It's because of me that Bram killed those women. I'm the reason he took Trey. He wants to hurt me. I knew him better than anyone," I said. "This side of him didn't show itself right away or all the time, but it was there, and I think I . . . God . . . I think I *encouraged* it. We used to play detective, and he cooked up crimes for my benefit. They were terrible sometimes. Violent. I didn't tell him to stop."

"Do you think Bram's the one who killed his father?"

"I don't know. Maybe he wants to show me just how evil he is. I mean, why is this happening now? Brett's bones have been out there for decades." I thought for a minute. "If Bram was the one who tipped off the police, he definitely knows something about Brett's death. But maybe he doesn't know everything. If that's the case, he could be using Trey to force me into doing the legwork for him. He might see it as a form of torture, too, me having to come back here and relive our childhood, knowing what I know about him now."

I touched my scar and watched Tim's eyes go hard and shiny. After holding it all in for so long, my need to unload on him was akin to releasing scummy water from a reservoir. I felt empty, but cleaner.

"If Bram's holding some kind of sick grudge against you for leaving him after he did this, *this*"—Tim motioned to my face—"that's on him."

"We were best friends," I said. "I think he saw me as the only sure thing in his life. I should have helped him fight whatever demons were setting up camp inside his head. Instead, I abandoned him." My breath hitched. Was that the kind of person I was? I thought of Suze and what she'd said about how I ended our friendship. Even Robbie knew it fell apart because I ditched her. But they didn't know why.

It took me years to realize Abe was the reason I was always so hard on Suze. He put a bug in my ear about her early on. *Suze is trouble. Stay away.* I didn't want to believe him, tuned out his warnings for as long as I could, but Abe was persuasive. Before I knew it I was noticing her faults, too, magnifying them in my mind until canceled plans became indefensible acts, and typical teenage bad behavior seemed deplorable. Abe didn't want to share me, that was the crux of it, so he poisoned the well. He governed me in ways I was ashamed to admit then, and that disgust me now. By the time he ran away and I got an untainted look at the life I'd lived, I was too guilt-ridden over what I did to Suze to make amends.

"He's why I became an investigator." I laid my forehead against the window and savored the cold as it fanned out across my skin. "I guess that makes this whole situation pretty ironic. I did this to protect people who can't—or won't—protect themselves, and because of that, he's out there hurting them."

"What makes people kill?" Tim said.

I knew the famed Four Ls, had learned them long ago. "Lust. Love. Loathing. Loot."

"No. I'm asking what makes a murderer. You said yourself it's in the blood. Abe was fighting demons even as a kid. Think back. Did he have dark impulses? Lie easily? Did he have a hard time distinguishing between right and wrong?"

Yes. Yes. Yes.

"You've convinced yourself that shunning him was the act that flicked the switch and turned a child into a sociopath. But Shane, you've got to acknowledge the wiring was already in place. He's a morally bankrupt criminal. Some people are just born that way."

"I know," I said thickly. "But, Tim, he's my cousin."

Tim leaned across the console toward me. His eyebrows were a straight line. "You're not like him," he said. "You never were. You didn't make him do what he did. But we can make him stop."

TWENTY-EIGHT

t was Tim's idea to go to Police Chief Harmison. He thought we should fill in local investigators on what was happening in the Thousand Islands, and the connection between our two cases. He said we could do it without revealing Bram was my cousin. For now.

We planned to stop at my parents' place only long enough to get some food in our stomachs, but when we got there Doug was at the kitchen table, flipping through a high school yearbook.

"There you are," my brother said, pushing aside the empty plate at his elbow. "And look, you brought a friend."

I made introductions, then turkey sandwiches on sourdough for Tim and me. The second my back was turned, Doug pressed the yearbook into Tim's hands.

"Some light entertainment while you eat. You can see how much Shana's improved," Doug said.

With the coffee brewing, I crossed the tile floor to deliver a shuto strike to his ribs.

"No fair, Chuck Norris. That shit hurts."

At the table, Tim laughed.

"Ignore my brother. What year is this?" I reached for the book. The answer was embossed on its thick, forest-green cover: 2000. Doug and Crissy's graduation year. I sat down and flipped to the individual photos of the grads. It was a miracle Crissy had managed to finish high school, but there she was in her cap and gown. I recognized several of their fellow grads as well, including Robbie. Blessed with those beautiful eyes, he'd been attractive when Crissy dated him, but in his senior year Robbie was scrawny. His awkward phase had started late. No wonder Crissy lost interest.

I should have stopped there, but I couldn't help myself. I leafed through the pages until I found my eighth-grade class. In his photo, Abe was doing his best to de-emphasize the hack-job haircut and crooked teeth. He could almost pass for normal. Two years later, he'd leave me with a defect of my own.

Doug closed the book, nearly catching my fingers.

"We can't pretend he never existed," I said.

"Actually, we can. His disappearing act was the best thing that ever happened to our family. Abe's dead to me," Doug said, "and you of all people should feel the same way."

I didn't like the way the photo was affecting my brother. I said, "Don't let him get to you."

"Don't let him *get to me*? He tried to kill you."

I touched my cheek, the scar as much a part of me as the nose on my face. "That's not what this was about."

"Like hell. He split your face open with a rusty nail. That should never have happened."

"I didn't see it coming. I couldn't have stopped him."

"It shouldn't have happened," Doug said, "because Abe was supposed to be gone."

When he was little, Doug developed a tell that allowed my parents to measure the potential force of his tantrums. There was a spot on the back of his neck that flushed when he started to freak out. Salmon-pink was manageable. Fruit punch meant trouble. I could see the spot now, at the base of his hairline. It was fire engine red.

"What's that supposed to mean?" I said. "Doug?"

He'd reached the peak of his anger and was coming down the other side. My brother looked at me for a long time before he said, "With Brett. Abe was supposed to leave with Brett."

"We know," I said, glancing at Tim. "Crissy told us. Brett was going to take the kids with him to Philadelphia, only Felicia found out."

"That didn't matter. Brett never showed up at the meeting place. He intentionally left them behind."

That's what Crissy had said, too. Except . . . "How would you know that?"

"I was there."

"Where, Doug? With Crissy? At the last place Brett was seen alive?" I stared him down, challenging him to come up with an excuse, any excuse, for such an egregious omission. Doug's jaw shifted. What my brother was about to divulge, he'd kept hidden for more than half my life.

"Brett told me he was planning on leaving with the kids," Doug said. "He needed help. I said I'd pick up Crissy and Abe and drive them out to where he was."

"To the boat launch?" Tim said. "Crissy told us she walked it."

"No. I drove her."

Something wasn't adding up. Doug knew things weren't right at the Skiltons, but he'd never shown any interest in getting involved. "Since when was Brett in the habit of calling you for favors?"

"He wasn't. I offered. You were too young," Doug said. "You didn't get it. Felicia was a disaster, Crissy was in a tailspin, and Abe . . ." He shook his head. "I didn't like the way he was with you. I didn't trust him, not ever."

Doug and I didn't get close until after Abe left town. I'd always assumed that up until my injury, I was alone in the knowledge that Abe was unstable. That wasn't the case, though. Doug had seen it, too.

My head swam. I didn't trust myself to formulate the questions that needed asking. I felt Tim's eyes pass over me before settling on Doug.

"Start at the beginning," Tim said. He took out his notebook, and the conversation shifted from a chat over lunch to a witness interview.

Doug took his time recounting what he knew. Well after

midnight, when we'd long since gotten home from the movie, Doug went to Crissy's house. He expected to find both cousins ready to go. Instead, he found only her.

Crissy was frantic. She didn't want to leave without Abe. Doug suggested they drive to the refuge to discuss the situation with Brett. He took Crissy to the designated meeting spot at the fishing access on Hook Road.

"I figured Brett would go back to the house for Abe, or come up with some other idea," Doug said. "But we couldn't find him. His car was there—he'd parked it at the boat launch—but he wasn't around. I thought maybe he'd gone to take a piss or something. So, we waited."

"How long?"

"Half an hour, maybe? The more time that passed, the more worried I got, but I kept telling Crissy he had to come back for his car. All his stuff was in there, packed right up to the ceiling. At one point we even searched around the tree line. Meanwhile, Crissy was losing it, going through denial, anger, fear. She was convinced it had all gone to hell. She said she couldn't go home, not now that the plan to desert Aunt Fee was out in the open. I tried to convince her to come back to our place, but she didn't trust Mom not to side with Felicia. No matter what I said, I couldn't get her to leave."

"So what did you do?" Tim asked.

"I went to get Mom anyway."

"You *left her there*?" I said. "Alone?"

"Yeah. And if you're hoping to make me feel guilty

about that, don't bother. I've had nineteen years to stew in my regrets."

Not knowing what else to do, Doug told Crissy he'd return to the house and try to sneak Abe out. By then, he said, maybe Brett would have returned.

"I got as far as the car dealership on the outskirts of town before I realized leaving her was a bad idea. She was hysterical by then—and I knew about her problem with drugs. She'd been using for a while," Doug said, "smoking a bowl in the woods, busting out the hash pipe at parties. I did a little of that myself for a while, so we were together pretty often. She never resorted to harder drugs, not as far as I knew, but I was worried she might have some scary shit on her and that she'd do something stupid. I was probably only gone fifteen minutes. By the time I got back, she was gone."

I blinked at him. "Gone."

"Brett's car was gone, too. I thought, okay, so Brett got back from wherever he was and they decided to leave without Abe. It's not like the man could show his face in town again after what he tried to pull. Felicia could have him arrested. I didn't like that they blew Abe off. Trust me," he said through his teeth, "I was very unhappy about that. But what could I do?"

I found myself nodding. What could he do? Brett and Crissy were gone. Only somehow, Crissy came back.

"So Crissy was reported missing the next day," Tim said. "Did you tell the police what you knew?"

"I figured Brett and Crissy were halfway to Philly by then. I had no reason to think otherwise, and I didn't want to rat them out. It wasn't until two days later, when Crissy was found, that I knew something went sideways."

Doug had been looking at Tim, but when his eyes pinged to me, I saw they were veined in red. "When Crissy turned up and Brett didn't, I had no idea what to think," Doug said. "She wouldn't tell me anything, not even when she tested positive for meth. My best guess was that she and Brett missed each other somehow, and she got desperate. Maybe she had the drugs on her. Took a hit and wandered off into the woods. Or maybe she met some tweaker on the road and didn't want anyone to know. I played out every scenario I could think of, but the bottom line for me was she was okay. What good would it do to tell everyone I was out there with her? You've gotta understand, I was sixteen years old. I didn't have a fucking clue what I was doing, but I knew it wouldn't look good if I admitted to driving her out of town."

"But didn't you wonder what happened to Brett?" My voice sounded oddly high to my ears.

"His car was gone," Doug said meekly. "I thought he went to Philadelphia. We all did."

I'd never considered the possibility there might be a downside to Doug's exceptional memory. He told the story like it was days rather than decades old, and that made it all the more unsettling. While I'd relied on him to sweep the cobwebs from my own mind, he'd been harboring this secret. It was like one of those gotcha moments from a detective drama—*I wasn't even at the quarry last night! Who said the body was found at the quarry?* There was no connection between Doug and Brett's murder until, suddenly, there was.

"Look," Doug said now, "I'm sorry I didn't tell you sooner. You keep a secret long enough and you forget it's there, you know?"

Again I nodded, but the truth was Doug never forgot anything.

It's funny how the mind plays favorites, jettisoning some memories while spotlighting others. Right then, mine was on my talk with Russell Loming. How he'd told me he'd sold drugs to a boy at the drive-in, and that the boy had been around Crissy's age. Doug had been at the drive-in that night. Doug and Crissy were born just a few months apart.

I stared at my brother. His brow was stitched, and he was looking down at the cover of the yearbook like he couldn't understand how it got there. By the time Tim's cell phone chimed, Doug's face was buried in his hands.

"It's a text from McIntyre," Tim said as he studied the screen. "We have a sighting at the river."

TWENTY-NINE

The transition from kitchen to outside world was jarring. Neither of us mentioned Doug, or questioned the wisdom of leaving Swanton without seeing Harmison, while I drove Tim back to the field to pick up his car. Somehow, we'd both decided to abide by an unspoken rule: put the baggage in the back and face forward. Now, the path forward led along three connecting routes to New York.

We three-way called Mac while we drove, Tim's car visible in my rearview mirror. She told us there had been a handyman working on Heart Island when Trey disappeared, something to do with the castle's pipes. He had given his statement to Tim already, but it wasn't until he heard the news report about a man dumping a tarp full of leaves in the river that he remembered something else about that day.

"The handyman saw a guy docked by the gazebo on the channel side," Mac said. "He thought it was castle staff, but he remembers there was a tarp spread on the floor of the boat, with something bulky underneath."

There was no record of a second worker at Boldt Castle that day, according to its manager. When Mac looked into the handyman's claim, she found the boat matched the description of a vessel that was stolen.

A memory bobbed to the surface of my mind: Tim and I chatting next to the coffee bar at Nelly's while his lady friend—*Kelly, was it?*—waited in the next room. An elderly woman named Miss Betty kept calling Tim about that boat. The thief had taken it from the RV park near the Price Chopper. The store that abutted Swan Bay.

"An hour ago," Mac said, "that boat was spotted at Dingman Point, docked outside the little rental cottages they've got over there. They're closed for the season, but the owner lives in one of them year-round. When he walked down to the water to investigate the boat, he was attacked by a man who fits Bram's description. Bram left him where he lay, and the owner—grandpa type in his seventies, lives alone—sustained a head injury. By the time he came to and emergency services got out there, Bram and the boat were gone. We searched the other cottages, and it looks like he and Trey might have been holed up in one for a bit. Bram looted the owner's fridge and pantry before he left."

"That's a good sign, right?" I said hopefully. "That food could be for Trey."

"Or it could be for him. With that composite sketch all over the news, he's gotta fly under the radar. Either way," she said, "we're going full-court press out there. I've been on this lead all day, and I'm not leaving anytime soon. The islands are deserted this time of year, and we've already got people out there looking. If that boat's on the river, we'll find it."

We agreed to meet at the station once Tim and I were back in A-Bay. Within seconds of us hanging up, Tim was calling me directly.

"Sol and Bogle have centralized all the data we've got on this," he said. "Witness statements, chronology of significant events, everything. It paints a pretty clear picture, so I'm thinking you should look it over and see if something jumps out. If anyone asks about your eval, or why you're wading through evidence when you're supposed to be suspended, make something up. They'll all be preoccupied with looking for Bram anyway."

"You want me to stay at the station while you and Mac search for him? Like hell," I said.

"The guy's a family member, Shana. He's your cousin."

"That only makes me want to put an end to this more."

"I don't doubt that, okay? You're probably more motivated than any of us, but have you thought about how big a problem your relationship could be if we actually find him? If we catch him, and he goes to trial, his attorney could use it against you. They could easily claim prejudice and bias. They'll pore over every interaction you've ever had with Bram—including what happened in New York. Do I have to remind you that the last time you had a chance to detain him you let him go?"

"Wow. So much for Mr. Understanding."

Tim made no reply. The rush of my tires speeding down the frozen highway filled the car. I was driving too fast, but my need to be back in the Thousand Islands had me wound up so tightly it hurt. I was tired of feeling divided between wanting to keep Bram masked and needing to see him exposed for his crimes. It was like battling a second personality for the upper hand; both had their claws out, and both had no intention of relinquishing control.

"It has to be me. I have to play by Bram's rules."

"Fuck his rules!"

"Yeah," I said, suddenly exhausted. "Fuck Bram. Except he's still got Trey Hayes. I never said I had it all figured out. I'm just trying to stay afloat."

My vision blurred, and the landscape blurred with it. Tim said he had another call coming in, and we hung up. I stole glances at him in the rear mirror after that. Saw his lips move when he answered the call, and go still when the conversation ended. It was a long time before he called me back.

"McIntyre again," Tim said. His voice was solemn. "They've got eyes on the boat. It's on the northeast shore of Deer Island, abandoned. There are buildings there. Places to hide."

I pulled in a breath. If Bram was on Deer Island, and Mac called in the cavalry, there was no telling how he'd react. He'd already attacked one person today; if he felt threatened, he could do a lot more damage. He wouldn't hurt me, though. Not yet. And as long as he wanted me alive to watch his plot unfold, Mac and Tim needed my help.

"Tell her to give the island a wide berth. Please, Tim. Don't let anyone tip him off."

"You're a stubborn woman, you know that?" he replied, but I knew he'd do what I asked. He'd had time to think it over, and his conclusion was inevitable. I was going after Bram with or without him, and we were better off as a team.

Easing the gas pedal downward, I said, "Tell her we're on our way."

THIRTY

By 5:00 p.m., all three of us were huddled on a police boat, hurtling into the icy wind. To my left, Boldt Castle was more visible than I'd ever seen it now that the trees surrounding the manse were stripped of their foliage. It was only a ten-minute boat ride from Heart Island, where Trey'd gone on his field trip, to Deer Island. Mac said she thought Bram hid in the cottages for a while, but had they been right under our noses on this island, too?

I never fully understood the magnetic draw of natural beauty until I started calling the North Country home. Even desolate and cold, the river put me in a state of awe. With no other boats around to disturb its numinous splendor, the surface of the water was a lustrous, level plane. We glided over it, past islands bordered by cliffs of gneiss and pink granite and crowned with eastern red and white pines, their trunks bent to dramatic angles by centuries of wind. Reflections of stone and cedar homes, all empty for the winter months, twinkled on the water like eventide ghosts. By the time we got close to our target, the sun was balanced on the horizon, and when Tim cut the motor the sound of geese calling echoed for miles. I could feel the water all around me, and it strengthened my resolve. This was a place unlike any other. And I wanted Bram out.

From our southwest vantage point, the forty-acre island appeared to be nothing but forest. I would have assumed it was uninhabited, and I would be right, but it wasn't always that way. When Deer Island was active as a summer retreat for Yale University's Skull and Bones Society, stewards served elaborate dinners to former American presidents while their fellow Bonesmen walked its bucolic trails and made use of its tennis court. Now, the place was just a pain in Tim's ass. In summer, local kids home from college liked to use it for parties. According to Tim, calling it a death trap was generous. Of the four original structures on the island, three now lay in ruins. Only the society lodge was still habitable.

That's where we found the stolen motorboat. Located on the channel side of the island, the lodge was the most visible of Deer Island's structures, its dock a neon arrow pointing the way in. I didn't like that at all. If someone was trying to hide, tying up here wasn't the way to do it.

Aside from the tarp, the boat was empty. There was nothing in it that appeared to belong to our missing boy or to Blake Bram. Stepping out of our own vessel, I transferred my gaze to the lodge. There was no smoke coming from its towering chimney. I pictured Trey Hayes in the jacket he'd been wearing the day he disappeared, which had been described to me as lightweight. It was a lot colder now than three days ago, and it seemed impossible that McIntyre and I had sat outside at Nelly's just last weekend. If Trey was here, this derelict building would provide little warmth.

Tim tied the police boat to the dock. McIntyre drew her weapon and a flashlight, Tim did the same, and with the two of them in the lead, we ascended the steps to the lodge's front porch.

All the while, I hammered away at my memories of Bram. What was the significance of this place? Proximity to Heart Island wasn't enough of a motivating factor. Why come *here*? Abe and I never spent time in a cottage in the woods or went to sleepaway camp. With its Canadiana style of architecture, all cedar shakes, swooping roof, and fieldstone, the lodge looked nothing like the homes in Swanton. The Bram I knew was meticulous in his planning. If he'd chosen Deer Island, there was a reason.

The decking creaked underfoot, and when Mac got to the lodge's massive door, she lifted two fingers. *Stop. Hang back.* Tim turned his head to look at me, and I registered his expression of surprise a second before I realized what I was hearing. Bird cries. An osprey, perched on the roof above us, shattered the silence with a strident screech. I scanned the woods for movement or a flash of color. Tim raised his eyebrows, and I nodded. *All clear.* McIntyre pushed open the door.

The lodge must have been impressive once, when the paint wasn't peeling and the woodwork wasn't cloaked in dust. It had soaring ceilings, and hulking beams some interior designers would surely sell their firstborn to acquire. Now, it looked like a frat house left to rot. Several windows were wide open, others smashed. Shards of glass, dried leaves, and crumpled beer cans littered the floor, and I was pretty sure the animal droppings scattered about the room didn't come from a dog. The place was dark and filthy and stank of mold. I flicked the nearest light switch. Nothing.

We spread out to search, Tim and I going one way while Mac went the other, all of us trying not to disturb the debris on the floor. The place felt unoccupied to me. Hollow. Despite all the rubble, it lacked substance. I felt sure there were no bodies inside this building but our own. None that were breathing, anyway.

McIntyre was down in the kitchen when Tim and I got to the second floor. There were bedrooms up there, lots of them. We searched them one by one. Because Tim was in front of me, he entered the room at the end of the hall first. "There's something in here," he said, and I called down for Mac to come upstairs. I barely needed to raise my voice. The silence on Deer Island was absolute.

McIntyre made her way up the cracked and crooked staircase to meet us. Neither Tim nor I had approached the object that lay on hardwood planks in the center of the near-empty room, illuminated by the beam from his flashlight. Tim didn't understand what we were looking at, but I did, and it paralyzed me. The object was the same size and shape as the cat in the woods. This time it wasn't wrapped in plastic, but cloth.

Mac's expression was complicated as she drew near it, a potent mix of bewilderment and fear. She pinched a fold of the gray fabric. There was an odd smell in the room now, a scent I knew was called Summer Meadow. Doing my laundry at Mac's house, I'd come to love it. In the lodge now, it made me gag.

My police academy T-shirt was one of my favorites. The last time I saw it, it was in my suitcase in the corner of Mac's living room. Now, it was here. When Mac pulled the fabric back, all three of us gasped. My shirt was wrapped around little Whiskey.

"*No.*"

Mac dropped to her knees beside the dog, and I stumbled forward, heaving. *Whiskey is here.* The lodge tilted and slipped toward the river. There were times when I thought about Bram's crimes and wondered how much farther he could take this. Now I knew. He'd gone into Mac's house, invaded her life and laid waste to her world. Visions of the bodies he left for me in Manhattan crowded the space behind my eyes, that gray skin and those bruises, matted hair, limbs akimbo, and vacant expressions. The ghosts of those women came up behind me and ran their cold fingertips down my neck. The panic I'd felt on Tern Island, the same all-consuming dread my ex-fiancé swore I'd never overcome, was back. *No,* I thought. *It never left.*

Mac's shaking hands hovered over Whiskey's body. There was blood behind his left ear and his eyes were closed, but Tim said, "He's breathing, we have to move fast," and bundled the dog into his arms. I listened to their boots pound down the hall, but still I couldn't move. Off in the distance, a boat engine rattled to life. I recognized the sound immediately, and in that moment it was the only thing that could have brought me to my feet. I could still hear Tim and Mac downstairs. They hadn't yet reached the door. I dragged myself upright, and I ran.

The path down to the river was firm and dry, but it wouldn't have mattered. Bram's bait had ensured we'd be far enough away from the dock that no amount of physical exertion would get us back there quickly enough. By the time we all reached the river's edge, Tim still clutching Whiskey in his arms, the stolen boat was in the channel and racing back toward A-Bay. As the sun slipped below the glittery horizon, I could just make out a single hooded figure sitting stoically inside.

In seconds Mac was on her phone, yelling at troopers on the mainland to get their asses to the river, but I think she knew, as I did, we'd find the boat empty. If Trey wasn't with Bram now, it was unlikely the boy was ever on Deer Island. The place had served its purpose.

I'd been warned.

THIRTY-ONE

The Riverboat Pub sat near the ferry dock at the edge of the St. Lawrence, but it was too late in the day to appreciate the water view, and I was too sloshed to notice it anyway. The ice in my third gin and tonic was cold against my bottom teeth, and the pungent scent of juniper stung my nostrils. Tim didn't say anything when my sips got bigger and I leaned into the bar's pleather bumper.

I'd never been out with Tim in town before, and was taken aback by the happy greetings and claps on the shoulder he got from the pub's patrons. Having grown up in A-Bay, Tim knew everyone—including my ex. I wondered if his reluctance to join me in my drunken haze could be attributed to the attention he was generating, or if it was something else. He didn't try to match my pace, not even when Matt gave him a beer on the house. He'd been nursing that same bottle for an hour.

As far as I was concerned, my keen desire to deaden the pain I felt was justified. I'd been desperate to go with Mac to the animal hospital. Whiskey's breaths were shallow, and he wasn't responding to her voice. When she told me she wanted to be alone with him, the rebuff sliced like a dagger to the heart. Tim had come back to Watertown with me, taking pictures of Mac's broken backdoor window for the B&E report, while I inched a zipper around my bulging suitcase and tried to tell myself she didn't blame me for what had happened to her dog. There was no way I was staying at her place anymore, not after what Bram had done. On the boat ride back to shore from Deer Island, I'd closed my eyes and hoped the rhythm of the waves on the hull would pacify me. Instead, my mind produced a picture show of friends and family in various states of demise. No matter how hard I tried to control my breathing and clear my head, I couldn't shake the visions of the people I loved left to die.

And now, I couldn't look Tim in the eye.

"You're gonna burn through your savings pretty quick at that inn," he said, rolling his bottle of Fat Tire between his palms.

"Sure, but it's within stumbling distance of this place. I call that money well spent."

"I don't think this behavior is healthy."

"Okay."

"Isn't your evaluation tomorrow?"

Fuck.

Gil Gasko had taken every opportunity to emphasize the

importance of this interview. I couldn't return to work without a formal all clear. After shooting a witness on my last case, I'd be lucky if I got reinstated at all. Weeks ago in Oneida, when I debriefed Lieutenant Henderson about Tern Island, he'd insisted that I focus on my mental health. Instead, I'd forced my way into not one new case, but two.

If I learned anything from my time with Carson, it was that I craved this job like a drug. I needed to be back at the station, rummaging through fresh case files while drinking coffee so strong it could beat Tim in an arm-wrestling match. What if Gil and Lieutenant Henderson deemed me unfit to return to duty altogether? If the past few weeks were any indication, I wasn't sure I could survive an extended suspension. Tomorrow was about demonstrating reliability and consistency. I was supposed to prove I was of sound mind and could be trusted to perform my duties, under even the most taxing of circumstances. How the hell was I going to do that?

I wasn't.

"I really thought we had him this time, Tim," I said.

"I know."

I plucked the lime wedge out of my drink and squeezed until it was a mass of dry pulp. "I could leave. If I went somewhere else, he'd follow me out of here."

"Maybe. But what about Trey?"

"Bram wants to hurt me, or punish me, or whatever, and that means nobody's safe while I'm around. So what am I supposed to do?"

"You focus on these two cases," Tim said. "Catch up with him before he can do any more damage."

I gave that some thought. "Every time we've gotten close to Trey, it's because Bram left a clue. If we haven't found him yet, maybe I missed something."

Tim said, "Okay, then let's talk through what you did find."

I pushed my drink aside and waved down Matt for a glass of water. "We found Trey's hat and the bloody message off Swan Hollow Road. The boat was stolen from Swan Bay. My shirt from the police academy—the place I went to after leaving Swanton—was on Deer Island. He's drawing parallels between Alexandria Bay and Swanton, my new town and our old one. Connecting the present with the past."

"If that's true, then you're probably right. There has to be more," Tim said. "You've got years of shared experiences."

I combed my memory of the past days for a cogent answer. "There was the missing persons poster at Smuggler's Cargo. It was in A-Bay, but related to Brett."

"Right. We've exhausted that lead. What else?"

"The note he left with the tooth. It said *The Truth Is Out There*, like from *The X-Files*. That was the movie playing at the drive-in the last night any of us saw Brett."

"Keep going."

The heat in the pub was dry and stale, and I felt a headache coming on. I closed my eyes. *What else?*

"We'll figure this out," Tim said. "We'll find Trey alive

and get Bram behind bars. You'll be reinstated, and I'll have someone interesting to talk to again. With all the bickering Sol and Bogle do, I'd rather share an office with Tweedledee and Tweedledum."

"Don't hold your breath," I said. "I still have to talk my way out of a suspension."

"I'm not worried. I've got your number, Shane. You may get off track now and then, but you play your cards right in the end."

"Cards." The word shot through me like an electric shock. The card was still in my gym bag. I'd found it after my class with Sensei Sam. It had the Three of Hearts on one side, and a picture of Boldt Castle on the other.

"Cards, Tim," I said. "The day I saw Bram at my karate studio may not have been his first time there. On Saturday I found a playing card in my gym bag after class. It's from a Thousand Islands deck—like the kind they have at the souvenir shops here in town. It's got Boldt Castle on it. The abduction site."

Tim tipped back his head to look up at the dusty ceiling tiles above us. "So what's the link to Swanton there?"

I knew the answer before he got the question out, couldn't believe it had taken me so long. "Brett was a gambler. He used to drive to Montreal and blow his paycheck at the casino. Everyone knew he did it—family, coworkers— except according to Russell Loming, he quit when they met some shady characters up there and got involved in dealing drugs close to home." I shook my head. "Abe must have known what was going on, that the gambling became a cover for drug trafficking."

An idea took shape in my mind. "The drugs. Maybe the killer was connected to Brett through drugs."

"So who are our suspects?" asked Tim.

"Loming. He's top of the list," I said, but when I did a mental about-face, I found myself looking at Felicia. "You were right before, we can't dismiss my aunt just yet, but I don't know what, if anything, she has to do with Brett's drug dealing. And there are two other people Brett was with that night whom I still haven't identified. One is the teenage girl seen with Brett in his car, the other is the boy Loming dealt drugs to at the drive-in right before Brett and Crissy went AWOL." A lump formed in my throat as I said it.

Tim was picking at the label on his beer. "Listen, don't slug me. Are you sure we can rule out Doug?"

I'd been doing everything in my power to avoid it, but now the image of my brother's face jostled for attention, the aggression I'd seen toward Abe—and, by proxy, Brett— terrible and real. I was closer to reconstructing the events that transpired the night Brett and Crissy disappeared, but there were still some cavernous gaps. What happened after Doug drove home to get Mom? Where did the meth in Crissy's bloodstream come from? Did Doug really not know what became of my cousin and uncle that night?

"He withheld evidence," Tim said gently. "Not just back then, but now. From you."

"He was trying to help Crissy."

"He's been sitting on a critical component of the case. You know as well as I do that can be a sign of guilt."

"He didn't know how much it mattered. It's not his fault."

To that, Tim had no reply. *Ask Doug* had been my life-long refrain. He was a master at summoning my memories, and I'd always considered the way he alloyed our recollections to be a form of magic. I couldn't count on his help anymore. He'd concealed so much, and his secrecy left me feeling both betrayed and afraid.

Tim was right; there was no excuse for Doug's behavior. The timeline of that night stood out hot and bright in my mind, and anyone could see he'd been involved in a crime, if only by omission. Whether it was against Brett or Crissy, and exactly how he factored in, I didn't know. I owed it to our victim to find out, but that would mean admitting the possibility of something I couldn't bear to be true.

It was a two-minute drive to the motel, but Tim insisted on coming with me. The rooms in the small motel overlooked Otter Creek, where the village of Alexandria Bay meets the St. Lawrence River. In the high season this strip of water is as busy as Church Street, boats from dozens of docks chugging toward the open water. Tonight, it was black and still.

At the front desk, I handed over my credit card and we carted my luggage through the parking lot, where I'd left the

SUV, and along an exterior corridor to my room. At the door, we stopped. This was the part where Tim, ever the concerned and thoughtful friend, would ask if I was okay and remind me I could call him anytime. His cottage was less than ten minutes by car. He'd point that out, too, and might even mention a guest bed and selection of calming herbal teas, even though he knew I wouldn't take him up on an offer to stay over. His hands were sunk deep in his pockets, his head cocked to the right. Shamefaced but still tipsy and a little cold, I hugged myself and prepared to receive his pity.

Tim leaned toward me.

His breaths were measured, but there was something in the hard lines of his body that spoke of urgency. One thing I know about Tim: when he's nervous, he swallows twice in a row. He did it now.

I can't be sure who moved first, but the energy between us was suddenly so high it propelled us toward each other, an inexorable force. All at once his hands were no longer in his pockets but on my waist, and my mouth was locked on his.

Tim took a step forward. His hipbones met mine, and my back met the motel wall. He smelled vaguely like gas fumes from the boat, but also peppery and sweet. In all the months we'd worked side by side I hadn't noticed this, not until my nose was buried in his warm neck.

"No. Tim, *no*."

It took everything I had to push him away. When I could

breathe again, I said, "We can't. He's watching. He's *everywhere*."

Tim stepped back from me, and his face went slack. I could sense his mind whirling as it searched for a cranny that would allow us to escape Bram's cruel trap. His mouth opened and closed a few times before he got the words out. "Dammit, Shana," was all he said before he turned and walked away.

After he was gone, I stared out at the dark parking lot, the marsh grass and cattails along the water, and the hulking aluminum boathouses that creaked and quaked in the wind. Somewhere, Bram was smiling to himself about this, reveling in the knowledge that forcing me to rifle through his old life was wreaking havoc on mine.

THIRTY-TWO

I was miles away from Swanton, far from my childhood home, but my mind was so addled that when I opened my eyes the next day, there was a second when I thought I was a teenager again. Many a morning I'd woken up with a hangover and a deep-seated feeling of regret about an illicit kiss or touch or make-out session at a party in the woods, the sweaty, smoky smell of boys with their hands on my body painfully fresh.

I felt no such compunction about what had happened with Tim—at least, not in the same way. *Tim.* His name sounded different now. He wasn't just a fellow investigator. Tim was the man I'd confided in, whose back had been warm and hard against the palms of my hands. I touched my fingertips to the place where he'd nuzzled my neck just as, on the nightstand, my phone buzzed. Suze's name was displayed on the screen.

"Robbie told me you interviewed Cheryl." Upbeat pop music played in the background, and my head pounded along with the rhythm. Suze was at the studio. "Now do you believe me? Cheryl wouldn't hurt a fly."

Through the gap between the motel curtains, I could see the peaks and towers of Boldt Castle on the horizon. Heart Island blended into the mainland behind it as if it were a peninsula and not a landmass all its own. I found the deception disconcerting. "You're probably right," I said, but I couldn't disregard the picture Felicia had painted of Brett with a young girl in his car. That would make any woman angry, and Cheryl had been counting on Brett to complete her family. "You and Cheryl are close, yeah?"

"As far as mothers-in-law go, I hit the jackpot," Suze said.

"And she never mentioned anything about dating Brett? You never asked about it?"

"No on both counts. Would you interrogate your husband's mom about ex-boyfriends from twenty years ago?" She paused. "So *did* they date? I asked Robbie, but he doesn't want to talk about it, and I don't want to pry."

"They did, for a few months before Brett made the decision to move. The thing is, he might have been dating someone else at the same time."

"Brett sure got a lot of action for a dude his age—hey, I get it," she said. "He was hot in an Owen Wilson kind of way, you know? Sweet but a little rough. How do you know there was someone else?"

I hadn't noticed it before, but Suze spoke of my uncle with atypical fondness, considering she'd only met him a couple of times. "My aunt told me," I said. "She saw them together at the drive-in the weekend Brett disappeared. And it gets worse. Apparently his woman on the side was underage."

"Yikes," Suze said without conviction. She sounded distracted. The background noise was picking up.

"Yeah. Anyway, now I've got to track down this rebel child. If you need me, I'll be interviewing every female student who attended our school in 1998."

"Good luck with that."

"Hey, you were at the movies that night." Suze had helped us look for Brett, if only half-heartedly. "Who'd you see there?"

"God, I don't know, it was so long ago. Crissy and Abe, obviously. Oh, and the Boisselle twins."

"Military haircuts, right?"

"Bad memories," she said through a laugh. "The short one kissed like a slug. I saw Robbie, too, and that super tall friend of his—Mitch, I think? Want to know a secret?" Her voice dropped low. "I thought Robbie was cute even then. He had no idea I existed, but I sure as hell noticed him. There were lots of times like that. It's weird, but sometimes he tells stories and I swear it's like he's pulling them straight from my own head."

"I know what that's like." I hoped she wouldn't hear the discomfort in my voice. Suze had described my experience with Bram to a tee. "Anyone else?"

"Well, Brett, of course."

"You saw Brett that night?"

"Sure. He saved my life from a swarm of killer mosquitos. The bugs were bad, so we talked in his car for a while."

I felt myself tense. "Suze," I said carefully. "Did you two kiss?"

"*He* kissed *me*—but just on the cheek. In retrospect, I guess that was his way of saying good-bye. I always liked him," she said. "Maybe that's because I associated him with Crissy. I totally idolized that girl. She finds that hilarious now, by the way, how I was always trying to dress like her. She was just so cool."

"Jesus, Suze," I said. "It's you. You're Brett's girl on the side."

Her laugh was light, a flip trill. "That's funny. He kissed my cheek, that's all! Shit, sorry, I've got to go. This class can't run long; I've got a date with Crissy right after."

I set down my phone and flopped back onto the thin motel pillow. The hard knot I'd felt in my chest for days had softened a little. Suze had nothing to do with Brett's death. There was no other woman; Felicia had seen my friend, a girl who looked older than her thirteen years, in an innocent moment.

It wasn't until I thought back to my youth with the wisdom of more than half a lifetime that I grasped the situation. Suze *had* emulated Crissy. She'd followed in my cousin's footsteps, even when they led to the darkest of places. Suze never wanted to hear me complain about Crissy's behavior, and threw her hands up at my disinterest in hanging out with my cousin. I'd seen it all happen without connecting the dots. It explained why she and Crissy had built a friendship as adults. Even as kids they'd had more in common with each other than Crissy and I ever would.

In the bathroom, I tore the flimsy wrapper off a plastic cup and chugged two glasses of lukewarm tap water before facing my reflection in the vanity mirror. The dark circles and puffy eyes weren't my concern. I'd just remembered that it was Thursday. The day of my psych exam.

When I imagined the day that would determine my future with the troop, I'd assumed I would get some rest on Mac's couch and spend an hour engaged in guided meditation courtesy of Gil Gasko's beloved app. Instead, I was dehydrated and dizzy, with a persistent thudding in my head. It was a two-hour drive to Oneida, and my appointment was at ten. I had to hustle to be on time, but when I got out of the shower, my phone was ringing again.

"How is he?" I said, terrified of McIntyre's answer.

She sighed. "He's gonna make it. They kept him overnight. I'm picking him up later today."

"Oh, thank God." But then why didn't Mac sound happy?

"No more secrets," she said in a voice I didn't recognize, a voice hard as flint. "That stops right now. What Bram did out there was personal. An attack on me is an attack on you. Why does he want to attack you, Shana? What the hell kind of history do you have with this guy?"

It was a miracle Whiskey survived Bram's violence, and the assault had happened because of me. I owed it to Mac to come clean. I owed her a lot more than that.

I told her then, everything I'd confessed to Tim and more. When I got to the part about my fear over what this news would do to my family, Mac was as practical as ever. All of this was Bram's doing, she said. Hiding that fact wouldn't make it untrue.

Keeping Bram to myself was futile and always had been. It didn't guarantee anyone's safety, because this game was unreliable. I knew that now—and in a way, it made everything just a little easier. No more weighing my actions against his, or tormenting myself with the misguided belief that my decisions could alter those of a madman. He didn't want me to win. His game was designed in a way that ensured I would lose. As far as Bram was concerned, I didn't stand a chance.

And maybe he's right, I thought as I pulled on a dress shirt and slacks, the same outfit I'd worn for my interview with the BCI lieutenant a month ago. On my own, I was beatable. What Blake Bram didn't understand was that by finally bringing Tim and Mac into my confidence, I was amassing an army.

THIRTY-THREE

B reakfast was two Tylenols, a cup of black instant coffee, and a few gulps of brisk November air. I got into my SUV and straight onto the highway headed south.

I drove with my window halfway down and my damp hair flowing behind me. The hilly landscape was speckled with dry snow, and the air tasted smoky. It made my throat ache. I was desperate for water but making good time, on track to be a few minutes early. I got as far as Adams before Fraser Harmison's name popped up on the car's dashboard screen.

"This is just a courtesy call," the police chief said, but a call meant news. It might even mean there'd been a development in Brett's case. "I wanted to tell you myself. We've taken Russell Loming into custody."

I was usually good at multitasking, could talk coherently while flawlessly following all the rules of the road, but my

294

concentration was immediately shot. "What happened?" I asked, focusing my eyes to the windshield. "Did he confess to killing Brett?"

"Not yet, but a witness has come forward. Does the name Ronnie Rockwell ring any bells?"

My mind was doing cartwheels, but I couldn't land a single one. I said, "Don't think so. Who is he?"

"*She* is a former coworker of Loming's. Retired now, but she worked the front desk for five of the same years Loming was at the factory, right up until the company folded."

The receptionist. "You're kidding," I said. "What does she know?"

"Seems all these news stories about your uncle sparked some memories about Loming, and she's had an epiphany. Apparently those two men were rabble-rousers, always chatting and flirting with the ladies—including her—so it was noticeably different after Brett left, especially since Loming vamoosed, too."

"What?" I brushed hair from my eyes and squinted at the road. "Where? When?"

"He failed to show up to work for a couple of days after Brett's supposed move. When he got back, he told Ms. Rockwell he'd been visiting some friends in Canada." Harmison cleared his throat to show me just how little stock he put in that claim. "Loming brought a new, expensive-looking watch back from that trip, too. Thing is, she's adamant he was always complaining about being cash-strapped."

Ahead of me, a Subaru was driving like it was a Sunday

in summer. I sped past it, wincing at the piercing wail of their horn. "What are you thinking?" I asked. "Loming used those days to make sure he'd covered his tracks?"

"We think he followed Brett out to Hook Road that night, stole the cash and the stash, and ditched his car somewhere. Loming was one of the few people who knew Brett was leaving that weekend, and he had a beef with Brett about money. With the drug business doing well, and Brett being the guy who set it all up, Loming wasn't happy he was leaving. Any of this square with what you know?"

I didn't have to think on that for long. Russell Loming had admitted he talked privately with Brett at the drive-in. I could see him using that time to make a last grab at the money he was owed, and getting angry when he failed. I told Harmison as much.

"Good," he said. "That helps. Loming already admitted to dealing drugs; it's just a matter of time before he fesses up about Brett, too. There's no hiding anything now—the whole town's already talking about him. Word travels fast."

"Sure does," I said.

I thanked the police chief for the update, and flexed my fingers on the steering wheel. My nails were short, the cuticles ragged. *Russell Loming.* I should have been relieved. No more worrying about Felicia's potential involvement in my uncle's murder, or agonizing over what else my brother might be hiding.

The receptionist's account was strong, Loming's behavior unarguably suspicious. As I absorbed Harmison's theory and called Loming's face to mind, though, I no longer saw a womanizer past his prime, but a man whose kitchen table had been set with colorful plastic dishes for his grandkids. I shook the picture from my head. *Be grateful, for Christ's sake.* Brett's killer had been found, and my family had nothing to do with the crime—at least, not this one.

With an hour to go and my brain in overdrive, I called my mother. She answered right away.

"Hi, sweetie," she said. Dishes clattered in the background. She was cleaning up the kitchen. "I was hoping to see you before you left again. Blink and I miss you these days."

"I'm sorry," I said, and I was. My mother and I hadn't talked one-on-one since that awkward conversation with Felicia, and I wasn't sure she'd forgiven me for insinuating her sister's guilt. "We had an emergency up at the river."

"The river? But isn't your evaluation today?"

"I'm on my way."

"Good. That's good." I waited for her to ask how I was feeling, if I was ready, but she let it alone. "I owe you an apology," she said instead. "I shouldn't have gotten angry with you the other day when you asked those questions about Fee. It's always been my job to defend her. I take it too seriously sometimes."

I suspected that was true. I wasn't sure I'd ever make sense of how much my mother overlooked about Felicia's condition back then. Maybe she, like me with Abe, hadn't wanted to see the ugliness we knew instinctively was there.

"I get it," I said. "I was out of line—and way off base. I guess you heard about Russell Loming?"

She clicked her tongue. "Can you imagine? Russell was a miscreant, but he and Brett were friends. Inseparable."

"That's the thing about money," I said. "It can come between anyone. How does Felicia feel?"

Her sigh was heavy, a full body release. "Grateful, I think. She's just happy to put this behind her. We all are. Your father and I are helping her organize a memorial for Brett. You'll come, won't you?"

Where would things stand with Bram by then? When my family learned who he was, there would be no public gathering to celebrate Brett's life. Shame and fear would send them into hiding from friends and neighbors. From him. I didn't know how to answer my mother. It didn't matter. In the background, voices spoke in low, urgent tones. "Hang on," said Mom. "Something's happening here."

The line went quiet. Before me, the road stretched over a hill so steep I couldn't see the other side. On the line, I heard my mother yip like a dog in pain.

"Mom?"

Like a camera coming into focus, my parents' kitchen sharpened in my mind, and what I saw hit me like a bucket of icy water. Bram had left Trey's tooth in my parents' mailbox. In A-Bay, he'd gone a step further and broken into Mac's cottage to take Whiskey. What if his need to violate the lives of the people closest to me had driven him back to my parents' place?

What if he was in their house right now?

"*Mom?*"

Trembling, I slowed my speed and pulled over onto the shoulder. Doug and my father were with her, I recognized the pitch and pattern of their speech, but the inflection was off. What I picked up in their voices now was alarm. I was hours away from Swanton. If Bram was there, I'd never arrive in time. *Not them. Not my family.* The hysteria I felt was blinding. I was about to hang up and plead with Harmison for help when Doug came on the line.

"Felicia just called," he said. "It's Crissy."

My heart seized. *Crissy.* I saw her full face and midriff-baring shirts, gum cracking between candy-scented lips. But no, that was Crissy at almost sixteen, the girl at the drive-in who dwelled in my memory.

In the background, a muffled sob. "What is it?" I said. "What happened?"

"She's at the hospital." Dismay bled through the cracks in Doug's voice. "She was found unconscious in her living room half an hour ago. It looks like an overdose."

THIRTY-FOUR

It was early afternoon when I got to St. Albans. I'd done the drive to Vermont and back so many times over the past few days it had become rote. That left me with nothing to do but worry.

There were times when I hated my mind for refusing to power down, and this was one of them. I'd missed my evaluation by hours, hit decline on three calls from my counselor. I would reschedule or . . . something. If they didn't reinstate me . . .

Don't think that way.

Focus on Crissy.

Eager as I was to get inside Northwestern Medical Center, I did a five-minute meditation session via Gasko's app before leaving my car. I'd been hospitalized after my abduction, checked over for physical injuries while the benzodiazepine in my blood was analyzed and recorded in my patient file, and the dichotomy between clean white sheets and unimaginable gore still sends my body into full revolt. As I approached the front desk for information, I held my breath against the odor of disinfectant spray, cafeteria food, and bodily fluids. It assaulted my senses anyway, and within minutes, a familiar woozy, weak-kneed sensation was back.

The elevator opened on the waiting room with a ding, and I spotted my parents sitting with Doug. Felicia stared blankly at the TV on the wall. The Food Network was playing on mute. My parents clambered up when they saw me, hugged me so hard it hurt. Doug did the same, and undeniably felt me stiffen in his arms. When I pulled back, he looked down at me with despair.

I turned to Felicia. "How is she?"

My aunt clasped my mother's hand.

"We're waiting to hear," said my father. "The doctors don't yet know what she took or how long she was unconscious."

A parade of potential side effects marched through my head. *Respiratory failure. Brain damage. Death.* "Who's got the boys?"

Mom's eyes drifted to her sister, and I regretted the question at once. "They'll go to a neighbor's after school," Dad said. "Standing plans for a playdate, thank goodness." I inferred the rest from the look on his face. *Not to their grandmother's. Crissy wouldn't allow it.*

Behind me, I heard the sound of the elevator again. This

time, the doors opened on Suze and Robbie. Robbie held a paper carrier warping under the weight of several to-go coffees and wore a sympathetic smile.

"It was Suze who found her," my dad said under his breath. "They've been here for hours."

Poor Suze. She had mentioned she'd be visiting Crissy today, must have walked into the house and found her unresponsive. My friend looked pale and shaken, and she placed a hand on her baby bump as she and her husband walked toward us.

"It was good of you to come," I said, hugging each of them in turn. It wasn't really my place to say it, given my superficial relationship with Crissy, but I didn't want Felicia to have to concern herself with doling out niceties.

"Any news?" Robbie asked as he distributed the coffees and urged everyone to sit down. When he got to Felicia, he gave her bony shoulder a quick squeeze.

"Not yet," said Dad.

"What happened?" I asked.

Doug said, "Nobody knows." But they did know. I could see it in the crinkle of their mouths and the creases under their eyes.

Based on my last two discussions with her, I'd already concluded that Crissy's blasé attitude about Brett's murder had been an act. Disaffected as she was, she'd been quick to dismiss her father's death, quicker still to deny any knowledge of the events leading up to it, when in fact she possessed more information about his last night than anyone save perhaps his killer. That secret had bubbled up in recent days, until she found herself drowning in guilt. I should have spotted it. I was intimately familiar with guilt myself.

"Felicia," I said, rousing my aunt from her torpor. "I know you don't see Crissy much these days, but was there any indication she was using again?"

"No." She said it with a note of surprise. "Crissy was clean, had been for years."

"It's true," said Suze, sweeping a strand of gleaming dark hair from her cheek. "She goes to an addiction support group every week—oh no, oh here, it's okay." Suze slid out of her chair and dropped to her knees before Felicia, whose shoulders had started to heave. In the seat next to her, Mom rubbed her palm in slow circles over Felicia's arched back.

"She doesn't even drink wine, right, Suze?" said Robbie. "But isn't this how it is with addiction? Even with a whole recovery plan, outpatient treatment, and behavioral counseling, stress can trigger the cravings. What is it they say? You're never an ex-addict, just an addict who hasn't used in a while."

A *relapse, then*. It happened, even to those with the best of intentions. "Has she slipped up before?" I asked.

"Never," Felicia said. "Once she made the decision to stop using, she swore she was done. How could she do this to herself? To the boys?"

A doctor in his sixties who walked with long, determined strides approached our group. As one, we got to our feet.

"I wish I had more news." His ID badge read Dr. Richard Klingemann, and in the photo under his name, he was grinning. "We've flushed the toxins from her system, but we won't know the extent of the damage until she regains consciousness. Brain injury is a very real concern. The blood work came back, and I can tell you the overdose was caused by opioids. A prescription drug is the most likely culprit."

"Was Crissy on any medication, Suze?" I asked. If anyone knew what Crissy was taking these days, it was her. "Any recent injuries she needed painkillers for?"

Suze shook her head. "Not that I know of."

"I don't get it," I said. "All those years without using, and now this? Crissy never had a problem with opioids, did she?"

Before Felicia or Suze could answer, Robbie said, "Drugs are drugs. In a negative emotional state, if they're desperate enough, an addict will take whatever they can get. The woman just lost her father for the second time. If anything was going to steer her off course, it's this."

I met his sad gaze, and held it. "I'm sure you're right," I said. "Hey, is your mother at home?"

"Sure. She's watching Erynn so we can be here." Robbie reached for his wife's hand.

"I'm going to Swanton," I said. "I'll be back in a bit."

"Seriously?" said Doug. "Now?"

Every neck twisted in my direction. They would think me heartless if I left, an ice queen of an investigator who sees cases in terms of losses and wins with no regard for human life. Already, I felt their expectations collapsing. *Too late now.* "Loming's in custody, but he hasn't been charged. It's going to take some effort to build a case against him after all these years. If Crissy did this because of the stress caused by Brett's death and this case, I can't just sit here doing nothing. I want to help the local police in whatever way I can."

"You won't get anywhere with my mother." Robbie's tone was apologetic. "She knows less about the night Brett went missing than anyone."

"You might be right, but I have to try." I shook my head. "I just can't believe Crissy would do this."

"Ah," my dad said, "but she did, poppet."

Felicia and I locked eyes, and hers began to fill with tears.

Maybe, I thought.

Then again, maybe not.

THIRTY-FIVE

Y ou're really racking up the miles," Tim said with undisguised awe when I called him from the hospital parking lot. "Isn't your car on a lease?"

"Just listen," I said, and explained what I needed him to do. He didn't say a word about last night, or cross-examine me about my missed evaluation, and for that I was grateful.

Erynn was napping when I arrived at Cheryl Copely's house. I'd interrupted her lunch, but she didn't seem to mind the company, so I sat with her while she ate a spinach salad and the vestiges of Erynn's neon orange boxed mac and cheese.

"I'm sorry about your cousin," she said. Suze had filled her in on what had happened when she'd asked Cheryl to babysit. I explained it was too soon to tell how Crissy would fare. While her stomach had been pumped, there was always the risk of long-term side effects. Upon hearing that, Cheryl lowered her eyes, and I knew she was thinking about Crissy's boys, just a few years older than Erynn.

I said, "I need to ask you some more questions about Brett."

Cheryl stabbed a cherry tomato with her fork and watched it ooze. "Be my guest. I'm not sure how much more I can help."

"You can start by telling me everything you know about Brett's involvement with drugs."

Cheryl set down her fork. "I don't know anything about that."

"I don't think that's true. You told me you insisted he quit gambling, and he did—but he traded one transgression for another, and you had to be aware of it. You were in a serious relationship, spending time at each other's homes. There's no way he could have hidden regular trips to Montreal from you, or the outings he took to Burlington and St. Albans. This is important, Mrs. Copely. Did you ever see anyone you know in possession of drugs that you believed came from Brett?"

"Oh, God." With trembling fingers, Cheryl reached for her glass of water. At that same moment, my cell phone rang.

"I need to take this," I said. "I want you to think very carefully about your answer. Can I borrow a room?"

Cheryl showed me to a guest room, and I closed the door behind me. I'd asked Tim to look up the Swanton Chamber of Commerce online and get a list of its employees. He'd called the business and spoken to its manager. "Left the office at ten and wasn't back until after noon," Tim said. "Which apparently is unusual for him."

"Call Harmison. Tell him to get some officers to the hospital right away."

"Will do." Tim paused. "And Trey?"

"I'm still working on that," I said, feeling my elation stutter. "I'll call you as soon as I know more."

Tim hung up, and I was left sitting on the guest bed in a room wallpapered in rosebuds, trying to process what I now knew to be true.

There was a part of me that felt Russell Loming could, in fact, be culpable, but I'd been too preoccupied with how he managed to pull off the murder to fully accept it. Between Brett, Crissy, and Doug, there was a lot of activity out at the refuge that Saturday night, and lots of comings and goings meant an enormous amount of risk. Loming could easily have been seen. If Brett confided in him at the drive-in about his intention to take his kids to Philly, Loming had to have known there would be witnesses at the fishing access. How had he executed such a perfect crime under such slippery circumstances?

When I talked to McIntyre about my frustration with Brett's case, she'd tried to allay my doubt in my abilities by reminding me the killer had a head start, and loads of time to prepare should they ever be questioned. Loming wasn't an idiot—yet he'd confessed to dealing drugs with Brett knowing full well Harmison and I would pursue that lead. It was just as Mac said: whoever killed Brett had years to prepare their response, nearly two decades to devise an escape plan. They'd be cool. Unflustered. And that described the individual I believed to be Brett's killer to a tee.

The playing card Bram left in Sam's studio had exposed the aspect of Brett's life I needed to examine, and that, in turn, led me to the person who had the most to gain from his demise. Someone who I believed was at the drive-in that night, who could easily lure Crissy into the woods, and who'd be able to persuade her to ingest a dangerous, highly addictive drug.

A tough conversation awaited me back in Cheryl's kitchen. I pulled open the door and plodded down the hall. But the kitchen was empty now and Cheryl's salad had been abandoned, curling leaves of spinach still on her fork. It was in the living room that I found her, sitting ladder-backed on the sofa. She wasn't alone.

The sight of him stopped me in my tracks. "I should have known you'd come," I said.

"Just checking in on Erynn." Robbie Copely's smile didn't reach his eyes. "What are you ladies talking about?"

"Just tying up some loose ends."

He nodded and rubbed his blond beard. "Poor Crissy. That's a hell of a thing. Who'd have thought she had it in her?"

I held his gaze. "To take all those pills, you mean?"

"Sure. What else?"

"You seem to know a lot about addiction. Recovery, too. When did you first start using drugs, Robbie?"

There was a chill in his eyes when he said, "What the hell kind of question is that?"

I turned to Cheryl. The woman's face had gone white as snow. "You need to be honest with me, Mrs. Copely. I'm pretty sure the motive for Brett's murder was related to the dope he sold. The person who killed him knew he was dealing, and either threatened to expose him or wanted a piece of the action. Do you know anything about that?"

"Of course not." Cheryl's voice was shaky, but she held her head high. "Robbie's an upstanding citizen of this town with a wife and a young child. He's the executive director of the Chamber of Commerce!"

"I don't doubt that," I said. "What about as a teenager, though? What was he like then?"

Cheryl's eyes flipped to her son.

"You don't need to answer that, Ma. This is ridiculous. Shana, I think you should go."

"You were soft on him," I told Cheryl. "You said so yourself. You gave him free rein to do what he wanted, not realizing he'd take it so far. You think it was Crissy who started him using, but he got there all on his own. For a while, he had it under control. Did things start to go down-hill before Brett left, or was it after, when Robbie siphoned Brett's drug supply? You knew," I said to Robbie. "You knew Brett was leaving. And you knew why."

Abe knew, too. He must have discovered his father was selling drugs at the drive-in. He'd seen something that night that I hadn't, and I finally thought I knew what it was.

In a small town like Swanton, secrets aren't secret for long. Robbie had heard—from a kid in his class, or a friend of a friend—that Crissy's father was dealing. I wondered if it was greed that made Brett oblivious to the risks, or if he'd planned to deliver his children from their free fall all along. Either way, the money would be too tempting to resist.

"My best guess is that you talked to Crissy at the movies," I said. "Russell Loming saw her with a kid your age, and I'm sure that if I showed him your school photo, he'd be able to ID you even now. You and Crissy were arguing. Maybe you wanted a hit, maybe she wanted the same from you. However it played out, Crissy let it slip that she was leaving town with Brett and Abe that night. She even told you where Brett was meeting them. So you went out there, knowing Brett would have brought his entire stash along with his other belongings. By the time my brother showed up at the fishing access with Crissy, Brett was already lying dead in the woods. All you needed to do was get rid of his car."

Cheryl clapped a pale hand over her mouth. "That's some story," Robbie said as he clasped his mother's shoulder, just as he'd done to Felicia at the hospital. He gave me a patronizing smile, but two fuchsia circles had formed on his cheeks.

"You do a convincing job of pretending it doesn't bother you that Suze and Crissy hang out," I said.

"It doesn't. I don't give a shit what Crissy does."

"I don't think she'd say the same about you. I thought it

was strange at first, the two of them getting close after circling each other's orbits for so many years, but Suze told me how it happened. They became friends shortly after you and Suze got together. After all this time, Crissy finally found a way into your head. Don't get me wrong," I said, showing him my hands. "I think she genuinely cares about Suze, but Crissy remembers more about that night than she's ever told anyone. She knows you regularly bought drugs from Loming, and that you had a hand in her doped-up adventure in the woods. She also knows you knew her dad was a dealer. If it makes you feel any better, I don't believe Crissy has a clear picture of what you did to her father, but when his remains turned up not far from the boat access where she last saw him, she pieced it together. She's a lot smarter than you think she is."

Robbie's lips were partially hidden by his beard, but I could read his expression through his wide, blank eyes. "I'd say that's when you started to panic," I went on. "It had to occur to you Crissy might remember you were at the boat launch, too. If she did, and she ever decided to tell Suze . . . well, desperate measures. I know you took an extra-long lunch today, Robbie, and I suspect I'll be able to find a neighbor who saw your car outside Crissy's house."

"Do you even hear yourself? None of what you're saying makes sense. I came here for lunch today—didn't I, Ma? I was here."

Cheryl bit her lip. I'd just seen her eat lunch alone. After a minute, though, she nodded. I pressed on.

"It doesn't take long to sneak a few pills into someone's coffee. Believe me," I said stolidly, "I know. But committing one murder doesn't make you an expert. This time you were sloppy. Suze must have told you my partner and I interviewed Crissy at work, and you knew they were meeting up today. Without having a clue how far we got with Crissy and what she told us, you were probably freaked. You couldn't have her exposing you as the person who gave her the meth, or revealing you were present at the crime scene that night. You saw your chance, and you took it. I'd say it's likely you'll be charged with both homicide and attempted murder."

"No." Cheryl's voice was little more than a squeak. There was a dull, dusty quality to her skin that made it easy to imagine what she'd look like dead.

"Still want to deny it, Robbie? You don't have to answer that," I said. "The chief of police will want to hear this all firsthand. For now, I just need you to know you have the right to remain silent, and that anything you do say can be used—"

That's when Robbie lunged.

They say it takes about seventy repetitions of a movement to develop muscle memory. Over the years I've had an opponent's arms around me hundreds of times, but all I could think of was my pitiful reaction when Sensei Sam challenged me in the dojo. I'd frozen that day, clammed up. And yet, when Robbie came at me with anger streaming from him like smoke, my body knew what to do.

Cheryl yelped as he shoved her aside and brought his

weight down on my shoulder, sending me staggering side-ways. A hot white flame of pain erupted in my upper arm. At the edge of my vision I saw Cheryl's horror-stricken face as she rushed from the room. *Erynn.* The kid was in the house, just down the hall, and her father was on a rampage. No sooner had I righted myself than Robbie's hands clamped my throat. There was a moment when the immense pressure on my windpipe sent my system into shock. Eyes streaming, I gaped at his face, red with outrage and rigid with determi-nation, and thought *I'm screwed.* But my hands . . . those were free.

I was barely conscious of the moment when my arm shot out, doubled back, and weaved over and under Robbie's un-yielding forearms. With my left hand I clasped the knuckles of my right and yanked upward with all my might. It was a basic self-defense move, a surefire escape plan I'd learned in maybe my second year of karate. It was all about leverage. The action wrenched his hands from my neck. I didn't waste any time capitalizing on his surprise. When he reached for me again, I braced his hand against my sternum, sank my weight, grabbed his neck with my right hand, and pulled. He yelped with pain as his wrist bent backward onto itself, and in seconds Robbie was on his knees.

If I'd had my cuffs and my weapon, our tussle would have come to an end. Instead, Robbie rose from the floor with the blind confidence of someone who knows they're doomed no matter what. It couldn't have been easy, spend-ing two decades congratulating himself on concealing a crime only to be exposed by a woman he still thought of as an inconsequential kid. He was about to be stripped of everything that mattered—his reputation, his job, his family—and as far as he was concerned, I alone was to blame. I was fighting a man who had nothing more to lose.

In Cheryl's tidy beige living room, we stood sweaty and panting, circling each other like hunter and prey. I brought up my fists and assumed the fighting stance I'd practiced in the safety of a studio. Robbie just laughed. His hands hung by his sides, weighted down by fists.

"Did you really think no one would find out?" I asked. "Even after you drugged Crissy? Even if you'd succeeded in killing her?"

Robbie gritted his teeth and said nothing.

"Your mother just watched you assault me. Her reaction to my questions corroborates my theory about your involvement in Brett's death. She's a witness to it all—and your kid's asleep in the next room. Come on, Robbie. Think this through."

But Robbie wasn't interested in being reasoned with. He swung at me but missed as I evaded his fist and caught his wrist with my left hand. With the fingers of my right bundled into the head of a snake, I struck at the hollow of his throat and kneed him in the groin. He doubled over, gasping for air, and my lips curled into a smile. I was feeling good, as nimble and alert as during my best moments in class, on those green-flag days when conditions are perfect and everything falls into place. I imagined it was Bram I was fighting, and that I had just one chance left. I was high on my success, luxuriating in the pure, clean power of my limbs. *Maybe I'm okay after all*, I thought. *Maybe I'm better than ever.*

The blow came from the left, an open-palmed strike that spun my head halfway around and obliterated my balance. My limbs unspooled like balls of yarn and I collapsed onto the carpet. There was a high-pitched ringing in my ear that made me think of those drive-in mosquitos, and I tasted the sharp tang of blood where I'd bitten a chunk out of my tongue.

Crouching to lean over me, Robbie laughed again, spittle flying. The sound left me cold. He said, "I wasn't going to kill him, all I wanted was his stash. But I'm not sorry I did."

I drove my right knee between his thighs a second time, rolled out from underneath him, and scrambled to my feet. I turned toward the kitchen—I needed a weapon, something to help me finish this—but Robbie caught me by the neck and hauled me back.

"Your whole fucked-up family's better off dead." His arm was wrapped around my shoulders, his breath hot on my ear. "It's pathetic. There were three of you out there, and it took you twenty fucking years to figure this out."

"Three," I croaked. "What are you talking about?"

"That weird little freak," said Robbie. "He showed up on his bike when I was in the woods with Brett. A few minutes sooner, and he would have seen everything."

This was it, the reason I was in Swanton. Abe saw Crissy

and Doug and Robbie on Hook Road that night. Abe knew Brett wouldn't leave him and his sister behind with Felicia—not after she hit him—and Abe needed me to figure out what happened next. I'd tapped away at the town's armor for days, desperate to hit upon a chink, and I'd finally found it. I was done.

The idea played out so beautifully in my mind I knew it couldn't fail. Just as I could have—should have—done in the dojo with Sam, I dropped to one knee. The movement put Robbie off balance, and for a moment he slackened his grip on my arms and was forced to lean forward. With my back to him, I summoned all my strength and thrust my fist upward toward his chin. His teeth slammed together with a sickening clack.

"Robbie."

Cheryl stood in the doorway, holding a sleeping Erynn against her chest. "Stop this. Stop this now."

Robbie's eyes alighted on his tiny daughter, and a look of horror washed over his face. Cheryl's chin quivered where she held it against the crown of the child's head.

"I called him," she said in a small voice. "The police chief. He's coming."

As I wiped saliva and blood from my mouth, Erynn opened her brilliant blue eyes.

From where he swayed in the living room, Robbie Copely closed his.

THIRTY-SIX

After Fraser Harmison arrived, made his arrest, and took my statement, I went home. I'd come to think of my parents' house that way again. It wasn't my only home, but my roots slinked under its foundation just as surely as those belonging to the maples in the yard. As always, Mac was right. Concealing Bram's crimes didn't magic them away. I could hide from my past in Swanton all I wanted, but it wouldn't cease to exist.

I slept fitfully that night, and when the alarm on my phone sounded at 4:00 a.m., I slipped into my jeans and flannel shirt in the dark and tiptoed out of the house to take the well-traveled road west once more. Before dawn the highway was eerily quiet, and I sped the whole way, imbued with a ham-handed dose of verve that I found profoundly satisfying until I remembered I wasn't done yet. I'd done what Bram had asked me to do. In this game, there was just one move left.

Tim's cottage sits on Goose Bay. I hadn't seen it in person, but I knew he'd topped out his budget on a 900-square-foot shack with no heating, and had done most of the renovation work himself. I arrived just as he was getting up, and Mac joined us soon after. Hot coffees in hand, we sat in the living room around the fire Tim had built in the potbellied stove. He'd cooked a batch of pancakes, and the house smelled like a sugar shack. I liked everything about his place, from the knotty pine walls to the stacks of books that didn't fit on his overstuffed shelves and the heavy wool blankets draped over the couch. The tiny house was Tim, through and through.

"Robbie Copely," he said, rolling his mug in his hands just as he'd done with the beer. "I'll be damned. Karate, huh?"

"Think Sensei Sam has room in class for one more?" Mac asked.

I smiled. "Maybe even two."

As they wiped the sleep from their eyes, I explained I'd given Robbie a grilling before leaving town. "Far as I can tell, the summer of 1998 was when he went from a casual drug user to a junkie." I'd seen the transformation in the pages of Doug's old yearbook, connected the dots based on Cheryl's attitude toward Crissy and her references to Robbie's reckless teenage years. "When Brett started dealing, and Robbie found out, he raided Brett's stash. Things were starting to get serious between Brett and Cheryl, so Robbie didn't worry about replenishing his supply. By then both Brett and Russell Loming had noticed the missing dope. Robbie was young and stupid, but it didn't occur to him that his access to the drugs might be compromised."

Then came the night of June 20th, when everything changed.

"Robbie confessed to approaching Brett at the drive-in," I said. "As soon as he found out from Crissy that Brett was leaving town, Robbie threatened to expose him to both Felicia and Cheryl unless he handed over the rest of his supply. Brett refused. He'd been dealing drugs to minors, even friends of his own children, but it was a means to an end, a way to save money for the move. In the meantime, Brett had cottoned on to both Crissy and Robbie's growing addictions. According to Cheryl, Brett was the first to notice Robbie's weight loss and sallow skin, while she remained in denial. Brett didn't want to be responsible for making things worse.

"He also suspected Robbie of the theft. That was one of the many reasons Brett had to leave Cheryl and Swanton behind," I said. "He couldn't stay and risk Robbie ratting him out to Cheryl and the police out of anger and spite. Like it or not, Brett had been actively fueling Robbie's habit. I'm sure skipping town seemed like the only solution. It would allow Brett to get his kids someplace safe, curb Crissy's drug use, cut Robbie off from his supply, and save his own ass, all at once."

"So where did the plan go wrong?" Tim asked, leaning

forward. The room shimmered with heat, and it gave his face a ruddy glow.

"When Brett arrived at the boat launch to wait for Crissy, Abe, and Doug, Robbie was already there. He hid in the woods and took Brett by surprise. Wielding the biggest stick he could carry, Robbie struck Brett from behind and dragged his body past the tree line where it wouldn't be seen. Robbie claims he didn't mean to kill him, though that won't be much comfort to Crissy and Felicia. His intention was to give himself enough time to clean out Brett's supply from his car."

"That car," Tim said. "What happened to it? Doug told us it was there when he and Crissy arrived at the meeting place, but later, when he came back, it was gone."

I took a sip of coffee. Heat shimmied down my throat. "After Doug left to get my mother, and Crissy was alone, Robbie approached her. He hadn't had time to dig through Brett's car, and he wasn't willing to give up his shot at the drugs. The details will all come out when Harmison does his interview, but I'm guessing Robbie convinced Crissy he was there on Brett's behalf and promised to bring her to him. That explains why both Crissy and Brett's car were gone when Doug got back. Robbie must have hidden his own car somewhere down the road and taken Crissy in Brett's instead. Here's what I do know," I said through a yawn. "Robbie offered Crissy meth. She'd been prowling for a hit of something at the movies—she was nervous about the plan to leave town, and Doug says she was an emotional mess—so she probably jumped at the chance. But Crissy had never done meth before, and Robbie was just as ignorant about the hard stuff. The dose was too heavy. He told her to snort it— easier that way, and whether he knew it or not, there's a greater likelihood of psychosis and hallucinations. He probably drove her around for a while, waited until she was good and looped. Then he walked her deep into the woods. Crissy was out of it by then, but not enough that she didn't detect danger. She tried to fight Robbie off and he hit her, like he did with Brett. They'd been friends, and even dated, and he basically left her for dead. He doubled back, and got rid of Brett's car."

Mac's eyebrow inched upward. "The lake?"

"Or the river," I said. "It was right there, easily the most convenient option if he wanted to ditch it. That kind of thing happens now and then, stolen vehicles recovered from the bottom of Lake Champlain or the Missisquoi. Once Brett's car was taken care of, Robbie walked back to his own and went home."

Scratching at his dark stubble, Tim stretched his arms over his head. "There's still one thing I don't get," he said. "Why was Crissy protecting Robbie? Even if she was fuzzy on the details, she had to remember Robbie gave her meth that night. The kid literally left her high and dry in the woods, and it took her two days to get out. Why didn't she report him to the police when the search party found her?"

"I'm hoping she can answer that." Would I ever have the chance to ask? Thinking of my cousin, the present-day version that lay prone in a hospital bed, tugged my mouth into a scowl.

Before I left Swanton for the third time that week, Harmison dispatched an officer to Robbie's house, where I suspected he'd find a near-empty bottle of oxycodone. Robbie had already confessed to sneaking the drugs, prescribed months earlier for his back spasms, into Crissy's mid-morning coffee.

"Back then, I'm guessing she kept quiet because she didn't want to risk getting in trouble," I said. "If she ratted out Robbie, he'd turn around and do the same to her. An abducted teen forced to use illegal drugs against her will is one thing. A teen drug addict on a bender is quite another. When everyone assumed she was taken against her will, she played along. It's likely Felicia put an end to that investigation because Crissy asked her to. I'm sure Crissy was afraid of what the cops would find out.

"As for Robbie's involvement in Brett's death," I said, "Crissy thought Brett went to Philly without her, remember? It wasn't until Brett's bones were recovered that she knew for sure taking meth and getting lost in the woods wasn't nearly the worst thing that happened that night. Even then, she had no proof. Robbie's well respected in town, he works for the Chamber of Commerce. Who would take Crissy's word over his? Sure, she cleaned herself up, but people don't forget the past that easily."

My lengthy report concluded, I heaved a breath. "I can't believe I missed it," I said. "Robbie was right in front of me. He has a history with Crissy. It was there all along."

"You figured it out in the end," Tim said. "That's what counts."

But his attempt at reassurance didn't find its mark. Sure, Russell Loming had been a strong suspect, and I had yet to hear an explanation for the missed days of work and new watch all those years ago, but I shouldn't have been so far-sighted. Meanwhile, Crissy's friendship with Suze had given me an uncomfortable tingle from the start. If I'd paid it more attention instead of letting my theories about Loming, Felicia, and Abe consume me, I would have unearthed Brett's murderer sooner.

A flaming log cracked inside the stove and settled with a sigh. In the clearing that doubled as Tim's front yard, it was snowing hefty flakes, the kind that would stick and become the Thousand Islands' first proper snowfall of the season. "So now what?" Tim said. "We did it. We know who killed Bram's dad. Where do we go from here?"

"If everything up to this point is any indication, we're still missing a link between what Bram's doing here and what happened to Brett," I said.

Now Mac was leaning forward, too. Her former career as an investigator had ended five years prior, but I knew she still missed the thrill of puzzling through cases. In the early morning light, her eyes blazed.

"What does Bram want?" she asked. "He roped you into investigating his father's murder. Why?"

It was an excellent question. I tried to imagine Bram that night, back when he was just Abe. Crissy had told him the plan to leave. He could have seen Russell Loming negotiating with Brett for his share of the money, Crissy arguing with

Robbie over drugs, Brett saying goodbye to Suze in his car. He might have overheard something that led him to believe Brett was in danger, and later, he snuck out of his house and rode his bike all the way to the refuge. How much had he seen?

"If Bram suspected something happened to Brett, he can't have been sure who hurt him," I said. "If he knew it was Robbie who killed his father, he would have gone after the guy himself."

"That's why he needed you to solve this," said Tim. "But why wait so long? Why now?"

I rubbed circles into my temples. "I don't know."

"It may not matter," said Mac. "You did what you were supposed to and identified Brett's killer. That should be enough to point us to Trey." She tapped her toe on the rug. "You collected accounts from a lot of people. What do they have in common?"

"With the exception of Cheryl, all of our witnesses interacted with Brett the same night."

"So what happened at the drive-in pretty much sealed Brett and Crissy's fates," said Mac.

"Totally. The conversations, the interactions—if it wasn't for that movie, nothing would have played out the same way." *The truth is out there.* "The drive-in is the common thread," I said. "Maybe that's the clue we're missing."

Tim sat up a little straighter. "You said his clues link the past to the present, right? There's a drive-in in A-Bay. Right on Route 26."

I felt my own spine go rigid. "All the key locations in this case have related to Swanton somehow. Swan Bay. Swan Hollow." I turned to face Mac full on.

She said, "It's worth a try. It'll be closed for the season, though."

"Let's check it out," I said. "Let's go right now."

I was ready to argue my case, but Tim and Mac were already setting down their mugs and crossing the room to retrieve their boots. They knew as well as I did it had taken too long to get to this point. Trey was four days gone, and that was four days too many.

At the door I said, "Hey, Mac. Happy birthday."

Barely managing a smile, she said, "I know what I want to wish for."

At first I couldn't work out why I hadn't thought of the drive-in myself. Carson had taken me all over A-Bay to familiarize me with my new home, and we'd traveled NY-26 many times, but drive-ins weren't his scene, and with its long, high wall separating the field and parking lot from the road, the screen was barely visible over the barrier. I didn't see it in its entirety until Mac turned onto a lane that cut a trail through a vast expanse of farmland. The chain that had been strung across the entrance by the star-spangled ticket booth lay coiled on the ground. It made a circular depression in the light layer of snow.

Though I saw no car, there were fresh tire tracks on the road, and they led to a low building that was part restaurant, part snack bar. Instead of turning into the parking lot, we drove past the property line. Once we were out of view of the canteen windows, we parked and stepped out into the cold. Above the trees the sunrise was orange and teal, a candy-colored smear across the sky. Tim and Mac checked their weapons, and we backtracked to the entrance on foot.

From the outside, the seasonal building looked as deserted as I'd expected. Its takeout counter had been boarded up for winter, and the windows on either side of the door were black. The handles themselves were wrapped in a chain and secured with a heavy lock. We jogged to the corner of the structure and tried to see inside, but the darkness was profound. When Tim reached for his flashlight, I put a hand on his arm. If Bram was in there, we didn't want to alert him to our presence until we had him in our sights.

At the side of the building, McIntyre made a sound like air escaping a balloon. Tim and I followed the wall around the corner, dividing our attention between the windows and the small grove of silver maples behind us. Was there movement out there? Transfixed, I assessed it, and wrote it off as the breeze.

Images of Bram's face at every age I'd known him flashed through my mind. At six years old, his tongue dyed cotton candy blue. At eleven, when the tilt of his teeth went from droll to disfiguring. Bram next to my mother, the two of them bent over the bathroom sink as she tenderly scrubbed mounds of suds into his oily scalp. Bram staring down at me while I trembled on the basement floor.

There would be another memory made today. What would I see when I looked at him this time? The collection of faces he'd worn through the years were different, but the malice that simmered beneath his smile never changed.

Beads of sweat formed on my forehead, and beneath my coat my underarms felt slippery. Tim was so close I could hear his breath, and I used its rhythm to regulate my own. Mac stood next to the back door, which I assumed led to the kitchen, and when we reached her she gave us a meaningful look. These handles were chained from the outside, too, but the lock was different. It looked brand-new. If Bram had been here, he was gone now. That didn't mean there was no one inside.

Tim reached for his flashlight once more, and together we circled the building, shining the light in every window. When we got back to the ones that flanked the entrance in front, he stopped.

"I think"—he said, then, more urgently—"*there*."

Days ago, when I first realized Bram was responsible for abducting Trey, I had decided I'd sooner surrender myself to my cousin than let a kid die. If I gave myself up, I reasoned, he might stop hurting others, and this senseless game could come to an end. The guilt I'd been carrying over the lives that were already lost would never go away, but others might be spared. *As sacrifices go*, I reasoned while shivering in the snow, *it's an honorable one.* There was just one thing standing in my way. Or more accurately, two.

In that moment, unarmed in the cold wind, my only concern was Tim and Mac. It wouldn't be easy, convincing them to let a psychotic criminal take me away. If they fought me on it, I'd retaliate. I didn't see any other option.

"Step back," Tim said, and with an almighty jab he brought the butt end of the flashlight down against the window. Again and again he struck the glass until, with a bright crunch and residual tinkle, the window shattered. He used his elbow to kick the remaining glass from the frame, and he and Mac raised their weapons. We were in.

Inside, the air was nearly as raw as out. The restaurant was done up fifties-style, with red retro diner booths and a black-and-white checkerboard floor, sparkly black tabletops and plastic condiment caddies. There was no time to let our eyes adjust. We followed the beam of Tim's flashlight to the items that had drawn his attention, empty soda cans and granola bar wrappers littering a table. We stole past the first few booths, and I scanned the darkness for movement, the floor for blood.

The fourth booth came up empty, and the fifth. Tim turned his face partway toward me and gave a small shake of his head.

An overwhelming hopelessness enveloped me then, a sense of failure and loss so intense it left me weak in the knees. I clamped my hand against the back of the nearest bench to steady myself. *What now?* Where would I go from here?

"Shana."

The flutter in Tim's voice whipped my head in his direction. He and Mac had reached the last booth. There, cowering in the far corner of the bench like a feral animal, was Trey Hayes.

"Jesus Christ," Mac said under her breath. Only one side of his face was visible, a single round eye and a cheek streaked with snot and tears. "I'll call an ambulance."

I said, "Hey, Trey. We're with the police. Everything's going to be okay."

The boy tried to make himself even smaller. He wouldn't look at me straight on.

"Are you hurt?" The trauma this kid had been through, my God. Bram had torn Trey's innocence from him like a strip of flesh. I knew his mouth must be aching from where Bram pried out the tooth, but I sensed there was something more to the child's pain. Very slowly I reached toward him, and after a while, Trey put his small, cold hand in mine. Tim's flashlight beam caught his face, and when the kid inched toward me, I sucked in a breath and had to swallow hard to keep from retching. A gash, long and wide, on the side of his face. A wound that would become a scar exactly like mine.

I looked down at Trey. I wouldn't let his disfigurement be in vain. This boy had been held captive by a killer, and like me, he'd survived. I'd learned a lot about Bram during those days, about his distrust of family, his malevolence toward women. He was a talker, always had been.

That meant Trey might hold the key to catching him.

"You must be freezing," I said. Though I was shaking, I took off my jacket and enveloped him in my warmth. "It's all right now. We've got you. But I need to ask you something. The man who took you. Do you know where he is?"

Trey shook his head, hard and fast.

"When was the last time you saw him?"

He burrowed into my jacket and squeezed his eyes shut.

"Okay," I said, nodding. "It's okay, Trey. Hey, Mac."

"Yeah?"

"You got your wish."

THIRTY-SEVEN

The day Robbie Copely is scheduled to be arraigned at Burlington's Costello Courthouse, I get to the station early. I make a pot of coffee for Solomon and Bogle and admire their decorating skills. With days to go until Thanksgiving, my investigators tired of waiting for the holidays and made a run to the local hardware store. Garlands of blinking lights are strung chaotically over the windows. Snowflakes and holly-shaped jelly decals have been slapped against the glass. Their efforts give the office a festive air, but they also remind me of a preschool where the kids are in charge of the ornaments.

In other words, I love it.

It wasn't easy, getting back to this place. Three days ago, I finally marshaled the courage to call Gil Gasko. I explained in detail why I'd missed my evaluation, which led to a lengthy discussion about my mental state. The concern in his voice was loud as a circus parade. He made me describe what he called my *constellation of kin*, their psychiatric history, the quality of those relationships, the events in which we'd been involved, and the impact they had—and were still having—on my life. After close to two hours on the phone, when he was satisfied I could recite the traumatic stressors I needed to avoid from memory, he sent me to Oneida.

There, it was much of the same—but thanks to Gil, I knew the answers to my supervisor's questions, and understood what the psychologist assigned to my case was looking for. Delusions. Hallucinations. Impaired communication. Short- and long-term memory loss. Did I engage in any obsessive behavior that interfered with my daily life? Was I experiencing problems with impulse control, or ongoing panic attacks? How would I rate their intensity, and what did I do to sate them? My responses were recorded in my file, already overflowing with psychometric data. I was a rat in a lab, but the torment was necessary, and I found I could muster the strength to weather it.

All of this resulted in a PTSD score and a mental competency rating that distilled my intellect and psychosocial functional status into a few key terms, and a diagnosis. It included the two best sentences I'd ever heard.

PTSD symptoms are not persistent enough to require medication.

PTSD symptoms are not sufficient to interfere with occupational functioning.

So here I sit, with a full inbox and a lot more to catch up

on once Tim and the others arrive. For the moment, the station is quiet, and before I can reconsider, I pick up the phone on my desk and dial Suze.

I don't expect her to take my call, am surprised when she answers after the first ring.

"Hey," I mumble. "Hi. It's Shana." Already I'm questioning the wisdom of approaching her so soon. After decades of lost time we somehow managed to rekindle our friendship, and now her husband is going to prison in large part because of me.

"Oh," she says, and there's a sluggishness to her voice I can only attribute to hours spent in tears. Mom told me Suze closed the dance studio, at least until Robbie's case goes to trial. "I didn't expect to hear from you," she says.

"Yeah. I wanted to . . . I don't know." *Grovel. Beg your forgiveness.* "Apologize, although that's nowhere near the right word for it. I am sorry, though, that things worked out this way. That it was me who had to do it."

"Oh." In the background I hear the sounds of a child at play. Little Erynn, whose daddy is gone now. "How is she?" I ask.

"Oblivious. Small mercies."

I nod to myself. Small mercies, indeed. "Look," I say, "I've been doing some research." *Some* was an understatement; I'd spent countless hours studying preschool inclusion programming options, trying to pick up where Robbie left off. "There's a center in Burlington that specializes in autism. They have an early childhood program that's supposed to be excellent. I'm sure it was on Robbie's list." Suddenly, my throat feels scrubbed raw. I swallow. No change. "I could send you some information."

Silence. "Oh," Suze says for the third time. "That's . . . sure. Thanks."

"I'd like to stay in touch. I know you might not be comfortable with that."

"No," she says, and my stomach drops. "No, I'd like that, Shana. It's not your fault. What Robbie did, that was real before you got here. It would have come out eventually."

"That's not much consolation."

"No, but we don't have to make it any harder than it is, either. I've been thinking."

"Yeah?"

"Next time you're in town, would you maybe like to get a coffee? You, me, and Crissy? The doctors say she's doing well, that she was . . . lucky. I think you'd like her if you got to know her better. She's not the same person she used to be."

Few of us are. I look out the station window at the road leading into Alexandria Bay. My family has changed. My friend, too. And with change comes opportunity.

"I want to show you something," Suze says.

My mobile phone vibrates on my desk, and I see she sent a text message. It's a video.

"This was last night," she tells me as I hit play. The video opens with a shot of Crissy and Felicia's street. It's lit up with Christmas lights, their reflection shimmering on Maquam

Bay. Every homeowner seems to have made an effort to wrap their pine trees or staple strings of lights to gutters, but it's Aunt Fee's house that stands out.

When she first described her plan to me, I pictured fat plastic Santas and gaudy wire stars strapped to the roof, but it turns out my aunt has an eye for décor. Lush green garlands studded with hundreds of white lights are draped over her windows and door. Her leafless trees have been swaddled in LED lights of periwinkle blue, and snowflake decorations hang from their branches, twirling and shimmering in the night breeze. I don't know who'll be judging the Chamber of Commerce contest now that Robbie's in custody, but I have a feeling Felicia's got this in the bag.

Already there are lookie-loos. Cars crawl past the displays, tiny faces mashed against windows and mittened hands patting excitedly against the glass. After lingering on the street for a moment, the camera swings around to face the sidewalk. What I see then is Crissy, walking toward Felicia's house with her boys in tow. The boys wearing excited smiles, the light already dancing in their eyes. They run ahead. When they get to their grandmother's neatly shoveled driveway, they stop.

She appears at her front door. Felicia's wearing pink, and a shawl with tassels. With one hand on her heart, she waves.

After a long moment, Crissy waves back.

"It's a start," says Suze. "I know they've got a lot of history to work through, but I'm always telling Crissy how special Erynn's relationship with Cheryl is. Maybe her boys can have that, too, someday."

"Yeah," I say softly. "Maybe they can."

As we say good-bye, I see Tim's car pulling into the lot. He gets out and flips up his windshield wipers. There's snow in the forecast again. That could work in our favor. Trey's parents have agreed to let us interview their son once he's recovered, and while we're running blind until then, fresh snow can leave tracks. Expose activity where there should be none.

I touch the barrels of the two travel mugs on my desk. Still hot. The coffee inside is good, an Italian blend I brewed at home, and in a minute, I'll hand one to Tim.

Regardless of the clues, there's really only one reason I found Trey: Bram let me. For the second time, my cousin allowed one of his victims to live, but he's still at large, possibly close. Tim and I have a lot to talk about.

The phone on my desk rings. "State police," I say. "BCI Senior Investigator Merchant."

"Hi, Shay."

A shiver darts down my back. "Bram."

"I guess you think you won."

My gaze flicks to the window. Tim stands on the path to the door, head down. He stopped out front to check an incoming text.

I say, "I don't want to play anymore."

That amuses him. When he speaks again, Blake Bram sounds pleased. "See, that's the problem. If you'd just kept playing back when we were kids, I wouldn't have needed to raise the stakes."

"What the hell do you want?" Try as I might, I can't keep the frustration and fury out of my voice. This game is nothing like the others.

"I guess I should thank you," he says, low and slow. "You found him."

Him. He's not talking about Trey now, but Robbie. I tunnel into every cranny of my mind, trying to parse his words. "You didn't know what happened to Brett?"

"I suspected."

And he needed me to complete the puzzle. "Why now?" I say, just like Tim did. It's illogical. Why let his father's remains rot out there all this time?

"He left me," Bram says simply. "He deserved what he got."

Brett did leave his family, but he also tried to make things right. Does Bram want me to appreciate how bad he had it? Use his childhood as an excuse for the destruction he's reaping now? Was he unable to show forgiveness even at twelve years old? All at once, I think I understand. He wants me to see what he's capable of, the brutal punishments he's willing to hand out. He was callous and delusional even then.

"You have to stop this. This is between us. No one else."

"Look in your purse," he says.

I turn to stone. My purse is on the floor under my desk. I pick it up. Spread it open.

Cards. A whole deck of them sit inside. *How?* My purse

has been by my feet for the last hour. Before that it was in my motel room, with me. I pull out a card at random. On the back, a black and white image of Eel Bay. I grab another. This one shows the Lost Channel.

The card I found in my gym bag belongs in this pack. Heart Island and Boldt Castle on the front, the Three of Hearts on the back.

Three hearts. Becca. Lanie. Jess. Three women gone, three hearts taken, and now here sits the rest of the deck. Bram isn't done, not even close.

"What—"

I stop. The line's gone dead. As I drag my gaze away from my purse, Tim opens the door.

"Morning," he says. "I just got the strangest text."

Acknowledgments

It was a joy working on this book with the amazing team at Berkley. Thank you especially to the brilliant Miranda Hill for committing to this story so completely and knowing exactly how to make it better, and to Brittanie Black, Elisha Katz, Erin Fitzsimmons, and Beth Partin for helping to polish and promote the Shana Merchant series. I'm deeply indebted to my eagle-eyed early readers Leila Wegert, Carol Repsher, Michelle Sowden, and Dorinda Bonanno, and always grateful to Jefferson County Sheriff Colleen O'Neill for answering my questions about the New York State Police and BCI investigators. To Bonnie and James Gombos, thanks for sharing your karate expertise. For your encouragement, savvy, and support, thank you Hank Phillippi Ryan and Wendy Walker; and for your generosity, thanks to the 2020 Debuts community of authors, Suzy Leopold, Barrett Bookstore, Finley's Fiction, the Darien Library, and Crime by the Book. As always, thank you to agent extraordinaire Marlene Stringer for continuing to champion my work after all these years. To Grant and my family, I'd be lost without you. Thanks for everything.

Tessa Wegert is a freelance writer whose work has appeared in *Forbes*, Huffington Post, *Adweek*, and *The Economist*. She grew up in Quebec near the border of Vermont and now lives with her husband and children in a hundred-year-old house in coastal Connecticut. Tessa writes mysteries set in upstate New York while studying martial arts and dance, and is the author of the Shana Merchant series, beginning with *Death in the Family*.

CONNECT ONLINE

TessaWegert.com

TessaWegertBooks

TessaWegert

TessaWegert

Ready to find
your next great read?

Let us help.

Visit prh.com/nextread

Penguin
Random
House